MAYBE LIFE IS THIS

MAYBE LIFE IS THIS

Inspired by True Events

Levon Aran

Maybe Life Is This

© 2025 Levon Aran

All rights reserved.

No part of this book may be reproduced, stored in a retrieval system, or transmitted in any form or by any means—electronic, mechanical, photocopying, recording, or otherwise—without the prior written permission of the publisher, except for brief quotations used in reviews or scholarly works.

This is a work of fiction. Names, characters, events, and places are either products of the author's imagination or used fictitiously. Any resemblance to actual persons, living or dead, is entirely coincidental.

ISBN: 979-8-89965-879-2

IMPORTANT NOTE TO READERS

This novel is inspired by true events, but it is a work of fiction. While certain elements draw from real experiences, the story has been significantly fictionalized. The characters, dialogues, and many of the events portrayed in this book are products of the author's imagination or have been materially altered for dramatic effect.

Names, physical descriptions, locations, and identifying details have been changed to protect privacy. Certain characters are composites, and some events have been compressed, expanded, or reordered. The emotional truth of the story remains authentic, but the specific incidents, conversations, and chronology have been reimagined through a creative lens.

Any resemblance to actual persons, living or dead, or to actual events, businesses, organizations, or locales is either coincidental or has been significantly altered for creative purposes. Where real places are mentioned, they serve only as backdrop for this work of fiction.

The author acknowledges that memory is subjective, and different individuals may remember shared events differently. This story represents one perspective, creatively reimagined, and does not claim to be a definitive account of actual events.

This book contains mature themes and complex emotional situations. It is intended for adult readers.

Dedication

To the love we hold on to, the
pain we carry, and the stories
we never forget and…
to remember it all too well.

ONE

THE OUTDOORSMAN AND
THE ENTREPRENEUR

The stars stretched endlessly above me as I sat beside my dying campfire, hundreds of miles from Tiraz and even further from answers. The desert night pressed in around me, bringing with it that profound silence that makes a person's thoughts sound like shouts. Out here, where the emptiness echoes like a heartbeat, I found myself questioning how a life so carefully built could feel so precarious.

Two things have always defined me: the thrill of building something from nothing and the untamed allure of the wild outdoors. Tonight, as I watched sparks dance toward the endless sky, these two worlds seemed further apart than ever.

I'm Darian Alister, and for the last decade, I've built the kind of life many dream about. Standing at six feet tall with weathered hands that betray my love of the outdoors, I straddle two distinct realms. Most people know me as the founder of Nexara Labs, an innovation hub where I mentor startups and invest in groundbreaking ideas. Just last month, I watched Maya, one of our youngest entrepreneurs, launch a solar-powered water purification system that could change lives across drought-stricken regions. We took an empty, abandoned factory in the heart of Tiraz and transformed it into a thriving center of innovation, where creativity and ambition collide daily.

I remember my father teaching me about the mountains when I was barely tall enough to carry my own backpack. "The wilderness doesn't care about your plans, son," he'd say, adjusting the straps across my small shoulders as the cool mountain air bit at our cheeks. "It only respects preparation and respect." Those early lessons shaped me, creating a perpetual tension between my drive to succeed in business and the peace I found in nature's embrace.

The satisfaction I find in my work at Nexara is undeniable. Yet there's always something pulling me away—an undeniable urge to escape the city, to shed the weight of meetings and deadlines and lose myself in the serenity of the wilderness. The tang of pine needles and the crunch of desert sand beneath my boots call to me with a clarity that grows stronger with each passing day.

That's where my Titanus comes in. More than just an off-road vehicle, it's my key to freedom, my confidant in solitude. The deep rumble of its engine changes pitch with the terrain—a mechanical symphony that accompanies my escapes into the unknown. When the noise of the city becomes too much, when the weight of expectations threatens to suffocate, I load my bow, camera, and essentials into that beast and drive until civilization disappears in my rearview mirror. Last year, when the Titanus rolled over on a remote trail, the frame held strong, and we both emerged with barely a scratch. Some might call my attachment to it absurd, but when you've trusted something with your life as often as I have, it becomes more than mere machinery—it becomes a part of your story.

My relationship with the wild has evolved over the years, much like I have. I used to hunt, finding meditation in the primal thrill of stalking prey, in the perfect stillness of waiting. But something shifted in me, a gentler wisdom taking root, and I traded my rifle for a camera, learning to capture the wildness without ending it. My traditional bow remains a constant companion though—not for hunting, but for the discipline of archery. There's something sacred in the ritual: the smooth pull of the string against calloused fingers, the perfect moment of tension before release, the whisper of the arrow cutting through air. Each shot is a conversation between precision and instinct, between who I am and who I'm becoming.

The same philosophy guides my fly fishing—catch and release only now. Standing thigh-deep in a mountain stream, the cold water pushing against waders, I find rhythm in the practice, poetry in the patience. When I feel the tug on the line, it's a momentary connection to something ancient and pure. I study each fish briefly before returning it to the current, watching it disappear like a secret back into the depths, carrying away a piece of my solitude.

Desert nights hold a special magic that seems to transcend time itself. As the sun sets, the harsh landscape transforms into something otherworldly, something that speaks to the deepest parts of who we are. The heat of the day bleeds into the sand, replaced by a cool breath that carries the scent of sage and stone. The silence out here has substance—it fills your lungs with each breath, makes the city's chaos feel like a half-remembered dream. My campfire pops and hisses, sending sparks toward stars that seem close enough to touch, each ember a fleeting moment of light in the vast darkness.

And then there's Nadia.

I met her ten years ago on a trail near the Velan Gulf, both of us chasing the perfect sunrise shot. She reached the ridge first, her camera already capturing the dawn when I arrived. Instead of claiming the spot, she smiled and shifted over, making room for us both to witness the moment the sun painted the world in gold. Something shifted in me that morning, watching her frame each shot with careful precision, her quiet focus matching my own. We spent hours trading photography tips and trail stories, and by sunset, we were planning our next adventure.

Those first two years were pure magic. We rappelled down hidden canyons, traced ancient paths through mountain passes, and shared sleeping bags under meteor showers. I remember one night in particular, caught in an unexpected storm high in the Kiran Range. We found shelter in a small cave, and while the wind howled outside, we talked until dawn about everything— our dreams, our fears, the core of who we were. Nadia wasn't just my partner; she was my best friend, my fellow explorer, my home regardless of where we found ourselves.

When she took the emergency doctor position at Shinar's coastal hospital, we saw it as another adventure to conquer together. The long stretches apart seemed manageable—we were used to challenging ourselves, pushing boundaries. Her work was vital, saving lives in a region that desperately needed her skills. I felt proud watching her thrive in the ER, her dedication matching my own drive to build and create. We bridged the distance with calls, video chats, and reunions filled with new discoveries.

But time has a way of changing things, even when you're not watching.

While Nadia was away, I found myself retreating more frequently into the wilderness. The Titanus became my constant companion, carrying me deeper into remote territories, away from the complexities of a life divided between city and coast, between ambition and connection. Out here, under the vast desert sky, everything seems simpler. Yet the answers I seek remain as elusive as the shooting stars that streak across the night.

The fire beside me has burned down to embers now, their glow barely competing with the starlight. Soon I'll pack up my gear, climb back into the Titanus, and start the long drive back to Tiraz. Back to the world of innovation and entrepreneurship, of deadlines and responsibilities. Back to everything I've built.

But something has shifted, like sand reshaped by desert winds, and I'm no longer sure where this path leads.

TWO

PATHS CROSSING

Today was one of those hot summer days—back-to-back meetings blurring into each other until time lost all meaning. By the time I got a moment to breathe, it was 6:00 PM, and exhaustion had settled deep into my bones. Still more to do. Nadia was coming home tonight after two weeks in Shinar, and I'd be picking her up from the airport. Her flight landed at 10:00, which meant another evening at the office—a routine we'd perfected over the years.

Our new apartment, the one we bought last year, nestled in the same neighborhood as Nexara Labs. The airport just a short drive away. I'd arranged everything to be connected, manageable. As if proximity could somehow make up for the growing stretches of absence between us.

Tiana, my personal assistant, knew the rhythm of these days by heart. She meticulously tracked Nadia's arrivals and departures in my calendar—a ritual we'd fallen into. I always drove Nadia to the airport, always waited to bring her home. And when she was away, Tiana knew I could pour myself into more mentorship hours, sometimes until 10:00 PM, filling the quiet evenings with work instead of emptiness.

The office was winding down, the familiar hum of laptops shutting off, bags being packed, voices growing softer as another day came to a close. That's when Tiana approached my desk, something different in her stance.

"Mr. Alister, are you going to stay here before you go to the airport?" she asked.

I glanced up, nodding. "Yes. And for tomorrow, are there any meetings early?"

"No, you're free until 10:00 AM," she replied, her voice carrying its usual efficiency.

Some of my colleagues called me Darian, others still used Mr. Alister. I didn't mind either way—at Nexara Labs, we built our culture on transparency and approachability. Leading by example meant working in a 1000-square-meter open space with glass walls, using the same desks and chairs as our 25 team members and the startups we mentored. Even my habit of scribbling thoughts directly onto glass desks with markers spoke to this philosophy of openness, of breaking down barriers.

As I scanned through my notes, a thought surfaced through the fog of exhaustion. "One more thing," I said, "our demo day is getting close. We need an all-hands meeting this week to finalize the guest and investor lists."

I was walking through the office, marker leaving trails of ideas across desks, when Tiana's voice pulled me back to the present.

"Do you have two minutes, Mr. Alister?" The hesitation in her tone made me pause.

"Sure," I replied, pulling out a chair and gesturing for her to sit. Something weighed on her mind—I could see it in the way she held herself, in the careful consideration behind her eyes.

She took a breath before speaking. "I should thank you for the last two years. You've taught me so much, especially about pushing beyond comfort zones, learning new things outside my role. As you suggested, I've been working with Lea, and I'm on track to become a paralegal expert sooner than expected."

The words hit differently than I'd anticipated. "Oh! That's... good news," I managed, keeping my tone firm. "Though I didn't realize it would happen so soon. We planned for the end of the year—still six months away." The unspoken message was clear: I wasn't ready to lose her yet.

"Yes, I understand," she said, her voice softening but carrying an undercurrent of determination. "But Lea needs more of my time than we expected. With 35 startups in our portfolio now, the legal work has grown significantly."

I could hear the careful balance in her voice—trying to honor both her commitment to me and her own future. The tension felt familiar somehow, echoing other parts of my life I wasn't ready to examine.

"Let's talk about this after demo day," I said, standing and walking her to the door. A clear end to the conversation, at least for now. But as I watched her leave, something nagged at me—how quickly things could shift, how people could outgrow the roles we'd carefully crafted for them.

Later That Night: At the Airport

The terminal lights buzzed overhead as I waited in the familiar space of baggage claim. Four more hours of work had left me drained, but this was our ritual—these late-night airport runs marking the rhythm of our lives. The arrivals board flashed Nadia's flight number, right on time.

When she emerged from security, pulling her suitcase behind her, her smile was automatic—the same one that had drawn me in years ago. Even exhausted from a grueling two-week shift, she lit up at the sight of me. Some things hadn't changed.

"You really didn't have to come, you know," she said as she slid into the passenger seat of the Titanus, but I could see the relief in her shoulders as she settled in.

"It's our routine," I replied, starting the engine. "Wouldn't feel right if I didn't."

We drove through the quiet streets, city lights blurring past the windows. These moments used to be filled with stories, shared experiences, plans for our next adventure. Now, comfortable silence stretched between us like a familiar blanket.

"How was your day?" she asked, breaking the quiet as we neared home.

"Busy," I said. "Back-to-back meetings. But it was good."

I glanced over at her, saw the way her eyes were half-closed, exhaustion finally catching up. "I missed you," I said, my voice softer than I intended.

She opened her eyes, looked at me, and for a moment, everything felt like it used to. "I missed you too," she said.

At home, she headed straight for the shower, and by the time I finished some work emails, she had fallen asleep on the bed—a familiar sight after her intense hospital shifts. I covered her with a blanket, pressed a kiss to her forehead, and retreated to my home office.

In the quiet of my study, I took out my favorite fountain pen— a limited edition with a golden nib—and opened my journal. This habit of writing had stayed with me since high school, a way to clear my head, to download thoughts and make space for whatever tomorrow might bring. The nib glided across the paper, smooth and sure, even as my thoughts wandered into less certain territory.

The Next Day

I arrived at Nexara Labs around 10:00 AM, my usual time. The seven-minute drive from home gave me space to think, to prepare for whatever the day might bring. Walking the length of the hall to my office at the far end, I could feel the energy of the space— the quiet hum of innovation, of ideas taking shape.

Coffee in hand, I settled into the rhythm of meetings and calls. Then I summoned Tiana to my office for our daily check-in.

"Here's what we have to do," I began, my mind already racing ahead. "First, I need a meeting with Edmund ASAP, and I'll go to his office—no online meeting."

Edmund Vance, founder and CEO of our primary investment company, held the final word on our board. Regular meetings with him were normal, but this time felt different.

"Is there anything wrong, Mr. Alister?" Tiana asked, concern edging into her voice.

"Nothing that makes you worry," I replied, and she understood the subtext—nothing to worry the team about. Their focus needed to stay sharp, especially now.

"Also about the demo day," I continued, "we have to book Hilton Hotel. They have the largest event venue that fits our guests. We haven't had demo day because of COVID for 2 years, and this time we have 20 startups to pitch and 5 AI products from the research lab to demo in the side fair. I'll do the pitch training myself, so you need to be efficient with my time."

That evening, I returned home to find Nadia preparing dinner. The domestic scene felt both familiar and somehow distant as we sat down to eat.

"We can't go on a trip this month," I said, the words coming out reluctantly. "I have a lot for the Demo Day."

"That's alright," she replied, her acceptance too easy. "We can visit the family sometimes then, and I can hang out with my friends too. They complain because I'm either not here or on a trip with you."

"Sounds like a good plan then," I said, focusing on serving chicken onto our plates.

"How was the work? How is the work of your new startup going? Do you still want to move that to Europe?" she asked, her voice carrying genuine interest despite her exhaustion.

"Definitely! I got all I wanted here and I'm in a comfort zone now. I need to challenge myself again and start something new," I replied, conviction building in my voice. "And as you know, the best place for this idea would be in Europe. I started the work with Rayan and also agreed to give him 10% besides the monthly payment that I do—in that case he'll reduce his salary and he'll code better as he owns equity in the company now."

"My lovely Darian!" Her eyes softened with pride and understanding. "That's what I love about you! You never stop dreaming and pursuing your dreams! I support you on that.... And don't worry about the costs, we are both making good money."

"I'm going to talk to Edmund soon. I asked Tiana to book a meeting with him," I said, the weight of what that conversation would mean settling in my chest.

As the CEO who had built such a successful firm, I couldn't just step down. I needed to plan carefully, find a successor before moving forward. That's what I had to do—start a new chapter of my professional life through my own work.

After dinner, we watched a movie together, falling into the comfortable routine we'd built over years. But as we headed to bed, my mind was already racing ahead to tomorrow, to changes I couldn't yet see clearly.

One Week Later

Nadia was back in Shinar, and work consumed my days. At 10:30 AM, I stood center stage in our office, overseeing pitch training for the upcoming demo day.

"Hello everyone! My name is Mahya from Revula AI solutions. Revula AI is a startup that helps sellers sell their product in a way that....."

"Stop there!" I cut through the air with my voice, striding toward him. I grabbed the paper from his hands, glanced at it, then deliberately tore it up and dropped it in the garbage can. The tension in the room was palpable.

"I asked you all not to write a full text and not to memorize everything! Do you want to get funded or not?"

"Yes," Mahya said, his voice barely audible.

"Then either listen or I will not let you pitch in Demo Day!" My voice was low but carried an edge sharp enough to cut through any remaining resistance.

The stakes were higher than they knew. Many people were waiting to see how our startups would perform. There were those who didn't want to see me succeed, who had tried to take me down. I couldn't let that happen—not now, not with everything else shifting beneath my feet.

Our team was getting ready, and my energy poured into delivering a great demo day. Every detail mattered. I corrected their pitches, refined their presentations, checked everything myself. With 20 startups in the new cohort waiting for their own pitch training after demo day for selection, the pressure mounted. These training and coaching sessions drained me completely, leaving me exhausted by the time I made it home each evening.

The responsibility weighed heavily. Each founder's dream, each team's future, rested partly on how well I could prepare them. It wasn't just about the pitches—it was about building something lasting, something that would continue even after I moved on to my next chapter.

Demo Day at the Hilton Hotel

The Hilton ballroom hummed with an energy we hadn't felt in two years. This wasn't just any demo day—this was our comeback, with 20 startups ready to prove themselves, including teams that had waited through the pandemic for their moment. The stakes felt higher, the air charged with a mixture of anticipation and nervous energy as investors, partners, and industry leaders filled the space.

Standing off to the side, I took in the scene. Rows of chairs faced the massive screen where each startup would present. Investors were already flipping through handouts, some networking in small clusters, others studying the booths set up around the perimeter. Years of work had led to this moment—not just mine, but every founder, every team member who had pushed through the challenges of the past two years.

Taking the stage, I felt the weight of the moment. "Welcome to Nexara Labs' Demo Day," my voice carried across the packed room. "It's been a long time since we've had this chance, and today, you're going to see 20 startups that are ready to change the game." I paused, scanning the audience. "We've got teams here from the past two years, and they've been working relentlessly to get to this point. Let's see what happens when innovation meets opportunity."

One by one, the startups took the stage. I watched each founder step up, their nervousness transformed into confidence through countless hours of preparation. They weren't just presenting products—they were telling stories of passion, of determination, of dreams taking shape. Investors leaned forward in their seats, pens moving rapidly across notepads, occasional nods showing their engagement.

Post-Presentation Networking

When the last pitch ended and the lights came up, the real work began. The energy shifted from the stage to the booths scattered around the room. I moved through the crowd, making introductions, fostering connections, ensuring the right conversations happened between founders and potential investors.

As I finished a conversation with one investor, I felt a tap on my shoulder. Turning, I found Melissa, a business consultant who had been increasingly present at our events. Her smile carried a warmth that suggested more than professional interest.

"Darian, this event is fantastic," she said, her voice carrying a practiced smoothness. "You really outdid yourself this time."

I nodded politely. "Thanks, Melissa. It's been two years in the making, so we wanted to make sure it was something special."

She stepped closer, her voice dropping to a more intimate tone. "You know, we really should get together sometime... outside of these events."

The suggestion hung in the air, unwelcome and clear. I glanced around, spotting a group of investors I still needed to speak with. "Actually, I've got to catch up with some business partners," I said, keeping my tone professional but firm. "I'll see you around."

Before she could respond, I moved toward the investor group, seamlessly sliding back into the rhythm of networking. These were the conversations that mattered—about partnerships, opportunities, and the futures we were building. The startups we had nurtured deserved every chance at success, and I wouldn't let anything distract from that.

That night, exhausted but riding the high of the event's success, I got home and posted some photos on my public Instagram. Nadia quickly reshared them as a story, her caption radiating pride and love.

Then I saw Melissa's tweet:

"What an incredible event at Nexara Labs today! Darian Alister has truly built something special. The company has helped develop so many groundbreaking technologies, thanks to his vision and the amazing startups under his mentorship. A true leader and an all-around great person. #Innovation #Leadership #Nexaralabs"

I stared at the screen for a moment. Melissa had been flattering me throughout the day, but seeing it broadcast publicly like this felt... different. Her words were all about me—the success I'd built, the company I'd led. It was as if she wanted the world to know just how much she admired me, and maybe more.

It was flattering, sure, but I knew better than to read too much into it. I quickly typed a brief, professional response thanking her for her support and refocused my attention on the follow-up work from the event. There were plenty of more pressing things to handle.

Over the years, I'd been approached by women who flirted, even knowing I was married—not only at work or parties, but also through my public social media accounts. Despite their persistence, I was grateful that the two weeks of distance each month had never led to any infidelity. I'd always had more important things to focus on—my work, my hobbies, and the passions that truly drove me in life.

Two Days Later

Our startup camp had a selection day approaching, and there would be pitch training for that too. I was preparing for a workshop when Tiana came to my office.

"Mr. Alister, your 1:30 interview is here—she's the one I told you about," she said, standing by the door.

I nodded, setting aside my work. "Send her in."

Tiana had discovered that the CCO of one of our partner companies had left, and consequently, his PA was going to quit. Now she was a candidate to be my PA.

Her CV sat on my desk as I read through it. I hoped to find someone better than Tiana, who, though good at her job, sometimes tested my patience with her slower pace. I moved fast—walked fast, acted fast, made decisions fast, often based on instinct. That's how entrepreneurs worked.

Tiana stepped out, and a moment later, Elina walked into the office, her professional attire and demeanor exuding confidence. She greeted me with a warm smile that somehow made the formal atmosphere feel more comfortable.

"It's a pleasure to meet you, Mr. Alister," she said, her tone polite but carrying a natural warmth.

I nodded in acknowledgment. "Please, take a seat," I gestured to the chair across from me.

As we began the interview, it was clear she had come fully prepared—both in presentation and presence.

"Let's start simply," I said. "Tell me about yourself and your background, freely. I'd like to get a sense of who you are."

She smiled, her posture relaxed but maintaining professionalism. "Of course. I studied for a bachelor's degree in art, but I never ended up working in that field. After my studies, I found myself drawn more toward administrative and operations roles. I started working in co-working spaces, handling day-to-day operations of shared and virtual offices. It was there that I really learned how to manage fast-paced, dynamic environments with different teams and clients. Then I also studied MBA at the university of Tiraz. My most recent role was as the personal assistant to the COO of the largest eCommerce platform in the country, which exposed me to the intricacies of high-level business operations and executive management."

I appreciated her honesty about the career shift. She spoke with clarity, comfortable with where her path had led her.

"The experience in co-working spaces sounds diverse," I said, genuinely interested. "What was it like working in that kind of environment?"

"It was incredibly dynamic," she replied, her expression brightening slightly. "Every day was different. I worked with entrepreneurs, startups, and established businesses, all using shared spaces. It forced me to be organized and adaptable because each client had different needs. From coordinating events to managing administrative tasks, I was always juggling multiple things at once. I also won the prize of the best receptionist of the year in that company."

Her background showed flexibility, and I could see how those experiences might transfer well to Nexara Labs.

"And from there, you moved on to being a personal assistant to the COO of the largest eCommerce platform," I noted. "That's quite a leap."

She nodded, her expression focused. "It was a huge step up in responsibility, but one I felt ready for. Working with the COO meant managing complex schedules, sensitive communications, and high-priority tasks daily. The pace was intense, but it taught me how to prioritize and stay calm under pressure, which I know would be valuable in this role."

I was impressed with how clearly she articulated her transition from co-working spaces to assisting a top executive. But I wanted to see where her aspirations lay.

"I understand you're considering another offer, too," I said, keeping my tone neutral.

"That's correct," she replied. "I've been offered a role in business development, which is something I'm interested in. However, the opportunity to work here at Nexara Labs, in such a fast-moving, innovative environment, is very appealing to me too. In fact, I need couple of days to make my decision."

I noticed her hesitation with decision-making, her apparent aversion to risk. It was clear to me.

"You know what? I might be able to make it easier for you. We have pitch training in two days. Maybe you just come and watch what we do here. It's different from what you have done before."

"That sounds good," she replied with a smile.

"One more thing!" She added, a note of determination entering her voice. "I have been working as an assistant for a long time and I am done being an assistant. That's why I am still thinking about other positions. It's important for me to change my position after years of working as an assistant."

"I suggest you first come to the pitch training and watch it for two hours, then we can discuss what we can do for you regarding your position. We both need to make a decision on that," I replied, measuring my words carefully.

I knew I needed an assistant. We were growing, and my current PA was moving to another department. I couldn't hire her for any other position—we simply didn't have the openings at the moment.

She stood, shaking my hand with a smile that lingered. "Thank you for the opportunity, Mr. Alister. It was a pleasure meeting you."

As she left, I sat back down, thinking over her responses. Her varied experience, from co-working spaces to assisting a high-level executive, combined with her interest in joining Nexara, made her a strong candidate. But there was something else—a quiet determination in her manner that suggested she wouldn't be content staying in one role forever. I was sure about one thing: both of us wanted this collaboration to start.

Two Days Later

The pitch training for selection day begins. I make some jokes along the way to reduce the founders' stress. About 30 people are sitting in the room, with me, Elina, and Sorvin in the front row. The first pitch starts, and the founder is only pitching to me, completely neglecting everyone else in the room. I point out the mistake and start pitching myself as an example.

After training, I asked Elina to come for a short talk.

"Mr. Alister, I really want to work here, but only don't want to have my position as PA," she said firmly, her earlier hesitation replaced with conviction.

"And you know we are looking for a PA," I replied, keeping my voice steady.

"I will do all PA work for you, but I need my position to be something else and also expect to do more work than just a PA's work. I want to learn and develop my career," she said, a slight edge of stress in her voice.

"In that case, I think we can come up with a position for you and you can start whenever you're ready," I told her while sipping my coffee. Something about her determination resonated with my own drive for growth.

"And regarding my salary?" she asked reluctantly.

"We will work this out, you know the market and we know it too. We have a package that you will receive in our offer letter," I said.

She said goodbye and I got back to my work, but something lingered in my mind. Her ambition, her unwillingness to settle— it reminded me of myself in ways I hadn't expected. The way she pushed for more than what was offered, yet remained willing to prove herself first. It was a quality I respected, even if it might make things more complicated down the line.

After Elina left the interview, I found myself replaying our conversation, struck by her quiet determination. Something about her measured responses and careful observations suggested depths I hadn't expected in a potential assistant. She had a way of listening that made you feel truly heard - a quality I'd always valued in Nadia.

THREE

TENSION BENEATH THE SURFACE

The scorching August heat pressed against the windows of Nexara Labs as we planned our upcoming team building retreat. Tiraz was experiencing one of its hottest summers, the kind that made the air shimmer above the pavement and turned every breath into a reminder of the season's intensity. Inside my office, the air conditioning hummed steadily, creating an artificial oasis from the oppressive heat outside.

Serena, our COO, had taken charge of organizing the retreat at one of the finest hotels in North Parin. I watched her coordinating with the team, her efficiency masking the underlying purpose of this trip—to address the subtle tensions that had begun to thread their way through our company culture. Every growing organization faces these challenges, I told myself, though lately the atmosphere felt different, charged with an energy I couldn't quite name.

I had already informed the team that Nadia would join us, though she would stay separate from the team building activities. Something in me needed that separation—needed to keep my wife away from the complex dynamics that had been developing at work. I insisted on booking and billing our room separately, creating a small but deliberate distance between my personal and professional lives.

When Elina approached my desk that afternoon, her presence sent a familiar warmth through my chest—a sensation I had been trying to ignore for weeks.

"Mr. Alister," she began, her voice carrying that slight hesitation I had come to recognize. "Unfortunately, I can't come to the team building."

I looked up from my papers, studying her face. The shy undertone in her voice contrasted with her usual confidence, and something about her vulnerability in that moment made my chest tighten.

"This is mandatory for all team members," I replied, keeping my voice firm despite the softness I felt creeping in. "We postponed it multiple times so everyone could join, and as a newcomer, you need to be there too."

She shifted slightly, her fingers fidgeting with the hem of her sleeve. "I am sorry to say that, but my grandmother lives with us and I am the one who takes care of her. She is 92 and needs me at home."

The genuine concern in her voice touched something in me. Here was another layer of her—the devoted granddaughter, the caretaker. I found myself wanting to ease her worry, to make her smile despite the situation.

"Alright then," I said, letting a playful tone slip into my voice. "Then you can guard our office and make sure no one steals our startups until we come back. Just make sure to let Serena know about it."

Her laughter, though soft, filled the space between us with a warmth that had nothing to do with the summer heat. I watched as the tension melted from her shoulders, the way her eyes crinkled slightly at the corners when she smiled.

"Sure. Thank you," she replied, and the gratitude in her voice felt like more than just appreciation for my understanding.

Trying to maintain professional distance, I shifted the conversation to work matters. "You need to talk to Tiana to speed up the onboarding. This is particularly for the board sessions."

She nodded eagerly, falling into the efficient assistant role that was becoming second nature to her. "Sure, we are doing our best. For now I am managing all calendars and meetings, and also your lunch orders." A small smile played at her lips as she added, "And Tiana told me that you don't like aubergine. Is there anything else I should do now?"

The fact that she had noted such a small detail about my preferences shouldn't have affected me, but it did. It spoke of an attention to detail that went beyond professional obligation.

"No, that's enough for now," I replied, my voice steadier than I felt. "I will ask for help if I need to."

Meeting with Edmund

The sound of my footsteps echoed softly in the long, marble-floored hallway as I made my way to Edmund's office, each step carrying the weight of years of shared history. I had rehearsed this conversation countless times in my mind, but now, with the moment actually upon me, my practiced words felt inadequate. How do you tell someone who has been more than just a chairman—someone who has been a mentor, a guide, almost a father figure—that you're about to upend everything you've built together?

The familiar scent of polished wood and aged leather enveloped me as I approached his office door. These corridors had witnessed my journey from an ambitious young entrepreneur to the leader I'd become, and Edmund had been there every step of the way. My hand hesitated for a moment on the heavy wooden door, my reflection in the polished brass nameplate showing a face I barely recognized—was this really who I'd become? A man who could walk away from everything he'd built?

Edmund sat at his desk, focused on a document, just as he had been during countless other meetings over the years. But this time was different. This time, I wasn't here to share success or seek advice—I was here to announce my departure. When he looked up, his eyes held that same penetrating intelligence that had guided us through our biggest challenges, and I felt a sudden, sharp pang of doubt.

"Darian," he greeted me with a nod, his voice carrying that familiar blend of authority and warmth that had always made me feel both challenged and supported. "Come in. Take a seat."

I closed the door behind me, the soft click feeling oddly final. The leather chair creaked as I sat down, a sound that had become as familiar as my own breathing over the years. Edmund's eyes studied my face with the same careful attention he gave to quarterly reports and market analyses. He had always been able to read me better than most.

"Edmund, I appreciate you taking the time to meet with me today," I began, fighting to keep my voice steady even as memories of our shared victories and challenges flooded my mind.

He leaned back in his chair, the afternoon light casting shadows across his face. "Of course. I get the sense this is important. What's on your mind?"

I took a deep breath, feeling the weight of my next words. This wasn't just about business—it was about trust, loyalty, and the bonds we forge when building something meaningful together. "I've been thinking about my next steps, about where I want to take things. I've come to a decision." My fingers gripped the armrests slightly tighter. "I'm planning to move to Europe to start my new venture. It's something I've been passionate about for a long time—building something from the ground up in a new market."

Edmund's expression remained neutral, but I saw the slight tightening around his eyes, the almost imperceptible shift in his posture. He had always been a master of composure, but I had learned to read the subtle signs over the years. This news had hit him harder than he was showing.

After a moment that seemed to stretch endlessly, Edmund spoke. "Europe," he repeated, rolling the word around as if tasting its implications. His voice carried the same measured tone he'd used years ago when I first pitched him the idea for Nexara Labs. "I knew you'd want to spread your wings eventually, but this... well, it's sooner than I thought."

The afternoon sun streaming through the window caught the silver in his hair, reminding me of how many years we'd spent in this very office, planning, dreaming, building. I could almost see the shadows of our younger selves, eager and uncertain, standing in these same spots.

"I know it's a big move," I said, leaning forward slightly, trying to bridge the growing space between us. "But it feels like the right time. Nexara Labs is stable now." I paused, choosing my next words carefully. "This new venture—it's something I've been nurturing for years. An opportunity to bring innovation into a new space." What I didn't say was that it was also an escape, a chance to rebuild myself away from the complications that had begun to entangle my life here.

Edmund clasped his hands together on the desk, a gesture I'd seen countless times before major decisions. "I can't say I'm not surprised, Darian." His voice softened slightly. "You've been the driving force behind so much of what we've built here. But if anyone can make a success out of this, it's you." He paused, and I could see him weighing his next words. "Have you considered the impact on the company? On the board?"

The question hit me like a physical blow, though I'd been expecting it. Edmund had always had a way of cutting straight to the heart of things. "I have," I replied, meeting his gaze steadily. "And I believe this move can benefit everyone. I'm not stepping away completely— I'll still be involved, just from a different vantage point. The new business will complement what we've built here."

Edmund studied me with the same intensity he'd shown when I first walked into his office all those years ago, barely more than an ambitious kid with big dreams. Now, the weight of his scrutiny felt different—heavier, loaded with years of shared history and trust.

"You've always been bold, Darian," he said finally, leaning back in his chair. "That's why you've been successful. I can't say I'm not disappointed, but I trust your judgment." His eyes held mine. "I just want to make sure you're prepared for what this means— for Nexara, for your team, and for yourself."

The unspoken question hung in the air between us: Was I really ready to leave everything we'd built? Was I running toward something or away from something?

"I am, Edmund," I assured him, though part of me wondered if anyone could truly be prepared for such a massive change. "This is a new chapter, but it doesn't mean leaving everything behind. It's about expanding what we've built, and I'll need your support, as always."

His expression softened almost imperceptibly. "You'll have it," he said firmly, then leaned forward, his voice dropping to a more intimate tone. "But before you go, I'll need you to find your own successor and onboard them properly. This isn't a decision you can take lightly—whoever steps into your shoes will need to carry the weight of what we've built, and I trust you'll choose the right person."

The responsibility of this final task settled on my shoulders like a physical weight. "I understand," I nodded, thinking of the complexities ahead. "I've already been considering potential candidates, and I'll make sure the transition is smooth." Though how I would manage this alongside everything else in my increasingly complicated life, I wasn't sure.

A small smile tugged at the corner of his lips—the same smile I'd seen when we'd closed our first major deal together. "Good. I've always believed in you, Darian. Just make sure you've thought through every detail."

I returned his smile, feeling a weight lift from my shoulders even as another settled in its place. "Thank you. I won't let you down."

As I stood to leave, I caught my reflection in the window—a man at a crossroads, about to step off the path he'd carefully built into unknown territory. But wasn't that what I'd always done? Wasn't that what had led me to success in the first place? Or was this time different, driven by forces I wasn't ready to fully acknowledge?

The heavy wooden door closed behind me with a soft click, and I stood for a moment in the marble hallway, letting the enormity of what I'd just done wash over me. One more bridge burned, one more step toward a future I couldn't quite see clearly. But there was no turning back now. There hadn't been for a long time.

After the Team Building

The team building retreat had been a success, though its aftermath left me with an unexpected hollow feeling. Watching Nadia interact with my colleagues had stirred something complex inside me—pride at how easily she won them over, guilt at how rarely I let her into this part of my life. She had always belonged in my world of adventure and wilderness; seeing her navigate my professional space with such natural grace made me question why I'd kept these spheres so separate.

Throughout the retreat, my phone had buzzed periodically with messages from Elina—always professional, always about investor meetings, yet each notification sent a small jolt through me. Her absence felt strangely conspicuous, like a shadow in reverse.

Back at the office, I called Elina in to debrief about the past three days. She entered with that careful grace I'd come to notice, her presence shifting the air in the room.

"So, how was the team building?" she asked, her voice carrying a note of something I couldn't quite place—curiosity? Regret?

"Very interesting. We all saw the unseen part of each other." I paused, then added, "You should be in the next team building." The words came out more like an invitation than a suggestion.

She looked down, fidgeting slightly with her sleeve. "Honestly, I have never been out of home for the night, except one trip that I had for work. As I live with my family, I try to be home especially for my grandma." The admission carried a vulnerability that made my chest tighten.

"I see." I shifted the conversation to safer ground. "Anyways, how was it when we were away? Any special news?"

After updating me about two startups needing assistance, she hesitated, her fingers tracing invisible patterns on her notepad. "There is something I want to talk to you about."

"Go ahead!" I tried to keep my tone light, professional.

"You know that I left the previous job because the CCO left the company. I want to tell you that I mostly choose people to work with, not the companies." Her eyes met mine with an intensity that made me want to look away, but I couldn't. "I chose this company because I want to learn a lot from you and I also need a stable job. I have heard about you and your talent and it's an honor to work with you."

The sincerity in her voice made something shift in my chest. "Alright! You just started to work with me."

Her next words caught me off guard. "There is a rumor that you are leaving the company."

"Who said that?" I asked, though I already knew the answer would lead back to Edmund.

"Some old colleagues who are working with Edmund told me about it," she confirmed.

I sighed, the weight of my recent conversation with Edmund pressing down. "That's not happening now, but to keep you informed, this is my long term plan, maybe for a year or so to step down."

"That's why I asked." She met my eyes directly, a smile playing at her lips that seemed to carry more meaning than it should. "I usually work with people and I don't want to lose working with you."

The moment stretched between us, heavy with unspoken implications. "You just started working here and don't know me that much..." I trailed off, aware of how false those words felt. "But don't worry about the future, here the system works well."

She wasn't finished. "One more thing, I didn't tell this in the previous work place that I've been working at. But I'm still working with the international company for some of their activities, but part time. I just told you this because I trust you too much."

The words 'trust you too much' hung in the air between us. I forced myself back into the role of employer. "But we usually don't like our employees to work somewhere else. Not to mention that you should also focus and try to get promoted where you work."

"It's not much, sometimes there are some small tasks," she said, her voice taking on a pleading quality that didn't suit her.

"Anyways, if you want to continue that for a longer term, you have to choose." I stood up, signaling the end of our conversation, needing to create distance before the air grew any thicker with things we weren't saying.

The next day, I noticed the changes immediately. Elina had moved her desk to the office next door, separated from mine only by a glass wall. Where Tiana had maintained professional distance, choosing to sit across the room, Elina had created a space that seemed designed to be in my orbit. The coffee machine's location gave her a perfect excuse to be there, to be seen, to be present in my peripheral vision all day long.

When I arrived the following morning, I found her desk transformed. She had brought in plants and flowers, adding life and color to the sterile office space. The gesture felt intimate somehow, as if she was slowly making her mark not just on the space, but on my daily life. Each flower seemed to whisper of something taking root that I wasn't ready to name.

Early October

The familiar rhythm of picking up Nadia from the airport settled over me like a well-worn jacket. These moments had defined our relationship for years—her returns, our adventures, the way we fell back into sync without missing a beat. As I drove her home, I watched her from the corner of my eye, noting how the hospital work had left its marks in the slight shadows under her eyes, the way she leaned her head against the window.

"No rest for the weary this time," I said softly, knowing she understood our pattern. After her shifts, we always sought refuge in the wilderness, as if nature itself could wash away the sterility of hospital corridors and the weight of her responsibilities.

While she showered, I moved around our kitchen with practiced ease, preparing dinner. The domestic silence felt comfortable, yet somehow different—as if the space between us had shifted in ways I couldn't quite name.

Over dinner, I found myself speaking with renewed enthusiasm about our upcoming trip, as if I could bridge any distance with plans and preparations. "I took the Titanus to the service shop and made it ready for the next trip. I talked to Adrian about a trip too." My voice carried the passion that always emerged when discussing our adventures. "This weekend we're going to see the beauty of forests, we'll go through mountains and go to the forest to the north and come back through the Tarvain Sea."

Nadia's face brightened, the exhaustion momentarily lifting from her features. "That's great! I need that after these two weeks of pressure." The simple way she said it reminded me of why we'd always worked—how she understood my need for escape and made it her own.

"It will be fun," I continued, automatically serving her favorite pieces of chicken, a gesture born from years of sharing meals. "But it's getting cold, so we need warm clothes. We'll stay one night in a hotel and two camp days. I also bought some wood so we can make a fire there."

Friday Afternoon

I left the office earlier than usual, my mind already on the journey ahead. Titanus sat waiting, packed full with camping gear, my camera, and traditional bow—tools of escape that had become symbols of our shared life. The familiar excitement of departure thrummed through me as I called Nadia.

"Hi darling! Don't be late as usual, just come down so we can drive more tonight!"

"Sure! I am ready!" Her voice carried that same anticipation that had marked the beginning of countless adventures together.

When I pulled up to our complex, she was already there, that smile I knew so well lighting up her face. Everything was loaded; we were ready to go.

"Let's go before the traffic on the highway gets built," I said, feeling the pull of the road ahead.

"Yes, and here's your coffee for the evening. We only need to buy water on the way." She placed my thermos in the custom-built console—one of many small modifications I'd made to Titanus over the years. The gesture spoke of our years together, how she'd learned every detail of my routines, my preferences.

As we headed west, the setting sun painted the sky in brilliant colors, threatening to blind me. Without a word, Nadia handed me my sunglasses, already cleaned, taking my regular glasses in exchange. "There you go," she said simply. This was us—the silent understanding, the thoughtful gestures, the way she anticipated my needs before I voiced them. I only wore my glasses for driving, and my sunglasses had prescription lenses—details she'd known and cared for throughout our years together.

The highway gradually gave way to smaller roads, and we stopped at our favorite gas station, the one with the coffee shop and the view that had witnessed so many of our journey's beginnings. Over cappuccino and cake, we sat in comfortable silence, the familiarity of the moment wrapping around us like a warm blanket.

As we continued on, the magical autumn colors began to emerge, the forest welcoming us into its embrace. We were heading to meet Adrian, and everything felt exactly as it should—the road stretching ahead, Nadia beside me, Titanus carrying us toward another adventure. This was our world, the one we'd built together through years of shared journeys and quiet understanding. I glanced at her, watching how she gazed out at the autumn landscape with the same wonder she'd shown on our very first trip together. These moments, just the two of us heading into the wilderness, were when everything made perfect sense.

After meeting Adrian and Mona, I quickly set up our radio frequencies for communication. This was our element—the mountain roads, the promise of adventure, the comfortable routine of preparation that Nadia and I had perfected over years of journeys together. We began our ascent through the mountains, and as we climbed higher, the world transformed around us. The autumn colors were almost overwhelming in their intensity, nature showing off her finest palette.

We stopped frequently for photos, falling into our familiar rhythm. While I scanned the trees for birds, my camera ready to capture any movement, Nadia explored the forest floor with the curiosity that had always drawn me to her. She had an eye for the smallest details—delicate mushrooms pushing through fallen leaves, intricate patterns in tree bark. Her face lit up as she discovered patches of wild berries and apples, the simple joy of foraging bringing out the child-like wonder in her that I'd fallen in love with years ago.

As we drove higher, the path narrowing beneath Titanus's wheels, I radioed Adrian. "We need to find a place, preferably a village house to stay tonight. It's better not to camp in tents, as wolves in this area are aggressive at this time of the year." The wolves were manageable—I'd once even tried to use myself as bait during a wildlife photography session in the snowy mountains—but I felt responsible for everyone's comfort and safety.

"Roger that! Whatever you say, I'll follow!" Adrian's trust in my leadership warmed me.

The sun began its descent as we navigated the unpaved mountain path, now barely wide enough for our vehicles. The sky erupted in colors so magnificent it seemed divine—sheets of fire painted across the heavens. I pulled over before darkness fell completely, stepping out into what felt like another world. The mountaintop stretched before us, trees adorned in yellows, oranges, pinks, and reds, their leaves dancing in the wind. The silence was absolute, broken only by the whisper of branches. I lost myself in the majesty of it all, the universe shrinking to this single perfect moment.

"Darian! Your coffee!" Nadia's voice, tinged with gentle exasperation, pulled me back.

"Oh, thanks! But why are you so loud?" I asked, accepting the mug from her familiar hands.

"You didn't reply what Adrian asked and you don't answer me either. What are you thinking about?"

"Nothing!"

"Tell me. What was that?" Her persistence was gentle, born of years of knowing when something moved me deeply.

"It was this scene that caught me. I was drowned in it," I admitted softly.

We shared coffee and Nadia's homemade cookies, the four of us huddled against the growing cold. As we continued our journey, I kept everyone entertained over the radio with jokes and occasional bursts of song, Nadia's laughter in the passenger seat beside me as familiar as my own heartbeat.

In the village, I found us a cottage through the local supermarket—something I'd learned through years of travel. I bought breakfast supplies too, always mindful of supporting local businesses. When we discovered our night's lodging came with an unexpected roommate—a mouse that scurried behind a cabinet—I watched Nadia's reaction with pride. She announced its presence calmly, the same unshakeable composure she'd shown when we'd encountered a snake near her feet once. Her steadiness in these moments only made me love her more.

While Mona's nerves got the better of her, leading Adrian to set up their tent inside the cottage, I had to confess to Nadia that I'd forgotten our instant tent.

"Do you want bad news, darling?" I whispered in her ear.

"What?" she asked, curiosity dancing in her eyes.

"I didn't bring the instant tent. We have to sleep with the mickey mouse!" I couldn't help but laugh.

Her response was perfect: "No, I only sleep here if that's Remy, the little chef mouse."

I promised her the mouse would make us breakfast, marveling at her spirit. This was what I loved most about her—her courage, her sense of adventure, her ability to find humor in any situation. She was more than just my wife; she was my true companion in every sense.

Looking at her now, I remembered all the times she'd refused to leave my side, even when I'd driven us along treacherous mountain roads with death-defying drops. Even when I'd shouted at her to get out, worried for her safety, she'd stayed, choosing to face whatever came together. Her loyalty, her sacrifice, her unwavering partnership—these were the foundations of our love.

As Adrian and Mona retreated to their tent, Nadia and I settled into our sleeping bags on the air mattress. The mouse might have the run of the cottage, but we had something better—each other, and another adventure to add to our collection of shared memories.

The Next Day

The next morning dawned crisp and clear as we ventured higher into the mountains, leaving the familiar paths behind. These were trails that even seasoned off-roaders rarely attempted, the kind of terrain that demanded respect and experience. I shifted the Titanus into 4WD low range, signaling Adrian to do the same with his Nissan. The ecosystem transformed around us as we climbed - dense berry bushes gave way to rocky outcrops, the air growing thinner with each turn of the wheels.

The wilderness had always been my sanctuary, a place where everything made sense. Up here, watching a golden eagle soar overhead through my camera lens, I felt that familiar peace settle over me. I captured shots of rock thrushes darting between the crags, their movements quick and decisive, so different from the complicated dance of human relationships I'd left behind in the city.

We spent two days embracing the simple rhythm of outdoor life - driving until we found the perfect spot to camp, grilling under star-filled skies, sharing stories around flickering flames. These moments reminded me of countless trips with Nadia, how naturally she fit into this world I loved. She had always understood this part of me, had helped shape it over our years together. The thought sent an unexpected pang through my chest.

By Sunday evening, exhaustion had settled deep in my bones as we made our way home. It had been a good trip, but something felt different now - as if the mountains themselves knew things were changing.

Monday morning found me at the office at my usual time, 10:30 AM, my head throbbing from the weekend's exertion. I made my way to Elina's room for coffee, the familiar routine now carrying new weight.

"Do you happen to have pain killers?" I asked, trying to maintain professional distance despite the concern that immediately flickered across her face.

"What happened, Mr. Alister?" The worry in her voice was impossible to miss.

"Just a headache. Long drive this weekend," I explained, watching as something soft and protective crossed her expression.

"You should be careful, Mr. Alister. I saw your Instagram page - your adventures look dangerous sometimes." Her smile held something more than casual observation, but I chose not to acknowledge it.

"Elina's herbal tea is better than chemical pills. I'll make you one," she offered, already standing.

I retreated to my office, immersing myself in emails until the door opened. Elina appeared with her infuser mug, steam rising gently from the pink cotton lamb's ear tea she'd prepared. The gesture was simple but carried weight - the kind of thoughtful care that was becoming increasingly harder to ignore.

"Here you are! Elina's medicine is better than chemical tea," she announced, setting it carefully on my desk.

"Thanks," I said, recognizing the familiar herb. "My mom used to make this for my coughs when I was young."

Her eyes lit up at this small shared connection. "Mr. Alister, you should remember that I am here too...?" She let the sentence hang, inviting me to complete it.

"You are here to...?" I repeated, trying to keep things light despite the intensity building between us.

"I am here to bring you peace of mind on everything," she finished, her voice carrying a conviction that made my chest tighten. "And I really mean it. I will do whatever it takes."

She remained standing, and I could feel her hoping for an invitation to stay. Against my better judgment, I offered one: "You may have a seat, Elina."

The joy that spread across her face was immediate and unguarded - pure as a child's. It was moments like these that made maintaining professional boundaries increasingly difficult. Her presence was becoming something more than just an assistant's role, and deep down, I knew I should address it. Instead, I let the moment stretch, watching as she settled into the chair, her eyes never leaving mine.

****

It was one of those demanding days that tested the boundaries of professionalism - two crucial meetings on the schedule, one with Elina accompanying me, and a high-stakes discussion with an investor I needed to handle alone. The weight of both responsibilities pressed against my chest as we navigated through the first meeting.

The conference room felt cool and impersonal, its glass walls reflecting the late afternoon light. I was presenting our startup's latest financial projections to a potential investor, carefully walking through each slide with the practiced ease of someone who had done this countless times before.

Seated at the far end of the table, Elina was ostensibly taking notes. But every time I glanced her way, I found her watching me—not the slides, not the investor, not her notebook—but me. Her gaze was so intense it was almost tangible, tracking my every movement, every gesture, every subtle shift in my expression.

When I adjusted my stance or turned to point at a graph, her eyes followed me with an almost magnetic precision. It was more than professional attentiveness. There was something deeper, something almost unnerving in the way she observed me.

The investor, a seasoned businessman in his fifties, was asking a complex question about our projected market expansion. As I began to answer, I was acutely aware of Elina's unwavering stare. For a moment, it felt like we were the only two people in the room, her eyes holding me in a gaze that seemed to strip away every professional veneer.

I cleared my throat, redirecting my attention back to the investor. But even as I spoke about market strategies and potential growth, I could feel her eyes burning into me—studying, consuming, understanding something far beyond the numbers on the screen.

When we finally stepped outside into the late afternoon air, Elina turned to me, her eyes alight with unmistakable admiration.

"Mr. Alister, you're simply incredible in meetings," she said softly, her voice carrying a warmth that made me slightly uncomfortable. "I've never seen anyone with such comprehensive knowledge. The way you handle everything, it's..." She trailed off, color rising in her cheeks.

I checked my watch, using the gesture to maintain professional distance. "You're too kind," I replied, keeping my tone measured. "It's 5:00 PM—you should head home. I have an hour before my next meeting, so I'll probably find a coffee shop to pass the time."

"Mr. Alister..." She hesitated, her fingers twisting together nervously. "I was wondering... Could I join you at the coffee shop? Only if I wouldn't be intruding, of course."

The request caught me off guard. In ten years of marriage, I'd never gone to a coffee shop with another woman without a clear business purpose or Nadia's knowledge. Something about her request made me uneasy, but I found myself reluctant to reject such a seemingly innocent professional courtesy.

"Of course," I heard myself say, though part of me knew I should have declined.

The coffee shop was quiet, the late afternoon lull creating an atmosphere that felt oddly intimate. We spoke about work, but I couldn't help noticing how Elina seemed to hang on every word, how her eyes never left my face, the way she leaned forward when I spoke. Though we never strayed from business topics, her attention felt more personal than professional.

Later, as I sat in my investor meeting, my mind kept returning to that hour in the coffee shop. Had I inadvertently encouraged something I shouldn't have? The memory of Nadia's trust weighed heavily on my conscience. Was there more to Elina's request than professional interest? I dismissed these thoughts quickly—we'd only discussed work, after all, and I had no interest in anything beyond our professional relationship.

That evening, driving home to Nadia, I pushed the afternoon's concerns aside. I told myself it was nothing - just coffee, just work - and I meant it. My life with Nadia was everything I wanted and needed. Still, a small voice in my head suggested that perhaps I should be more careful about maintaining professional boundaries with Elina in the future.

Late October

The office hummed with the usual late-day energy, investor meetings filling my schedule. Elina was in her room when she suddenly packed up and left - her characteristic quick stride carrying her through the hallway. There was something admirable about her efficiency, the way she never wasted a moment. A text buzzed on my phone as I continued my meeting:

"Mr. Alister, my brother told me that my father is sick and I had to go."

I read the message during a pause in the investor's presentation, quickly typing back: "Sure, let me know if you need any help."

By 8:00 PM, the building had emptied except for a few dedicated founders. The silence felt heavier than usual as I tried calling Elina. No answer.

Two Days Later

A cloud of worry hung over the office. Elina's absence and silence created an unexpected void - her efficient presence missed more than anyone had anticipated. The lack of communication stirred both concern and frustration in me; as her boss, I needed to know what was happening.

The unknown caller's voice trembled as she delivered the news: "Hi Mr. Alister. I am Elina's friend... Elina's father passed away and she can't even talk. She asked me to call you and tell you that her absence was because of this."

The words hit me with unexpected force, memories of my own father's death rising unbidden. "Really? Is she OK now?"

"No, she is terrible. Not talking to anyone."

"I understand her," I said softly, the weight of old grief pressing against my chest. "Just tell her not to worry about here at all. Let me know if there is anything I can do. When is the funeral?"

"It was today."

After arranging for flowers and support through HR, learning the ceremony would be held in another town, I headed home. The day's heaviness followed me.

At 7:00 PM, I called Nadia - our daily ritual of me waking her for her shift. Her voice, warm and familiar, filled the line: "Hello darling. How was work?"

"Are you wearing clothes or what? You are so far?" I couldn't help smiling at her distant voice.

"Yes, getting ready," she replied, closer now.

"Now it's better. How are you?"

"I am tired. And you? How is my Darian?" The tenderness in her question wrapped around me like a comfort.

"Not good. Elina's dad passed."

"Oh, I am sorry. How is she now?"

"I don't know. She is shocked and not talking to anyone." My voice caught slightly, remembering my own devastating loss.

"Make sure to go there for condolences," Nadia urged gently. "You are really lazy in such cases and I have to always push you."

"OK. Don't worry. Actually, she reminded me of the day that my father died. I understand her." The memory of that pain, still sharp after all these years, made me empathize with Elina's silence.

"I don't know what to say," Nadia whispered.

"I know. Now just go and focus on patience. I hope there won't be any accident patients for you tonight."

"Me too. Thanks darling. Talk to you soon. Miss you."

"Miss you too."

As I hung up, the parallels between Elina's loss and my own sat heavily in my chest. Not because of any romantic connection, but because grief has a way of bridging distances, of making us recognize our shared humanity. Still, it was Nadia's voice, her gentle concern, that anchored me in the present, reminding me of the love and stability we'd built together.

****

When I was barely a year old, my father moved us to the outskirts of Parin, where the mountains met the sky and a crystal-clear river carved through our land. The property sprawled across 6,000 square meters, bordered by the rushing waters on one side and a winding road on the other. My father, a distinguished chemistry professor at the University of Parin, found his true self not in the sterile confines of laboratories, but in the raw beauty of the wilderness.

I can still feel the weight of that first cartridge he made specially for me when I was seven. His hands, steady and sure, guided mine as he taught me to shoot. "Remember, son," he would say, his voice carrying the quiet authority I grew to cherish, "this isn't about the shot—it's about respect for the land and everything in it." Those words etched themselves into my soul, becoming as much a part of me as my own heartbeat.

Every weekend brought a new adventure—fishing in the early morning mist, tracking game through dense forests, or simply sitting in comfortable silence as he taught me to read the language of the wild. While other children played with toys, I was learning to tie flies, to understand wind patterns, to move through the forest like a ghost. My father wasn't just teaching me skills; he was showing me how to see the world through eyes of wonder and respect.

We were inseparable, my father and I. He wasn't just my parent—he was my mentor, my best friend, my window into a world that felt more real than anything within four walls. His laugh would echo across the river as I struggled with a particularly stubborn fish, his pride evident in the way he'd clasp my shoulder when I finally succeeded.

Then, when I was twenty-two, the unthinkable happened. A heart attack took him from me in an instant, leaving behind a void that seemed to swallow everything else. The river's song turned hollow, the mountains lost their magic, and for years afterward, I found myself unable to form deep connections with others, especially romantic relationships. The world had lost its center, and I was adrift.

But grief has a way of reshaping us. In the depths of my loss, I made a silent promise—to make him proud, to build something meaningful from the ashes of my pain. I threw myself into my studies, channeled my energy into personal development, driven by the ghostly echo of his encouraging voice in my head.

Twenty years passed, and I thought I had made peace with his absence. Then Elina's father died, and suddenly, I was that lost twenty-two-year-old again, watching helplessly as someone else's world crumbled. Her pain mirrored mine in a way that broke through walls I didn't even know I still had, creating a connection I wasn't prepared for—one that would change everything.

****

After hanging up with Nadia, I took a long shower, letting the hot water wash over me as memories of my father flooded back - his laugh, his steady hands teaching me to shoot, the way he'd wake me before dawn for our fishing trips. Twenty years had passed, but grief has a way of making time collapse.

I was settling onto the couch, trying to distract myself with TV, when my phone lit up with a WhatsApp message. Seeing Elina's name, I felt a surge of relief - not personal, but professional concern finally easing.

But as I read her words, something shifted. The raw honesty in her message stripped away our usual professional dynamic, revealing the universal language of loss we both understood too well.

"I know what you feel. I'm happy that you got your energy back to reply," I wrote, my tone softer than our usual exchanges.

"You have no idea, Mr. Alister! My dad was a great person. He was kind. He had helped many people and he was too young to go." Her words carried a pain I recognized intimately.

"I know how you feel. I have been there myself. Mine was even worse. My father was my best friend and I was reminded by this news about that. But this is life." As I typed these words, I felt the old wound in my chest opening slightly.

Our conversation flowed naturally, the shared experience of loss creating a bridge neither of us had expected. When she mentioned wanting to visit the cemetery but having no one to take her, something in me responded to that lonely echo I knew too well.

"I can come and take you there," I offered, remembering my own solitary visits to my father's grave. "I wanted to come anyway. I will come and take you to the cemetery."

"Tomorrow is Sunday and you have your normal plans," she protested gently.

"Don't worry, I will come for a short visit. I wanted to come to your home." The words came easily, born from genuine empathy rather than any deeper attachment.

We talked longer than I expected, our conversation flowing from grief to memories, from pain to small moments of connection. I found myself sharing things about my father I rarely discussed, hoping it might help her feel less alone. Her responses revealed a depth I hadn't noticed before - not romantic interest, but a genuine human connection forming through shared pain.

As she excused herself to return to her guests, I felt strangely protective - not as a man towards a woman, but as someone who understood the overwhelming nature of loss.

"Send me the location and address, I will be there tomorrow 11:30 A.M.," I told her.

"Sure Mr. Alister."

"Good night!"

"Good night."

As I set my phone down, I thought of Nadia, grateful for her steady presence in my life. She had been my anchor through my own grief, and now she was encouraging me to support someone else through theirs. I hadn't realized then that this moment of shared vulnerability would eventually crack open something deeper - something that would challenge everything I thought I knew about love and loyalty.

Sunday Morning

Sunday morning arrived with a heavy stillness. I sat in Titanus, still caked with mud from my last off-road trip, and called Nadia. As always, her voice carried warmth and understanding.

"I'm taking Elina to her father's grave," I explained.

"Of course, you should go," Nadia said softly. "She needs support right now." Her empathy, her immediate concern for others, was one of the countless reasons I loved her. I felt a twinge of guilt for not sharing the full story of my conversations with Elina, something I'd never hidden from Nadia before.

On the Tiraz-Kavignar highway, my mind drifted to my own father's death. The raw wound of loss that, even after twenty years, had never fully healed. Perhaps that's why I felt compelled to help Elina through this - I understood the void she was facing.

When I arrived at her home, she stepped out looking almost unrecognizable - diminished somehow, as if grief had physically altered her. This wasn't my capable assistant anymore; this was someone stripped bare by loss.

"Hi, Mr. Alister. Thank you for coming," she said, her voice thin and fragile.

"Hi, Elina." Words felt inadequate in the face of such sorrow. We shared a silence as heavy as the gathering clouds above us.

The cemetery stretched before us, a vast field where every mound told its own story of loss. The fresh grave - her father's final resting place - stood out against the weathered plots, its earth still dark and unsettled. Like a wound that hadn't begun to heal.

I had visited countless graves before, mostly to photograph the birds that found peace among the stones. But this was different. This was raw, immediate grief - the kind that changes people forever.

Elina stopped at the edge of her father's grave, staring down as if trying to make sense of something senseless. Then, in a moment that would stay with me forever, she sank to her knees. Her body seemed to crumple, all pretense of composure falling away as she lay beside the mound. She pressed her cheek into the damp earth, arms stretching across the grave as if trying to embrace what she had lost.

I stepped back, then further back, crossing to the other side of the cemetery road. This wasn't my moment to witness, yet I couldn't look away. Her fingers dug into the mud, shoulders shaking with silent sobs. The grief pouring from her was primal, unrestricted - the kind I remembered all too well from my own father's death.

Her whispered words carried on the wind, though I couldn't make them out. Private things, meant only for him. She pressed her lips to the soil as if she could somehow reach him, her face etched with a pain so pure it made my chest ache. In that moment, I saw myself at twenty-two, facing my own father's grave, feeling that same desperate need to hold onto something already gone.

She stayed there, her body pressed against the fresh earth, whispering words that seemed to come from somewhere deep inside her. I watched as her fingers dug into the soil, desperately clinging to what remained of her connection to her father. Her knuckles turned white with effort, as if she could somehow reach through the ground and touch him one last time.

"Papa," she whispered, her voice carrying on the wind, "I'm sorry. I'm so sorry." Her words dissolved into quiet sobs as she pressed her lips to the earth, leaving traces of lipstick on the soil. Each whispered word seemed to carry years of unspoken feelings, of moments that would never come again.

The pain etched across her face was unlike anything I'd ever witnessed—raw, primal, unreserved. This wasn't the composed professional I knew from work. This was a daughter stripped bare by grief, a child saying goodbye to her father far too soon. Something in my chest tightened as I watched her, remembering my own father's death, understanding the desperate need to hold onto something—anything—that remained.

Her fingers traced patterns in the dirt, perhaps writing messages he would never read, or maybe just trying to memorize the feel of the earth that now held him. Every movement seemed to carry the weight of finality, of understanding that this moment would never come again.

Just when her sobs had quieted to gentle hiccups, a woman approached—another mourner, her high heels sinking slightly into the damp ground. She looked down at Elina with that particular expression people wear when they think they know better about how grief should look.

"Dear," the woman said, reaching down to touch Elina's shoulder, "you shouldn't be lying there." Her voice dripped with condescension masked as concern.

Elina's body tensed under the stranger's touch. She lifted her head slowly, her face a map of mud and tears, mascara running in dark rivers down her cheeks. Her eyes, when they met the woman's, held such depths of pain that the stranger took an involuntary step back.

Something protective stirred in me then—something I hadn't expected to feel. I moved forward, crossing the distance between us in long strides. The stranger retreated as I approached, perhaps sensing she had intruded on something sacred.

When I reached Elina's side, she looked up at me, and in that moment, something shifted between us. Her eyes, though swollen from crying, held a vulnerability I'd never seen before— a trust that made my heart ache in a way I wasn't prepared for.

She reached for my hand, and I helped her up, supporting her weight as her legs trembled beneath her.

"Thank you," she whispered, her voice hoarse from crying. Her fingers gripped my arm, leaving muddy prints on my sleeve, but I didn't care. "Thank you for being here."

Standing there, with her tear-stained face turned up to mine, I felt the first stirrings of something deeper than sympathy, something that would eventually change everything. But in that moment, I was simply a man supporting a grieving woman, offering what comfort I could in the face of unbearable loss.

I brushed a streak of mud from her cheek with my thumb, a gesture that felt more intimate than I'd intended. "You don't need to thank me," I said softly, my voice catching slightly. "I understand."

And I did understand—more than I wanted to admit. In her grief, I saw echoes of my own, and something in me began to shift, like tectonic plates moving imperceptibly beneath the earth's surface. Though I didn't realize it then, this was the moment everything began to change.

I'll help edit this section to emphasize that Darian maintains professional boundaries and only begins developing feelings after seeing Elina's profound grief over her father's death. Here's my suggested revision:

The drive back was silent, heavy with the weight of shared grief. As I glanced at Elina, I saw my own loss reflected in her tears— the memory of losing my father still sharp after all these years.

She stared out the window, lost in her thoughts, hands clasped tightly in her lap as though trying to hold herself together.

When we reached her home, she hesitated, then turned to me, her voice barely above a whisper. "Mr. Alister... would you... would you come in for just a cup of tea?"

The vulnerability in her voice caught me off guard. In that moment, I saw not my assistant or even a friend, but simply a daughter who had lost her father—someone who needed not to be alone with her grief. Her eyes held a quiet desperation that stirred something deep within me, memories of my own sleepless nights after my father's passing flooding back.

But I knew maintaining boundaries was crucial, especially now when we were both emotionally raw. "Thank you, Elina," I replied gently, choosing my words with care, "but I think you should get some rest. You've been through a lot today. I just wanted to make sure you got home safely."

She nodded slowly, forcing a small smile that didn't reach her eyes. "You're probably right," she said, her voice wavering. "Thank you again, for everything. It... it really meant a lot."

There was a pause as she looked down, her hands twisting together. The light from her house cast a warm glow behind her, contrasting sharply with the shadows of grief that seemed to envelop her. Something shifted in my chest—an unexpected ache, a recognition of shared pain that transcended our professional relationship.

"Take care of yourself, Elina," I said softly. "And remember, if you need anything, I'm just a call away."

She looked up at me one last time, her eyes glistening. "Goodnight, Mr. Alister."

As I watched her walk away, shoulders heavy with the burden of loss, I felt an unfamiliar pull—not of attraction or desire, but of profound empathy. The image of her lying on her father's grave stayed with me, stirring memories of my own grief, creating an unexpected bridge between us that would slowly, inexorably, change everything.

That night, driving home to Nadia, I couldn't shake the feeling that something fundamental had shifted—not in my marriage or my feelings, but in my understanding of Elina. I had seen past the professional facade to the raw humanity beneath, and in her grief, I recognized echoes of my own heart.

Two Days Later

Our team planned to visit Elina's house to pay their respects, and they asked me to join them. I declined, citing an important meeting as the reason, though the truth was more complex. Having already seen her in such a raw, vulnerable state at the cemetery, I felt a need to maintain professional boundaries. Something about that day had shifted something in me - seeing her grief had awakened an empathy I hadn't expected to feel.

In the days that followed, I found myself thinking about her more often than I should. Our conversations, initially meant to offer support during her mourning, began to take on a different quality. When Nadia was away, our late-night text exchanges grew longer, more personal. I told myself I was just being a supportive boss, a friend helping someone through their grief. But there were moments when the line between professional concern and personal connection began to blur.

Elina returned to work after a while, carrying herself with a quiet strength that caught me off guard. I watched her settle back into her routine, noticing small changes in her - a newfound depth in her eyes, a maturity that grief often brings. During this time, I found myself going out of my way to help her, perhaps more than was necessary for a boss or even a friend.

Our conversations deepened, especially during those night-time exchanges. She began to open up about her family dynamics, her complicated relationship with her brothers, and most significantly, her father. The way she spoke about him revealed layers of complexity I hadn't seen before - sometimes with love so pure it made her voice tremble, other times with a pain so deep it seemed to echo through her words. She would share stories of his kindness, then in the next breath, reveal wounds that still hadn't healed. I found myself wanting to help her find peace with these contradictions, to help her forgive not just her father, but perhaps herself as well.

When Nadia was home, I maintained appropriate boundaries, keeping our interactions professional and brief. I didn't hide these conversations from Nadia - there was nothing to hide, I told myself. We were just colleagues, friends perhaps, nothing more.

But sometimes, in quiet moments, I caught myself wondering why I felt the need to justify these interactions at all.

A small voice in the back of my mind warned me that something was shifting. Our conversations had grown more frequent, more intimate than they should be. I tried to rationalize it - she was grieving, she needed support, I was just being kind. But deep down, I knew that the comfort I found in our talks, the way I looked forward to her messages, suggested something more complicated was beginning to take root.

Yet I pushed these thoughts aside, focusing instead on my solid marriage with Nadia, our years of love and trust. Still, I couldn't shake the nagging worry that these innocent exchanges were slowly leading somewhere I hadn't intended to go.

More Work Engagement

After Elina's father passed away, I found myself drawn to support her through her grief. Having lost my own father at a young age, I recognized the deep pain she carried. At first, it was purely empathy - a desire to help someone experiencing a loss I understood all too well. I began engaging her in more tasks, not just as my assistant, but as someone I wanted to see grow and heal through meaningful work.

She was always the first one to arrive at the office, her dedication unwavering even through her grief. I started coming in earlier too, telling myself it was to prepare for the day, but perhaps subconsciously seeking those quiet morning moments when the office belonged to just us. The cultural gap between us was apparent - she came from a corporate background, all structure and formality, while our startup world thrived on controlled chaos and innovation. I found her adjustment challenging yet endearing.

I began setting aside time for special training sessions, drawing diagrams on my desk as I explained business models, startup dynamics, and fundraising strategies. While I regularly mentored others, with Elina, these sessions felt different. I caught myself spending extra time ensuring she understood every concept, watching her eyes light up with comprehension. Her grief had awakened something protective in me, though I wasn't ready to acknowledge it was becoming more than just mentorship.

One day, I decided to share something I hadn't told anyone else - my plans for Virelio, a new venture I'd been quietly building. The company was more than just a business idea; it represented my dreams of expanding to Europe.

"You know, Elina," I said carefully, "remember when I mentioned having long-term plans?"

She looked up from her notes, a hint of curiosity crossing her face. "Yes, I recall. I've been too shy to ask about it, but I'm curious."

As I described the platform - an AI-driven marketplace - I watched her expression. She absorbed every word with an intensity that made me slightly uncomfortable, though I couldn't say why.

"Good," she said with a light laugh that didn't quite mask her genuine interest. "Maybe I could get some shares and help with the project?" Though she played it off as a joke, I caught the hopeful undertone in her voice.

"We can discuss that sometime after finishing our work here," she added quickly.

"I would be glad to," she replied, her eyes brightening in a way that made me glance away.

Later that week, we met at a coffee shop outside the office. I offered her compensation for helping with documentation - no shares yet. True to her nature, she agonized over the decision, taking time to think and consult before accepting. We began with a monthly payment arrangement.

The new venture meant longer hours together, our days stretching from early morning until midnight. During investor meetings, I began noticing things that should have warned me about the shifting dynamic between us. She would watch me intently as I spoke, her gaze never wavering even when I fell silent. At first, I dismissed it as professional attention, but deep down, I knew something was changing. I chose not to acknowledge it, perhaps because I wasn't ready to face what it might mean for my marriage with Nadia, whom I still deeply loved.

The lines between professional mentorship and personal connection were beginning to blur, though I wasn't yet willing to admit it to myself.

Mid-November

I was planning a trip to Ravenia with Nadia and my beloved Titanus - an ambitious journey of over 2000 kilometers through snow-covered mountains. These trips had always been our thing. For years, Nadia and I had explored the wilderness together, finding pieces of ourselves in every mile we covered. She wasn't just my wife; she was my adventure partner, the one who understood my need to chase horizons.

Lately though, work had been consuming me. The new business venture meant longer hours, fewer moments together. But Nadia, with her quiet strength, never complained. She simply adjusted, supported, waited. When I finally told her about the Ravenia trip, her eyes lit up with that familiar excitement I'd fallen in love with years ago.

"Just like old times," she said, already pulling out maps, planning our route with the meticulous care I'd come to rely on. Her enthusiasm was contagious, reminding me of countless adventures we'd shared. Nobody understood the rhythm of these journeys like Nadia - she knew when to talk, when to sit in comfortable silence, when to hand me coffee without being asked.

The route I'd chosen was treacherous - narrow mountain passes notorious for their winter dangers. But Nadia and I had faced worse together. We'd built our relationship on trust, on knowing that whatever challenge lay ahead, we'd face it side by side.

When I informed Elina about my upcoming absence, asking her to handle the office logistics, something shifted in her expression.

Since her father's death, I'd noticed a new vulnerability in her, a fear of loss that seemed to haunt her.

"You shouldn't go, Mr. Alister!" The worry in her voice was raw, unfiltered.

"Don't worry, I'll be fine," I assured her, trying to keep things professional.

"No! Please!" Her voice cracked slightly. "I'll arrange meetings so you can't go!" She attempted to mask her anxiety with humor, but I could see the genuine fear beneath.

"Why are you so worried, Elina?" I asked, surprised by the intensity of her reaction.

"I..." she hesitated, fingers twisting together nervously. "I lost my dad, I lost my previous boss... and I don't want to lose you." The words tumbled out, heavy with meaning I wasn't ready to acknowledge.

"I'm unbeatable," I said softly, trying to lighten the moment. "I'm always careful."

Something in her eyes made me pause - a depth of emotion that went beyond professional concern. It stirred something unexpected in me, a feeling I quickly pushed aside. I had a wife waiting at home, planning our next adventure. I had no right to feel anything else.

Some Days Later

I was in the middle of the building, engaged in conversation with a group of startup founders - one of those casual moments that helped build the community feeling at Nexara Labs. Our HR manager approached, her expression professional but warm.

"Mr. Alister, do you have a moment?" she asked.

"Of course," I replied, excusing myself from the group.

"Elina's birthday is on the December 1st, and as usual, we're planning a small celebration," she explained. "Given recent events with her father's passing, I wanted to check if you'd like us to do anything special, since she's your PA."

I considered this carefully. Elina's grief was still fresh, and I'd seen how it had affected her work ethic and determination. Since her father's death, I'd found myself paying more attention to her wellbeing, feeling a growing sense of responsibility for her healing process. Still, I wanted to maintain professional boundaries.

"No," I replied after a moment. "Let's keep it consistent with how we celebrate everyone else."

The next day, I was at the prestigious city mall with Nadia, our fingers intertwined as we window-shopped. My mind drifted to Elina's recent gift to me - "The Archer," a thoughtful choice that showed she paid attention to details. Since her father's death, our conversations had deepened beyond work. She'd confided in me about her struggles, like when her brother tried to fill their father's shoes, attempting to control her movements. I'd shared these conversations with Nadia, who understood my role as both boss and mentor.

"I should get something for Elina's birthday," I mentioned to Nadia, feeling slightly uncertain. "She's been through a lot lately."

Nadia squeezed my hand supportively. "We can find something here."

"Any suggestions?"

"Maybe perfume?" Nadia offered. "That's usually safe for ladies."

"No," I said quickly, too aware of how personal that might seem. "What about a fountain pen? She's always admired my handwriting and collection."

Nadia's eyes crinkled with amusement. "I knew it! You just wanted an excuse to visit your favorite store."

"Guilty," I laughed, pulling her close. "Maybe we'll find something for you too." Her smile, warm and genuine, reminded me why I'd fallen in love with her in the first place.

In the store, Nadia helped me select a pen for Elina. When she pointed out an expensive, ornate model, I hesitated. It felt too intimate, too significant. Instead, we chose something professional yet thoughtful - along with two more pens for ourselves, making it feel more like a shared experience than a personal gift.

On December 1st, during the office celebration, I gave Elina the pen. "Please keep this between us," I said quietly. "I don't usually give personal gifts to employees."

But her excitement was impossible to contain, and soon everyone knew. Looking at her joy, I felt a subtle shift in my chest.

"You're terrible at keeping secrets," I teased, trying to lighten the moment. Her laughter echoed through the office, and for a second, I forgot about professional boundaries and proper distances. For just that moment, I saw her not as my PA or a grieving daughter, but as Elina - complex, resilient, and somehow beginning to matter more than I'd intended.

Early December

I was preparing for a trip to Ravenia with Nadia, my partner of over a decade. The journey would take us northwest for 12 days, through mountain passes and snow-laden villages. It was a chance to reconnect, to remember why we had chosen each other all those years ago. Before leaving, Elina, my assistant, expressed concerns about the dangerous winter routes, but I assured her it was nothing Titanus and I couldn't handle.

We started our journey at 10:00 PM, just after a board meeting. Nadia sat beside me, her presence as comforting as always. The way she navigated for us, anticipated my needs, and shared comfortable silences – it was all so familiar, so right. We crossed the border at midnight, heavy snow forcing us to stop at the first village we found. In our small hotel room, Nadia and I talked late into the night, sharing stories and dreams like we used to.

The next morning brought crystal-clear skies and breathtaking views. Each mountain pass revealed another stunning vista, and I watched Nadia's face light up at every turn. We celebrated her birthday in a tiny mountain village, the snow falling softly outside our window. It felt like the early days of our relationship, when every moment together was an adventure.

Throughout the trip, I received occasional messages from Elina – mostly professional updates about the office. But one message stood out: a photo of my empty office chair with the caption, "Everyone is missing you so much, Mr. Alister." Something in those words gave me pause. Since her father's death, I'd noticed her growing attachment to me, and it worried me. She was vulnerable, seeking connection in her grief, and I needed to maintain clear boundaries.

The final night of our journey brought treacherous conditions – deep snow and thick fog that tested even my experience. Nadia remained calm beside me, trusting me completely as she always had. When we couldn't find an open hotel, we spent the night in Titanus, huddled together in the back where I'd built a makeshift bed. Despite the circumstances, there was something perfect about it – just us, safe in our own world.

Returning to the office, Elina greeted me with unexpected enthusiasm. She jumped up from her desk, her eyes bright with more than just professional welcome.

"Hello, Mr. Alister! Welcome back!"

"Hi, Elina. Nice to see you with such energy," I replied, keeping my tone neutral.

"How was the trip?" she asked, something almost hungry in her gaze.

"It was amazing! A few challenges, but absolutely worth it," I said, thinking of the precious time with Nadia.

"This place isn't the same when you're not here," she said softly, her words carrying weight I wasn't ready to acknowledge.

"Thank you. That's very kind of you," I replied, deliberately professional.

I saw something in her eyes then – a depth of feeling that unnerved me. I quickly looked away, busying myself with work. The trip had reminded me of everything I had with Nadia, everything I'd built. I couldn't let anything threaten that, not even the growing pull I felt toward Elina's vulnerability and warmth.

But something had shifted during those days away. Whether I wanted to admit it or not, Elina's presence in my life was becoming harder to ignore, and the careful distance I'd maintained was beginning to crumble.

As she left my office, I found myself watching her go, wondering when exactly her presence had begun to feel less like that of an assistant and more like something I couldn't—or shouldn't—name.

FOUR

UNSPOKEN TRUTHS

January arrived with a relentless pile of work, casting long shadows across our days at the office. Elina remained dedicated in her role, present at every meeting, managing logistics with precision, and coordinating details that kept our venture moving forward. Her calm efficiency had earned her the position of co-founder, a 10% stakeholder in our growing enterprise. But something had shifted between us since her father's passing - a subtle change in the air that I couldn't quite name.

I found myself watching her more closely now, noticing things I hadn't before. The way her hands moved decisively across her notebook during meetings, the quiet strength in her voice when she spoke to clients, the flicker of vulnerability that sometimes crossed her face when she thought no one was looking. Her grief had carved a space between us where understanding could grow, and I recognized in her pain echoes of my own loss years ago.

Our days fell into a rhythm of strategy sessions and planning meetings. The conversations that had once been strictly professional began to carry undertones of something deeper. We'd find ourselves lingering, sharing thoughts over Discord or exchanging messages on WhatsApp during the nights Nadia was away. At first, I told myself it was just work, just the natural flow of two people building something together. But gradually, those exchanges drifted into personal territory - small confessions, quiet observations, moments of shared understanding that felt increasingly dangerous.

I thought often of Nadia during these times, of our years together, of the life we'd built. The guilt would creep in during quiet moments, reminding me of promises made and a love that had sustained me for so long. Yet there was an undeniable pull toward Elina now, a connection forged in shared grief that was slowly transforming into something else entirely. The ease of her presence, the natural rhythm we'd fallen into - it all hovered on the edge of something neither of us dared to name, but both could feel shifting beneath the surface.

That Night

It was late when the WhatsApp notification lit up my screen. Elina's message caught me off guard: "Mr. Alister, I am single and lonely."

The confession felt oddly personal, crossing the professional boundary we'd maintained. As her mentor and boss, I felt obligated to offer some comfort, but wanted to keep appropriate distance.

"Don't worry. You'll find someone soon," I replied neutrally. "You're young, driven, and talented—anyone would be lucky to have you."

"Doesn't feel like it. Seems like no one wants to be with me," she responded, vulnerability seeping through her words.

I should have left it there, maintained that professional line. Instead, I made what I thought was a harmless joke: "If I weren't married, I'd date you myself." The moment I sent it, I regretted it—it was exactly the kind of comment that could be misinterpreted.

She sent back a smiley face, then a playful sticker of a mustachioed character offering a rose. Grateful for the light turn, I played along: "Maybe Mr. Mustache will propose to you one day."

The next day at work, I mentioned Mr. Mustache once or twice, keeping things professional but friendly. That evening, though, she messaged again.

"Mr. Alister! How's it going?"

"Fine," I replied, my thoughts on Nadia, who was away at work. "Been home alone all day. Went to the archery club and practiced for five hours. I'm exhausted."

"That's amazing," she wrote back. "I love everything about your lifestyle—the archery, nature trips, camping, even your handwriting. You have this way of doing everything perfectly."

Her admiration made me uncomfortable. "Thank you, but I think you might be exaggerating."

"Not at all. You're a real hero. In meetings, you're practically a superhero."

I shifted in my chair, increasingly aware of the direction this conversation was taking. "It's just years of experience, mistakes, and plenty of books," I deflected. "You'll be even better when you're my age."

She changed topics abruptly: "Today was rough. I got some work done this morning, but by evening, I just felt down. I'm drinking a glass of wine that my ex left here months ago."

"Wine's nice, but I try not to drink too often," I replied, hoping to keep things casual.

"I don't either. Tonight was just one of those nights." There was a pause before she added, "Mr. Alister?"

"Yes?"

"They say people are most honest when they're drunk."

My finger hovered over the phone. I should end the conversation now, I thought. But I didn't. "Yes, I've heard that."

"Then let me be honest," she typed. Another pause. "I love you so much. I would do anything for you. And I mean anything."

The words hit me like a physical blow. Before I could respond, another message appeared: "I want my future 'Mr. Mustache' to be just like you. Exactly like you. I mean, exactly, exactly like you."

I stared at the screen, my thoughts racing to Nadia. Ten years of love, adventure, and trust. I couldn't—wouldn't—jeopardize that.

"Everyone's unique," I wrote back carefully. "No one's going to be exactly like me."

"I know," she responded. "But that doesn't change what I feel."

We kept talking until nearly 3 a.m., but I maintained my distance, kept my responses measured and professional. Still, as I lay in bed afterward, I couldn't sleep. Not because I felt the same way—I didn't, I told myself firmly—but because I knew something had shifted. A line had been crossed, and I wasn't sure how to uncross it.

I thought of Nadia, probably just finishing her night shift at the hospital. I should tell her about this, I thought. But I didn't. I told myself it was nothing, that I could handle it professionally. That Elina's feelings would pass.

I was wrong.

The Next Day

"Sorry, Mr. Alister, I fell asleep during our talk," her message read the next morning.

"No worries," I replied, maintaining the professional tone that had defined our relationship. Her words from the night before lingered uncomfortably in my mind—not because I reciprocated her feelings, but because they complicated the careful boundaries I'd always maintained at work.

On Monday, we returned to the office as if nothing had happened. I threw myself into meetings and deadlines, grateful for the distraction of work. But beneath the surface, I knew we needed clarity—not for any personal reason, but for the sake of our professional relationship and the company's wellbeing. That evening, I suggested we meet somewhere outside the office, neutral ground where we could address what had been said.

We drove separately to a quiet spot halfway to her home, by a lake I often visited when I needed to think. The cold air pressed against my skin as I got out and joined her in the passenger seat of her car. For a moment, we sat in silence, the weight of unspoken words filling the space between us.

"We need to talk about that night," I began, careful to keep my voice steady and professional.

Elina looked down, her face flushing. "I'm embarrassed," she said softly. "Not just because of what I said, but because you're married. I never meant to put you in this position." She paused, twisting her hands in her lap. "But even though I'm ashamed of saying it... it was true."

Something in her vulnerability stirred an unexpected protective instinct in me—the same feeling I often had when mentoring younger employees through difficult times. Without thinking, I reached out to pat her hand reassuringly, a gesture I immediately recognized as perhaps too familiar.

She let out a gentle sigh, and looking at me with an openness I hadn't seen before, said, "Mr. Alister's hand is always warm."

The simple observation created an intimacy I hadn't anticipated. Her gaze held more than just admiration—there was a raw honesty that made me uncomfortable yet somehow unable to look away. Her fingers tightened around mine briefly, and in that moment, I felt the first hairline crack in my professional facade.

We sat there, my hand still covering hers, neither of us speaking. I told myself this was just comfort offered to a valued employee, just as I would support any member of my team going through a difficult time. But somewhere deep inside, I recognized this as a moment that would alter the careful boundaries I'd maintained for years.

As we sat in silence, my thoughts drifted to Nadia—her unwavering support, her understanding, the life we'd built together. The guilt of this moment, however innocent it might seem, weighed heavily on me. I gently withdrew my hand, creating the distance that propriety demanded.

Yet something had shifted, subtle but undeniable. The careful walls of professionalism had developed a tiny fissure, one that would, in time, grow into something neither of us could have anticipated.

Two Days Later

The need to discuss Virelio, our new startup, brought us together again. We needed privacy, somewhere away from curious eyes. A coffee shop was out of the question; as a known figure in the business community,

I couldn't risk being seen alone with a woman who wasn't my wife. The speculation would be inevitable and damaging—not just to me, but to Nadia.

When Elina mentioned that Nadia was away and suggested meeting at my home, my first instinct was to refuse. It crossed a line I'd never breached before, inviting another woman into the space Nadia and I shared. But the practicality of the suggestion and the importance of our work eventually won out over my misgivings. Still, as she parked her car nearby and slipped into mine for the drive through the parking structure, I felt a gnawing discomfort.

Entering the passcode to our home felt like a betrayal of sorts. Each number I pressed seemed to echo with the weight of what I was doing. As we stepped inside, I was acutely aware of Nadia's presence in every corner—her books on the shelf, her favorite throw draped over the couch, the subtle scent of her preferred candles lingering in the air.

Elina moved through the space, her eyes taking in every detail with obvious curiosity. "This is exactly what I imagined your home would look like. Very 'Mr. Alister,'" she observed.

Near the entrance, by the kitchen, stood the custom-built bar I had designed, framed by photos from my wildlife excursions. A large shed antler mount adorned the living room wall, engraved with leaves and set above photos of Nadia and me. I watched as Elina's gaze lingered on those photos, something flickering across her face before she quickly looked away.

"Did you hunt that deer yourself?" she asked, clearly trying to move past the moment.

"No," I replied, grateful for the shift in focus. "I buy shed antlers from villagers. It gives them a way to make money without poaching. I also donate to red deer conservation efforts."

She nodded, but I noticed how she avoided looking at the photos of Nadia and me again. The guilt I'd been suppressing surged back. This was our home—mine and Nadia's—and despite the innocence of this meeting, something felt wrong about having Elina here.

I led her to my home-office quickly, hoping to keep things strictly professional. The space was even more reflective of my personal tastes, with its red deer antler chandelier and wall of books. She seemed to take it all in, nodding with a soft smile.

"Now this," she said, "this is definitely Mr. Alister's space."

"Yeah, I spend a lot of time here," I replied, trying to maintain a casual tone while steering us back to business.

But as we settled in the living room to go over our work, I couldn't shake the feeling that something had shifted. The professional distance I'd maintained was beginning to blur, despite my best efforts to keep it intact.

"Coffee, tea, or something cold?" I offered, falling back on the safety of hospitality.

"Coffee would be great—and a glass of water," she replied.

I led her to the bar where my coffee setup was displayed, grateful for the distraction of brewing. "Chemex, cappuccino, espresso, Americano, or latte?"

She laughed, surveying the equipment. "This is practically a café. I'll take 'water-coffee,'" she said, using our joke for an Americano. The familiar banter made me smile despite myself, and as I prepared our drinks, I felt some of the tension ease.

But it was temporary. As we sat reviewing our plans for Virelio, I couldn't ignore the growing weight in the air between us. Even the music I queued up—a playlist from a recent trip—seemed to highlight rather than dispel the tension.

When she returned from the bathroom, she sat closer to me on the couch than she had before. The space between us felt charged with something I wasn't ready to acknowledge. Outside, the sky had darkened, and a quiet settled around us that felt dangerous in its comfort.

The music filled the room, wrapping around the silence between us. Slowly, I reached out, taking her hand in mine, feeling the warmth of her fingers as they intertwined with mine. We looked at each other, eyes meeting, the unspoken growing with each passing second. For a brief moment, we leaned closer, our breaths mingling, but then stopped, the weight of everything catching up with us.

"This is wrong," she whispered, her voice a mix of longing and restraint.

"I know," I replied, sighing, as I looked into her eyes. The words hung between us, their meaning undeniable.

The next track began, "In This Moment We're Infinite" by Clara Hale, one of my favorite songs. The melody seemed to understand, the lyrics adding depth to the silence.

"In the quiet between heartbeats, Time slows down, the world retreats. It's just us in the stillness here, Holding close what we both hold dear."

The song seemed to pull us closer, the words echoing the tension and tenderness we'd both tried to keep hidden. I leaned in, guiding her gently down onto the couch until she lay beneath me. We hesitated, lingering in that fragile space between decision and regret, the melody carrying us beyond words. And then, finally, our lips met, and it was as if the world around us dissolved.

A warmth bloomed inside me, unfamiliar and overwhelming - a trembling that reached deeper than any sensation I'd known before. Her taste was achingly soft, yet it stirred something primal and urgent within me. The kiss transported me somewhere I'd never been, somewhere that felt both electrifying and terrifying in its intensity. I found myself opening my eyes, needing to witness her face in these stolen moments - her eyes closed, completely surrendered to what was happening between us. The sight of her quiet rapture sent waves of guilt and desire crashing through me. Watching her, seeing the pure vulnerability there, made me feel simultaneously more connected and more lost than I'd ever been.

In that kiss, time didn't just stop - it shattered, leaving us suspended in a moment that felt both eternal and heartbreakingly finite. The music played on somewhere distant, but all I could feel was her, and all I knew was that we had crossed a line that could never be uncrossed, stepped into territory that would forever change everything we thought we knew about love and loyalty.

"This was just fun and meant nothing more," she whispered, but her voice trembled with the weight of the lie. Her eyes told a different story - one of longing, fear, and something deeper that neither of us was ready to name.

"I agree," I replied, the words tasting bitter as they left my mouth. We both knew it was a facade, a desperate attempt to deny what had just passed between us. The truth hung heavy in the air - this wasn't just fun, and it meant everything.

The Next Day

The next morning, I arrived at the office at 7:30, the first rays of dawn barely warming the empty halls. The familiar space felt different somehow, charged with the memory of yesterday's kiss. I chose this early hour deliberately, needing the solitude to wrestle with the storm of emotions threatening to overwhelm me. Each step through the quiet building echoed with questions I wasn't ready to answer.

The usual comfort of my morning routine - the smell of fresh coffee, the gentle hum of computers coming to life - now felt like a façade, a thin veneer of normalcy covering the seismic shift beneath. I found myself touching my lips unconsciously, the ghost of her kiss still lingering there, a constant reminder of how quickly everything could change.

When she arrived, we performed the careful dance of professionalism - polite nods, casual greetings, the exchange of mundane work details. But beneath this choreography of normalcy, electricity crackled in every shared glance. Her smile, when it came, carried worlds of meaning - secret, knowing, slightly shy but tinged with something that made my heart race. I caught myself watching the way she moved, how she tucked her hair behind her ear, the slight tremor in her hands as she arranged papers on her desk. Each small gesture seemed loaded with significance, speaking volumes in our new language of unspoken understanding.

The weight of guilt pressed heavily against my chest - thoughts of Nadia, of promises made and lives intertwined, threatened to suffocate me. Yet I couldn't deny the magnetic pull I felt toward Elina, the way my body seemed to know exactly where she was in the room at all times. We were like two planets caught in each other's gravity, trying desperately to maintain our separate orbits while being inexorably drawn together.

In the harsh fluorescent light of the office, yesterday's kiss felt both impossibly distant and startlingly immediate. Every time our eyes met,

I saw the same question reflected back at me - what happens now? But neither of us had the courage to voice it, to acknowledge the trembling possibility that hung in the air between us.

The rhythm of my days began to revolve around these stolen moments. I found myself arriving earlier and earlier, sometimes before dawn, telling myself it was for the quiet, for productivity. But in truth, it was for those precious minutes when the office belonged only to us. Elina would already be there, her presence as constant as the sunrise, greeting me with that soft smile that seemed to hold secrets only we shared. The scent of fresh coffee and the gentle click of her heels on the marble floor became the soundtrack to my mornings, replacing the familiar comfort of breakfast with Nadia.

Work became my excuse to stay late into the evening, long after others had gone home. I told myself it was dedication to the company, but my heart knew better. These stretched hours were threads in a tapestry of moments with Elina, each one pulling me further from the life I'd built with Nadia. The guilt of these choices sat heavy in my chest, yet I couldn't seem to stop myself from seeking more time, more connection.

Our days developed an intimate choreography. Client meetings and investor visits became opportunities for shared glances and whispered observations. Walking through factory floors, I found myself hyperaware of her presence beside me, the way she'd lean in slightly when speaking, how her hand would occasionally brush against mine. Each touch, however brief, sent electricity through my veins, making the mundane feel magnetic.

The drive home became an extension of our day, a liminal space where professional boundaries blurred into something more dangerous. We'd find quiet parking spots in the city's forgotten corners, where streetlights cast soft shadows and the world beyond our bubble seemed to fade away. Her car became our confession booth, where words flowed easier in the darkness. Our hands would find each other almost unconsciously, fingers intertwining as if they'd always known this dance.

Time behaved differently in these moments - hours compressed into minutes, yet each second seemed to stretch infinitely. We talked about everything and nothing - her dreams, my fears, the complexities of life that seemed simpler when shared. Even our silences felt intimate, loaded with unspoken understanding that made my heart ache with both joy and guilt.

The pattern deepened with each passing day, like water wearing grooves into stone. Morning coffee, shared looks across meeting rooms, evening drives - these moments became the framework around which I built my days. My late returns home to an empty apartment (when Nadia was away) or quick excuses about work demands (when she was there) became more frequent. The weight of these deceptions pressed against my conscience, yet the pull toward Elina grew stronger, like a tide I couldn't resist.

Each day added another layer to our connection, building something that felt both profound and precarious. The early mornings and late nights became more than just time - they were spaces where we could be ourselves, where the complications of our situation could be momentarily forgotten in the simple act of being together. Yet beneath every shared smile, every gentle touch, lurked the knowledge that we were writing a story that could shatter multiple lives - including our own.

Mid January

The fluorescent lights of the airport terminal cast harsh shadows as I waited for Nadia. For the first time in our decade together, I felt a strange heaviness in my chest. Something had shifted during her absence - not in my love for her, which remained as steady as ever, but in the careful boundaries I'd always maintained in my life. The memory of my recent conversations with Elina weighed on me, carrying a complexity I hadn't anticipated.

"Have you ever had an affair before?" Elina had asked one evening, her voice carrying a vulnerability that made my chest tighten. The question had caught me off guard - not just because of its directness, but because until recently, I would have dismissed the very possibility without a second thought.

"No, never," I'd replied truthfully, my voice steadier than my thoughts. My marriage to Nadia had always been my anchor, our love built on years of shared adventures and unwavering trust.

Elina's response had come softly, laden with emotion that seemed to fill the space between us. "I really don't want to be your first cheat. But these feelings... they're so strong. Being with you, talking to you - it helps me feel less lost. I know it's wrong, but I can't seem to stop."

Her honesty had stirred something unexpected in me - a connection I hadn't been looking for but couldn't seem to ignore. The way she looked at me carried a weight of emotion that both drew me in and filled me with guilt.

Now, watching Nadia emerge from the crowd, I felt the full weight of these complicated emotions. My wife's smile still warmed me to my core, her presence as familiar and necessary as breathing. I helped her with her bags, trying to focus on the present moment rather than the confusing tangle of feelings I'd developed during her absence.

In the car, seeking to bridge any distance that might have grown between us, I mentioned something I knew would bring us back to familiar ground. "Nurak, the bird, is back again," I said, thinking of the rare crane that had become a symbol of our shared appreciation for life's precious moments. "Do you want to go see it?"

"You know my answer, darling," she replied with that smile that had first captured my heart years ago. Her immediate enthusiasm reminded me of why we worked so well together - how she understood and celebrated the things that mattered to me.

As we made plans to see Nurak with friends, I found myself studying Nadia's profile in the dim car light. The bird's annual return had always represented hope to me - survival against impossible odds. Now it seemed to carry new meaning, as if nature itself was offering commentary on the delicate balance of relationships, on how easily something rare and precious could be lost through carelessness.

The familiar drive home felt different somehow, weighted with unspoken thoughts. I loved Nadia - that hadn't changed. But something else had taken root in my heart, something that had started as simple connection but was slowly transforming into feelings I wasn't ready to name. The guilt of these emerging emotions sat heavy in my chest, even as I tried to convince myself they meant nothing.

We left in the early evening, snow dusting the roads as we drove through the mountains. The familiar comfort of these trips - the way Nadia would lean into the curves, how she'd instinctively reach to adjust the heat before I needed to ask - felt somehow different tonight. There was a heaviness in my chest I couldn't explain, thoughts pulling me away from the present moment even as Nadia remained steadfastly by my side.

She leaned over at one point, her eyes bright with that childlike excitement I'd always loved. "Can we stop for soup? You know, from that little roadside place?" Her voice carried the warmth of countless shared memories - all the times we'd pulled over at similar spots, sharing simple meals that somehow tasted better because we were together.

I hesitated, something unfamiliar and cold settling in my chest. The thought of stopping, of delaying our journey for something so trivial, irritated me in a way it never had before. But Nadia's hopeful expression - the same one that had made me fall in love with her all those years ago - won out. We pulled over, and despite my barely concealed impatience, she ordered her soup with familiar delight.

As we resumed our drive, I noticed the change in her first - the way her face paled, how she shifted uncomfortably in her seat. She pressed a hand to her stomach, trying to hide her discomfort, but I knew her too well not to notice.

"Are you alright?" The words came out sharp, brittle, nothing like the concern I should have felt for my wife's wellbeing.

"I think it was the soup," she whispered, pain evident in her voice. She leaned back, trying to find a comfortable position, still attempting to protect me from her discomfort as she always did.

Something inside me snapped - not the gentle concern of a husband, but a cold anger that surprised even me. "You just had to have that soup, didn't you?" The words felt foreign in my mouth, cruel in a way I'd never been with her before. "I warned you, Nadia. Now you're sick, and we have to get up early tomorrow. You're ruining everything just because you wanted a bowl of soup. You just eat and eat without thinking of the consequences!"

The moment the words left my mouth, I saw something break in her eyes - not just hurt, but confusion, as if she was seeing a stranger wearing her husband's face. Tears welled up, catching the dim light of the dashboard, and she turned away, pulling her coat closer like armor against my unexpected cruelty.

"Darian," she said softly, her voice carrying years of shared love and trust, now wavering with uncertainty, "is this really you?"

The question hung in the air between us, heavy with implication. This wasn't about the soup - we both knew that. Something had changed, was changing, and neither of us knew how to name it. She silently took a pill for her stomach and lay down, turning her back to me. The physical distance between us seemed to mirror something deeper, a chasm opening that I wasn't ready to acknowledge.

I drove through the darkness, the familiar hum of Titanus's engine unable to drown out the echo of my harsh words. Each glance at Nadia's turned back was a reminder of how far I'd strayed from the man she'd married - the man who would have held her hand through her discomfort, who would have been concerned rather than angry. The guilt settled heavy in my chest, but beneath it lurked something else - a restlessness I couldn't explain, thoughts that kept drifting back to the office, to conversations I shouldn't be having, to a connection I shouldn't be feeling.

Sleep eluded me that night, my mind replaying the hurt in Nadia's eyes. Ten years of marriage, of adventures, of complete trust - and for the first time, I'd made her question who I was. The realization kept me awake until dawn, staring at the ceiling, wondering when I'd started becoming someone I didn't recognize.

The Next Day

Dawn crept through our hotel window, painting shadows across Nadia's sleeping face. I watched her for a moment, my heart heavy with a familiar love that now carried an unfamiliar weight. When I kissed her forehead, whispering an apology, her eyes fluttered open with that same unconditional acceptance I'd always known. She didn't speak, just nodded - a gesture that spoke volumes about the years we'd built together, about her endless capacity to understand. That quiet forgiveness cut deeper than any anger could have.

As we prepared for our day searching for the Nurak, I noticed how carefully she moved around me, as if afraid to disturb the fragile peace between us. The morning light caught her wedding ring as she packed her camera, and for a moment, I was transported back to the day I'd slipped it onto her finger, full of certainty and dreams. Now, those same dreams felt like they were shifting beneath my feet, transforming into something I couldn't quite recognize.

The wilderness around us was stunning - the kind of raw beauty that had always brought us closer together. But today, even as we walked familiar paths, something had changed. There was a new distance between us, invisible but palpable, like a shadow I couldn't quite shake. I watched her photograph a distant bird, her movements precise and passionate as always, and felt a deep ache in my chest. This was the woman who had built her life around my dreams, who had never asked for more than I could give. Until now.

When we stopped for lunch, sitting on sun-warmed rocks overlooking the valley, she turned to me with that gentle smile I'd fallen in love with years ago. "Remember our first trip here?" she asked, her voice soft with memory. "We got so lost, but you made it feel like an adventure."

I nodded, throat tight with emotion. Every shared memory now felt precious and precarious, weighted with the knowledge of what was growing in my heart - unbidden, unwanted, but undeniable.

Later, back in the village, I found myself reaching for my phone, composing a message to Elina about our day. It was innocent enough - just updates about the trip, the birds we'd seen, the challenges we'd faced. But as minutes ticked by without her response, I felt an unfamiliar anxiety building in my chest. Each glance at my phone, each moment of silence, brought with it a revelation I'd been trying to deny.

Sitting there in the growing darkness, Nadia's steady breathing beside me as she dozed, I finally faced the truth I'd been running from: I was in love with Elina. Not just attracted, not just drawn to her vulnerability or her grief. It was deeper than that - a connection that had grown slowly, imperceptibly, until it could no longer be ignored. The realization didn't come with excitement or joy, but with a profound sense of loss - for the simple certainty I'd once had, for the uncomplicated love I shared with Nadia, for the man I'd thought I was.

I looked at Nadia's sleeping form, this woman who had been my north star for so long, and felt tears prick at my eyes. She deserved better than this divided heart, better than a husband who found himself falling for another woman. Yet here I was, caught between the life I'd built and feelings I couldn't control, watching everything I thought I knew about love and loyalty shift like sand beneath my feet.

The worst part wasn't the guilt, though that was crushing. It was the realization that I couldn't undo this, couldn't un-know what I now knew about my own heart. As I sat there in the darkness, my phone silent and accusing in my hand, I understood that I had crossed a line within myself - one that would change everything, whether I wanted it to or not.

FIVE

SILENT CROSSROADS

As January faded into February, I found myself caught in an undertow of emotions I hadn't seen coming. What had begun as pure empathy for Elina's grief - a connection forged through our shared experience of losing fathers - had slowly transformed into something more complex, more dangerous. The change had been so gradual that I barely noticed it happening, like watching shadows lengthen across a afternoon.

Each morning, I arrived at the office earlier than before, telling myself it was just to get more work done. But I knew, in some quiet corner of my mind, that I was really seeking those moments when the office belonged to just Elina and me. The silence before others arrived felt charged now, heavy with things we weren't saying.

When I drove Nadia to the airport that February morning, the familiar goodbye ritual felt different. Instead of the usual ache of temporary separation, I felt an unsettling flutter of anticipation. The guilt hit immediately - how could I feel anything but sadness at watching my wife leave? This was Nadia, my partner of ten years, the woman who had stood beside me through everything. Yet here I was, already thinking about the unstructured hours ahead, the time that would now be filled with Elina's presence.

Our days began stretching longer, work discussions flowing seamlessly into personal conversations. We justified every extra hour with talk of the new venture, Virelio, but beneath the professional veneer, something else was growing. The comfort I found in her company had deepened into a connection that frightened me with its intensity.

The only sanctuary I maintained was the archery club - my private space where I could think clearly, away from the confusion Elina's presence stirred in me. But even that last boundary began to waver when she spoke my name for the first time.

"Darian," she said one evening, her voice soft but deliberate, "could I join you at the archery club?"

The sound of my first name on her lips sent an unexpected shiver through me. After months of "Mr. Alister," this simple shift felt monumental. I tried to keep my voice steady as I replied, "Of course. Do you think you'll enjoy it?"

"Yes, and I think I could be good at it," she said, her voice carrying a certainty that made me look at her more closely.

That evening at the club, watching her step onto the shooting line in her work clothes and heels, I felt an unfamiliar tightness in my chest. She drew attention immediately - not just for her formal attire among the casual sportswear, but for the natural grace with which she approached everything. As I helped position her hands on the bow, showing her the proper stance, I found myself hyper-aware of every point of contact between us. The professional boundaries I'd maintained for so long felt paper-thin.

The days began to blur together, each one filled with increasingly intimate moments that I tried to justify as purely professional. Work discussions would stretch late into the evening, our conversations drifting from business to personal matters with dangerous ease. Something was shifting between us, like sand beneath my feet, and I found myself powerless to stop it.

During those long evenings at the office, I caught myself watching her more often than I should - the way she moved with quiet confidence, how her eyes lit up when she mastered a new concept, the subtle changes in her voice when she spoke to me versus others. These observations made me uncomfortable, yet I couldn't seem to stop noticing.

In the following sessions, I found myself wanting to nurture her newfound passion for archery. Before I could fully consider the implications, I gave her one of my own bows, along with a set of arrows and a target. The gesture felt more intimate than I'd intended - sharing something that had always been uniquely mine, a part of my identity I'd kept separate from everyone except Nadia.

Snowy Baharvan

When snow blanketed Tiraz and Baharvan, something shifted. During one of Nadia's hospital rotations, I suggested a weekend practice session. Early that morning, I drove to Baharvan, the quiet suburb where Elina lived. The town lay peaceful under fresh snow, pine and oak trees glistening in the morning light. As I pulled up, Elina emerged from her house, and the smile she gave me made my chest tighten with emotions I couldn't quite name.

"Hi, Elina," I said as she settled into the passenger seat, bringing with her the subtle scent of her perfume.

"Hi, my life," she replied softly, her voice carrying a warmth that caught me completely off guard.

Her words hit me like a physical force. No one had ever called me that - "my life" - and the raw honesty in her voice made it impossible to dismiss as casual affection. The intensity of her feelings was written in every glance, every word. She spoke of a love so consuming that she would accept any terms, even remaining in the shadows, if it meant being part of my life. The purity of her devotion both thrilled and terrified me.

Here's my suggested revision to maintain emotional depth while keeping the progression natural:

"It's a beautiful day, isn't it?" I said, trying to ease the intensity that had settled between us after her words.

"Yes," she replied with a soft smile, her eyes taking in the snow-laden trees. "I told you Baharvan would look magical in the snow."

I started the car, and then felt her hand slide over mine where it rested on the gearshift. The touch was gentle but deliberate, and I found myself adjusting to drive with my left hand rather than pulling away. The warmth of her fingers against mine felt dangerous in its comfort.

"You know," I heard myself say, the words coming before I could really think them through, "I've never let anyone else drive the Titanus. Not even..." I caught myself before saying Nadia's name. "Would you like to try?"

Her eyes lit up with that spark of confidence I'd come to admire. "Just pull over and see," she replied, a challenge in her voice.

To my surprise - and secret pleasure - she handled the manual 4WD as if she'd been driving it for years. Her natural ability with the Titanus stirred something in me; this vehicle had always been my sanctuary, my escape, and watching her command it with such ease felt like worlds colliding.

We found our way to a hidden coffee shop she'd chosen, tucked away in Baharvan's winding streets. As we settled into a quiet corner, laptops open but forgotten, I realized how easily we'd slipped into this comfortable intimacy. The guilt was still there, a constant presence, but it was increasingly drowned out by the simple pleasure of being with someone who seemed to understand parts of me I hadn't known needed understanding.

Our laughter echoed through the coffee shop, drawing curious glances from other patrons. I fell into my habit of renaming dishes - something I usually kept to myself but found myself sharing with her. "I'll have the 'Soup,'" I said with mock seriousness, referring to my elaborate breakfast order. Her eyes crinkled with delight at our private joke, and I felt that familiar warmth spread through my chest.

Something about being here, in this hidden corner of Baharvan, made everything feel different. Each shared laugh, each inside joke, seemed to build another brick in the wall separating this reality from my life with Nadia. The guilt was still there, but it was becoming easier to push aside, lost in the simple joy of these moments that felt like they belonged to just us.

When the waitress came back confused about the "Soup" order, Elina jumped in to translate, already fluent in my peculiar menu language. The easy way she navigated between my world and the real one made my chest tighten with emotions I wasn't ready to name. These weren't just shared jokes anymore - they were becoming the foundation of something deeper, something that both thrilled and terrified me.

The Lines Begin to Blur

After Elina's father's death, something shifted in our dynamic. The shared understanding of loss created a bridge between us that I hadn't anticipated. Each morning, I found myself arriving earlier at the office, telling myself it was just to get more work done. But there was something about those quiet moments before everyone else arrived - the way the morning light caught her smile as she handed me coffee, the gentle way she'd inquire about my evening.

Our conversations deepened beyond work, flowing into personal territory with an ease that should have worried me. She began leaving small gifts on my desk - a book about archery she thought I'd enjoy, homemade pastries that reminded her of something her father used to make. Each gesture carried a weight of meaning I wasn't ready to acknowledge.

One particularly difficult morning, when memories of my own father felt overwhelming, I found myself sharing stories I'd never told anyone but Nadia. Elina listened with an intensity that made the rest of the world fade away, her eyes holding mine with understanding that went beyond sympathy.

"Sometimes," she said softly, "I wake up forgetting he's gone. Then it hits me all over again."

I recognized that pain, remembered how it had hollowed me out at twenty-two. Without thinking, I reached across my desk and squeezed her hand. The touch lasted only seconds, but it felt like crossing an invisible line.

The weekend at the villa happened almost naturally - a celebration of a successful project that somehow turned into just the two of us. I brought my pistol, telling myself it was just to teach her something new, just as I would with any colleague. I'd also picked up burgers from my favorite place - thick, juicy doubles that seemed too large to handle.

"Here, like this," I said, standing behind her at the makeshift shooting range we'd set up. My hands covered hers as I showed her how to hold the pistol properly, adjust her stance. The proximity sent my heart racing in a way I hadn't expected. She was a quick learner, her determination evident in every focused shot.

Later, as we sat on the terrace with our burgers, she laughed at how impossibly large they were. "I don't think I can fit this in my mouth," she said, eyeing the towering creation.

"Here," I said, demonstrating how to compress it slightly. "We'll take a bite together on three." Our eyes met as we counted down, and something about that shared moment - both of us trying to manage these enormous burgers, laughing as sauce dripped everywhere - felt startlingly intimate. The synchronicity of our movements, the shared laughter, the way her eyes crinkled with joy - it all felt both perfectly natural and terrifyingly significant.

As evening approached and the sky painted itself in twilight colors, our conversation flowed effortlessly, punctuated by comfortable silences that felt dangerously intimate. When she spoke about her family, her dreams, her fears, I found myself drawn into her world in a way I hadn't expected.

Driving her home that evening, I caught myself watching her profile in the fading light. She was everything she'd always been - kind, brilliant, family-oriented - but somehow more. The realization sent a jolt of guilt through me as I thought of Nadia working at the hospital miles away.

Valentines Day

Valentine's Day arrived like an accusation. Nadia had returned home the night before, and for the first time in our decade together, I felt no flutter of anticipation at her homecoming. Instead, there was only a hollow ache in my chest, a reminder of how far I'd strayed from the man I used to be.

Standing in the jewelry store, I studied the display cases with a growing sense of disconnect. The earrings I chose for Nadia were perfect—exactly what she would love, selected with the practiced knowledge of years together. Yet as I turned to leave, something pulled at me, an invisible thread I couldn't ignore. I found myself turning back, drawn to another display case.

"I need something else," I told the salesperson, the lie forming easily on my tongue. "For my... sister."

The necklace I chose for Elina—three interlocking hearts in 24-karat gold—felt weighted with meaning I didn't dare acknowledge. As I tucked it into my car's trunk, hidden like the feelings I was harboring, guilt pressed against my chest like a physical thing.

That evening, I returned home to find Nadia had transformed our space into a Valentine's haven. Red hearts dotted the walls, and handmade decorations—the kind that had once made my heart swell with love for her thoughtfulness—adorned every surface. She'd even recreated elements from our first Valentine's Day together, a detail that now felt like a knife twisting in my gut.

The collection of books she'd gotten me—ones I'd mentioned wanting months ago—showed how attentively she still listened, how present she remained in our marriage even as I drifted away. Her eyes shone with love as she presented them, and I felt myself shrinking from that pure devotion.

"I have a lot of work to finish," I said, the words tasting bitter in my mouth. I gave her a quick kiss, an echo of the passion we once shared, before retreating to my laptop. "Let's celebrate and then I need to get back to it."

The sadness that flickered across her face was like watching a candle being snuffed out. She accepted the earrings with a quiet thank you, but her fingers lingered on my hand as if trying to hold onto something she sensed slipping away.

The next morning, when Elina picked me up for the board meeting, the contrast was stark. Her presence filled the car with an electric energy that made my skin tingle. She held my hand as she drove, occasionally bringing it to her chest or pressing her lips against my knuckles. Each gesture felt like a secret language, one that spoke directly to the heart I was trying to deny.

"Pull over," I said suddenly, overwhelmed by the need to give her the necklace burning a hole in my conscience.

When I handed it to her, her face transformed with joy. "Oh my god! This is... this is beautiful. I didn't get you anything, my love."

"You've already given me more than I could ever ask for," I replied, the truth of the words frightening me. "This is for you, for everything."

Her kiss was full of promise and possibility, and as we continued to the meeting, she kept my hand pressed against her heart. The gesture felt both right and terribly wrong.

That night, Nadia's words cut through my defenses like glass. "My Darian isn't here anymore," she whispered, her voice heavy with understanding. "I know your look. I know those eyes. They talked to me all these years, and now they're silent. Something is wrong."

She suggested marriage counseling, and I agreed, hoping it would ease her suspicions. But as I sat there, watching tears gather in the eyes of the woman who had been my adventure partner, my best friend, my home for so long, I knew I was already lost to another shore.

Snowy Weekend Trip

The weekend trip with friends that followed felt like an attempt to outrun my own shadow. I found myself stealing moments to message Elina, each secret exchange both thrilling and damning. In a moment alone, I wrote her name in the snow with a stick—a childish gesture that somehow captured the reckless abandon of my feelings. I photographed it before erasing it, another secret to add to my growing collection.

When Nadia mentioned wanting to meet her ex, something twisted inside me—hope mixed with shame. For a moment, I wished she would find solace elsewhere, absolving me of the choice I was too cowardly to make. I shared this with Elina, who laughed softly, secure in her place in my heart.

But the next day in counseling, Nadia's eyes met mine with devastating clarity. "You're hiding something," she said, revealing her comment about her ex had been a test. "I know you are."

A friend's words echoed in my mind: "Darian, do you know why people lie?"

"Because they're afraid?"

"Yes. They're afraid of the truth."

Sitting there, watching the woman I had built a life with search my face for traces of the man she married, I realized I had become someone I never thought I'd be—a man afraid of his own truth. I had fallen in love with someone else, and no amount of denial could bridge the chasm that had opened in my marriage. The life Nadia and I had built together was crumbling, and I was the one holding the sledgehammer.

Later that evening, as we sat in our living room—the same space where we'd shared countless intimate conversations over the years—Nadia's words struck me like lightning.

"I need to tell you something," she said, her voice steady but her hands clasped tightly in her lap. "What I said about meeting my ex... it wasn't true."

The admission hung in the air between us. I sat very still, feeling exposed under her careful gaze.

"I said it to see your reaction," she continued, her eyes never leaving my face. "And your response told me everything I needed to know."

My throat went dry. I thought back to my earlier conversation with Elina, how I'd shared Nadia's supposed plans, even feeling a twisted sense of relief. Now that relief turned to ash in my mouth.

"What do you mean?" I managed, though I already knew.

"The Darian I married would have been hurt, would have fought for us," she said softly. "But you... you seemed almost hopeful. Like it would solve a problem for you."

Her perceptiveness cut through my defenses. This was the woman who had known me for over a decade, who could read the smallest changes in my expression, who had weathered countless adventures by my side. Of course she would see through my attempts at deception.

"I don't know what you're talking about," I said, but the words sounded hollow even to my own ears.

Nadia's eyes filled with tears, but her voice remained steady. "Yes, you do. Something's changed. Someone's changed you." She paused, letting the weight of her words sink in. "I've known you too long, loved you too deeply not to see it."

The silence that followed was deafening. Outside our window, the city lights twinkled as always, but inside, our carefully built world was cracking at its foundations. I wanted to deny it, to reassure her, to be the man she had married. Instead, I sat there, trapped between the truth I couldn't admit and the lies I couldn't maintain.

"I think we need some time," she finally said, rising from her seat. "Some space to figure out what's happening to us."

As she walked away, I remained frozen, realizing that my silence had spoken volumes. The woman who had once been my everything had just offered me an opening to fight for our marriage, and I had let it pass. The guilt of this moment would haunt me, adding another layer to the complex web of emotions I was tangled in.

Later that night, as I lay awake in our guest room, I thought about how skillfully Nadia had exposed the changes in my heart. She had always been intelligent, intuitive—it was one of the things I had fallen in love with. Now those same qualities were unveiling the very things I was trying to hide. The irony wasn't lost on me: the woman who knew me best was watching me become someone she didn't recognize at all.

***

The snow in town was getting heavier, transforming the urban landscape into something softer, more intimate. The white blanket muffled the usual city sounds, creating pockets of silence that seemed to invite confession. That morning, when the snowfall was particularly thick, I noticed Elina hadn't brought her car to work. The sight of her standing near the entrance, snow gathering on her shoulders, stirred something protective in me that I wasn't ready to examine too closely.

"I'll drive you home," I offered, the words coming easily, naturally. Her smile in response held a warmth that made my chest tighten - a feeling I'd been experiencing more frequently since that day at the cemetery, when I'd watched her pour her grief into the earth that held her father.

The drive was quiet, peaceful. The snow created a cocoon around us, as if we were suspended in a world of our own. I found myself driving slower than necessary, savoring the comfortable silence between us. These moments had become precious somehow, charged with an understanding that had grown from shared pain into something more complex.

As we neared her home, neither of us made a move to end the moment. She leaned slightly toward me, her presence filling the car with a warmth that had nothing to do with the heater. The scent of her perfume mingled with the leather of my car seats, creating an intimacy that made my heart race. I could feel her eyes on me, carrying all the words we hadn't dared to speak.

When my phone buzzed, Nadia's name lighting up the screen, guilt twisted in my stomach. She needed a ride home from the hospital - a simple request from my wife of ten years, the woman who had been my adventure partner, my constant support. But in that moment, with Elina's warmth beside me, I couldn't bring myself to leave. The lie came too easily: I was far away, caught in a late meeting, the traffic too heavy to reach her.

The weight of that decision followed me home later that night. Nadia's hurt was palpable, her silence filling our apartment with unspoken accusations. The disappointment in her eyes should have crushed me - and part of me knew it would, later, when I lay awake remembering the love and trust I was slowly betraying. But in that moment, my thoughts kept drifting back to Elina, to the way she'd looked at me with such complete understanding, such absolute acceptance.

I stood in our kitchen, the space Nadia and I had shared countless meals and conversations in, and felt like a stranger. The photos on our walls - adventures we'd shared, mountains we'd climbed together - seemed to watch me with judgment. But the pull I felt toward Elina had grown beyond my control, born in the shared understanding of loss and grief, transformed into something that both thrilled and terrified me.

My Mom's Sickness

My mother has always shared a profound bond with Nadia, seeing her not just as a daughter-in-law, but as the daughter she never had. Their connection ran deep – through years of shared experiences, quiet understanding, and mutual care. Nadia had been there through all of my mother's health struggles: the open heart surgery to replace two valves, the delicate brain procedure, and now this new challenge with her digestion that required extensive testing.

I was driving to the service shop with Titanus when my phone rang. Nadia's voice, usually so steady, carried a weight that made my heart stop.

"Darling, I need to tell you something," she began, her medical training evident in how carefully she chose her words. "Mother needs surgery immediately."

"What is it?" I gripped the steering wheel tighter. "Just tell me straight."

"Colorectal cancer..."

The words hit me like a physical blow. I pulled over, my vision blurring as memories flooded back – my father's sudden death, the weight of loss that had shaped so much of who I'd become. Not again, I thought. Not another parent.

"Darian? Are you there? Talk to me, love," Nadia's voice anchored me back to the present.

"Yes," I managed, forcing the word past the tightness in my throat. "I'm just... processing."

"Listen to me," she said, her voice taking on the gentle but firm tone she used with patients. "We have the best doctors here. I've already spoken with Dr. Rehan. We need to act quickly, but we're going to fight this together."

Within a week, thanks to Nadia's connections and expertise, we had mother admitted to a private hospital and surgery scheduled. Watching Nadia navigate the medical system, advocate for my mother, and still find time to support me emotionally reminded me of why I'd fallen in love with her. She was my rock, steady and unwavering when everything else felt uncertain.

Yet even as we faced this family crisis, professional challenges mounted at work. Tensions were rising with board members and investors, including Edmund. They were pushing to bring in new people – people who lacked the vision and expertise I knew were crucial for Nexara Labs' future. I found myself fighting on multiple fronts, determined not to let the company I'd built fall into the wrong hands.

At work, I buried myself in meetings and strategy sessions, channeling my worry into productive action. During breaks, I'd call Nadia for updates about my mother, drawing strength from her calm reassurance and medical insight. Our evening conversations, though brief due to her hospital schedule, kept me grounded. She understood my fears without me having to voice them, offering the quiet support that had always been the foundation of our relationship.

The stress began taking its toll, manifesting in sleepless nights and constant tension. I found myself spending more time at the office, where at least I could feel in control of something. Elina, ever-efficient, helped manage the increasing workload, her presence a steady constant during this tumultuous time. Having experienced her own loss so recently, she seemed to intuitively understand the weight I carried, though I maintained professional boundaries in our interactions.

Through it all, Nadia remained my anchor, balancing her own medical duties with caring for my mother and supporting me. Each night as we talked, whether in person or over the phone, I was reminded of the depth of our connection – how she could read my silences, anticipate my needs, and offer strength when mine faltered. In those moments, despite the storms raging around us, I knew we would weather this challenge as we had every other: together.

Late February

The promise of spring hung in the air, but I barely noticed. My thoughts were consumed by the complexity of emotions I never expected to feel. Looking back, I could see how things had shifted so gradually - Elina's quiet admiration in meetings, her dedication that went beyond professional duty, the way her eyes followed me even before her father's passing. I had noticed but chose to ignore it, maintaining professional distance. But that day at the cemetery had broken something in me - not because of her grief, but because I finally saw her completely, beyond the walls I'd carefully built.

After taking Nadia to the airport, I felt the familiar twist of emotions - guilt tangled with a relief I couldn't justify. My thoughts inevitably drifted to Elina, to stolen moments and unspoken words.

My mother's successful cancer surgery should have commanded my full attention - we were incredibly fortunate, especially with Nadia's early detection. She had always been our family's guardian angel, caring for everyone with that quiet competence I'd fallen in love with years ago. The thought of her dedication only deepened my shame.

Work provided little escape. Board meetings for both startups and Nexara Labs had become battlegrounds, with investors pushing for changes I couldn't accept. The upcoming team-building retreat loomed, adding another layer of complexity to an already overwhelming schedule.

Yet amid this chaos, I found myself seeking moments with Elina with an intensity that scared me. She had become my anchor, though I knew she should be anything but. Whether driving to meetings together, her hand finding mine with a certainty that felt both wrong and inevitable, or stealing away to quiet coffee shops where we could pretend the world outside didn't exist - these moments had become my refuge.

During a brainstorming session, tension surfaced when I supported Kamila, a promising young employee. That afternoon, Elina led me to her car, her face tight with barely contained emotion.

"You think because I accept sharing you with her, I'd be fine with anyone else?" The hurt in her voice cut deeper than anger would have.

"What do you mean?" I asked, though I knew.

"The way you looked at her, spoke to her - like she mattered." Her voice cracked slightly.

"Elina," I said softly, reaching for her hand, "I've only ever betrayed Nadia once - with you. Kamila is family, like everyone at Nexara Labs. I'm her mentor, nothing more."

She collapsed into my arms then, and I held her, knowing I should step back but unable to let go. The line between right and wrong had blurred so gradually, I hardly knew where it lay anymore.

Early Special Birthday

Later that week, after a company off-site retreat, I found myself driving through the narrow streets of Baharvan, anticipation building in my chest. These private moments with Elina had become precious to me, stolen fragments of time where we could just be ourselves, away from the weight of our complicated situation. I'd arranged a private celebration, another moment to add to our growing collection of secrets.

When she messaged asking me not to come to her street, instead sending a pin location in a quieter part of the neighborhood, I understood. We'd become experts at this careful dance of discretion, finding quiet corners of the city where we could briefly let our guard down.

I pulled up to the spot she'd indicated, a quiet corner where two streets met beneath the spreading branches of an old oak tree. The evening light filtered through the leaves, creating patterns that reminded me of the way happiness and guilt now intertwined in my life - light and shadow, joy and remorse.

Then I saw her.

She emerged from a small confectionery shop, and the sight of her made my heart swell with a familiar ache. Her arms were full - a carefully balanced cake box, two blue balloons dancing above her head in the gentle breeze, and a small bag that she held close. But it was her face that captured me completely. Her eyes sparkled with that special joy she reserved just for me, the one that made me forget, if only for a moment, about the promises I was breaking.

As she walked toward me, each step bringing her closer, I felt that now-familiar surge of emotion - love mixed with guilt, happiness tangled with shame. The way she moved, the grace in how she balanced her precious cargo, the sheer delight radiating from her - it all reminded me why I'd risked everything for these moments.

The streetlights had just begun to flicker on, casting her in alternating light and shadow. Her happiness was infectious, pure, making me temporarily forget the complexity of our situation. In that instant, there was only Elina, walking toward me with love in her eyes and blue balloons dancing above her head.

As she reached the car, her smile widened into that special expression I'd come to cherish. "My love," she said softly, the words both warming and haunting me, "I hope you like surprises."

I stepped out to help her, and as our hands met in the transfer of the cake box, I felt that familiar spark - the one that had led me down this path of no return. The blue balloons caught the last rays of sunlight, their surfaces gleaming like captured pieces of sky, witnesses to another moment in our hidden love story.

As we settled into the car, those balloons bobbing gently in the backseat, I couldn't help but think they were like our relationship - beautiful but fragile, floating in a space between reality and dreams. Despite the guilt that never fully left me, despite thoughts of Nadia that haunted quiet moments, I knew in my heart that I was helplessly, irrevocably in love with Elina. The complexity of loving two women differently but deeply had become my daily reality, a weight I carried even in our happiest moments together.

After settling in at the place I'd rented for the night, I moved to the small kitchen with familiar ease. The ritual of making coffee for us had become one of our special moments. I took out the coffee equipment I'd brought along - I never trusted rental places to have proper tools - and began the careful process of brewing.

"You spoil me," she said, watching me from where she sat cross-legged on the floor, surrounded by the blue balloons she'd brought. "No one makes coffee like you do."

The wine she'd chosen - a bottle of red she'd been saving for a special occasion - breathed on the counter while I worked. The aroma of freshly ground coffee filled the space between us, mixing with the sweet scent of the cake she'd brought - my favorite, dark chocolate with a hint of orange.

We shared the cake straight from the box, passing a single fork between us, laughing at the intimacy of it. The wine loosened our usual restraint, and soon we were trading stories and secrets, the kind that only emerge in those precious hours when the world feels far away.

The next morning, Elina arrived early at our meeting place, golden sunlight just beginning to spill across the city. She carried a bag from my favorite café, the aroma of fresh croissants mingling with the crisp morning air. The simple gesture - remembering exactly how I liked my coffee, bringing fruits she knew I favored - spoke of an attention to detail that made my chest tighten.

"Good morning," she whispered as I opened the door, her eyes bright with an emotion that mirrored my own. The thermal flask she handed me was still warm, like the flutter in my chest at seeing her.

We settled by the window, sharing breakfast in comfortable silence as the city slowly awakened below. The quiet felt sacred somehow, each stolen moment precious and fleeting. Sunlight painted patterns across the bedsheets, turning ordinary moments into something that felt like magic.

"I couldn't sleep," she admitted softly, curled beside me on the small couch. "Every minute away feels like forever now." The vulnerability in her voice made my heart ache.

Without speaking, I removed my watch - the one that had marked countless moments of my life, through marriage and career and everything between. The leather strap showed years of wear, telling its own story of time passed. With deliberate care, I took out my pocket knife and began to carve an "E" into the leather.

Each stroke felt momentous, like I was inscribing something far deeper than just a letter. The morning light caught the fresh marks in the leather, making them shine like something precious. This wasn't just an initial - it was a declaration, a promise, a secret testament to what we'd become to each other.

"This is your sign," I said quietly, meeting her gaze. The emotion in her eyes made my voice catch. "We're bound to each other now— you're my second wife."

She didn't speak, but her fingers traced the carved letter with such tenderness it made my chest hurt. The 'E' wasn't perfect - slightly uneven, raw at the edges - but somehow that made it more beautiful, more real. Like our love - unconventional, complicated, but undeniably true.

In that moment, the world beyond our room ceased to exist. There were no witnesses to this private ceremony except the morning sun, no rings exchanged - just a carved initial and the weight of unspoken vows between us. Every time I would check the time now, I would feel this moment, this promise etched not just in leather but in my heart.

She leaned against me, her breath warm against my neck, and we watched the sun climb higher over the city we'd made our own. In the quiet of that rented room, we'd created something that belonged only to us - not sanctioned by law or tradition, but sacred in its own way.

My Birthday

The morning of my birthday arrived with a weight I couldn't name. Nadia had come home early from her hospital shift, determined to make the day special as she always did. Her dedication, once so deeply moving to me, now filled me with a guilt that threatened to consume me. I watched her preparing breakfast, her movements filled with the familiar grace that had captivated me for a decade, and felt the sharp sting of knowing I was slowly breaking something precious.

At work, colleagues gathered for a surprise celebration. Among the gifts was one that made my heart stutter - a Black Lamy fountain pen, perfectly wrapped. The exact pen I had shown Elina months ago, one I had admired but never purchased.

"This is from all of us," Elina announced, her voice carrying a warmth that seemed to reach past my skin and settle somewhere deeper.

Our eyes met briefly, and in that moment, I saw everything we couldn't say aloud. She had remembered. Such a small detail, yet it spoke volumes about how carefully she had been watching, listening, understanding.

The day continued as planned. Nadia had arranged lunch at my favorite restaurant, a quiet place with warm lighting and soft music. We sat across from each other, and I found myself studying her face - the gentle curves I knew by heart, the kind eyes that had witnessed so many of our adventures together. Our conversation felt hollow though, words failing to bridge a gap that grew wider with each passing day.

Back home, I saw the effort she'd poured into the decorations. Blue balloons hung from the ceiling, matching the theme of the cake she'd ordered - a three-dimensional fisherman perched on top, a loving nod to my passion for the outdoors. The setup bore an uncanny resemblance to Elina's recent decorations, and the parallel made my chest tight with conflicting emotions.

We lit the candles, cut the cake, and Nadia handed me a box. Inside lay a sleek pair of sunglasses, exactly the kind I'd mentioned needing for off-roading trips. Her thoughtfulness, once so precious to me, now felt like another weight added to my shoulders.

"Thank you, Nadia," I said, placing them on the table. My attempted smile felt brittle, and I turned quickly to my laptop, seeking escape from the storm of emotions threatening to overwhelm me.

"Try them on," she suggested, hope threading through her voice.

"I will later," I replied dismissively, already retreating behind my screen.

The silence stretched between us until Nadia's composure finally cracked. "Is this it?" she asked, her voice low but sharp. "Your birthday, your gift, your wife... is this all you have to say?"

I remained silent, pretending absorption in my work while my mind raced. She deserved better than this half-presence I was offering. The love we'd built over years of shared adventures and quiet moments - I was watching it crumble, and worse, I was the one holding the hammer.

The next day at our counseling session, the words I never thought I'd speak fell from my lips: "Maybe it's best if we divorce."

Nadia's sharp intake of breath cut through the room. "You're serious?" she whispered, her voice trembling with disbelief.

"I don't know what else to do," I admitted, the truth of it aching in my chest. "We've tried everything, and nothing feels... right anymore."

Before her return to work, I suggested a desert trip - one last grasp at the connection we'd once shared so effortlessly. The endless landscape stretched before us, but instead of finding peace in the familiar terrain, we found only echoing silence and unspoken accusations.

I couldn't stop myself from messaging Elina, seeking moments of connection that felt electric compared to the deadened air between Nadia and me. I tried to be discrete, but Nadia wasn't blind to my divided attention.

"Who are you texting, Darian?" she asked one evening by the fire, her voice carrying a resignation that hurt more than anger would have.

"Work," I lied, the word bitter on my tongue. "The team has questions about the upcoming board meeting."

She didn't press further, but her silence spoke volumes. As we drove home, the tension between us was a living thing. I watched her staring out the window and knew that every glance at my phone, every moment of distraction, had been another crack in the foundation of our marriage. The guilt was overwhelming, but not enough to stop me from destroying something that had once been beautiful.

Nadia's Departure

The morning of her departure felt surreal. Ten years of love and adventure hung in the air between us as I loaded her bags into the car. Each movement felt heavy with memory - countless airport runs, always together, always returning to each other. But this time was different.

The drive to the airport was wrapped in a silence that ached. I caught glimpses of her profile against the window, seeing traces of the woman who had stood beside me on mountaintops, who had trusted me through treacherous paths, who had built a life with me piece by piece. My hands tightened on the steering wheel, fighting the urge to turn around, to choose the familiar comfort of our shared life over the consuming passion that had upended everything.

At the departure gate, Nadia turned to face me. The morning light caught her eyes, and for a moment, I saw every sunrise we'd chased together, every quiet moment we'd shared in the wilderness. Her strength, even now, took my breath away.

"Take care of yourself, Darian," she said softly. There was no bitterness in her voice, no recrimination - only a profound sadness that cut deeper than anger ever could. She had always been the better person between us.

"You too," I managed, unable to meet her gaze. The weight of my choices pressed against my chest, making it hard to breathe. Part of me wanted to reach for her, to apologize, to rebuild what we had. But I knew it would be cruel to offer false hope when my heart had already chosen a different path.

She lingered for a moment, as if giving me one last chance to choose differently. Then, with the quiet dignity that had always been her hallmark, she turned and walked away. I watched her disappear into the crowd, taking with her a decade of shared dreams and trust.

The drive home felt endless. My reflection in the rearview mirror showed a man I barely recognized - someone who had broken the most sacred promises for a love that had consumed him like wildfire. The guilt was there, heavy and real, but so was the undeniable pull toward the future I had chosen. Every mile marker seemed to ask if it was worth it - trading the steady warmth of a decade-long love for the intense flame that had ignited with Elina.

Back home, I stood in our - my - apartment, surrounded by the life Nadia and I had built together. Her absence felt physical, like a presence in itself. Photos of our adventures still lined the walls, each one a testament to the love we had shared. I thought of removing them, but couldn't bring myself to erase those memories. They were part of who I was, even if I was becoming someone new.

In the days that followed, I threw myself into work, into my new life, trying to outrun the echoes of Nadia's quiet goodbye. The pain was there, a constant companion, but so was the certainty that I couldn't have chosen differently. My love for Elina had become as essential as breathing - unstoppable, undeniable, even in the face of everything it cost.

Yet in quiet moments, when the city slept and my thoughts wandered, I found myself remembering Nadia's last look - not accusatory, but understanding, as if she had seen this coming long before I had admitted it to myself. Those moments brought waves of guilt sharp enough to steal my breath, but they couldn't compete with the magnetic pull toward the future I had chosen, toward Elina and the all-consuming love that had rewritten everything I thought I knew about myself.

Parin's Year End

The year in Parin starts in early April. As the final days approached, the city bustled with traditional cleaning and preparation for spring. But for me, time had taken on a different quality - measured not in days or hours, but in moments with Elina. While others cleaned their homes and made preparations, I found myself increasingly drawn to her presence, our time together becoming the axis around which my world turned.

My hand still ached from that desert trip with Nadia weeks ago - the last real connection I'd shared with my wife before everything began to shift. The injury came from gripping the Titanus's steering wheel too tightly through rough terrain, and now required physiotherapy. When Elina learned my doctor was an attractive young woman, her reaction revealed the depth of her feelings.

"Why a beautiful physiotherapist?" she teased, but I could hear the undercurrent of genuine concern in her voice. "Do you think her looks will heal you faster?"

"She's just a good doctor," I laughed, but something in Elina's expression made my heart tighten. Without asking, she began massaging my hand herself, her touch gentle yet purposeful. It became our daily ritual - her fingers working to ease my pain, but also creating an intimacy that went far beyond physical comfort.

One evening, as her hands moved across mine with practiced tenderness, I suddenly interrupted her mid-sentence:

"Swifts arrived!" I exclaimed, pointing to the sky where the birds cut through the air with their distinctive whistles.

"I'm in the middle of talking, and you're distracted by birds?" Her laughter held no real reproach, only affection. I couldn't help sharing my passion for these remarkable creatures - how they spent ten months of the year in constant flight, eating and sleeping on the wing, their lives an endless journey. As I spoke, I watched her face, saw how she absorbed every word, genuinely interested in this window into my soul.

"To me, swifts are messengers of spring," I said softly, watching her eyes follow their flight. "When they return, they bring the promise of new beginnings."

"You never cease to amaze me," she replied, her fingers intertwining with mine. "The way you find passion in things most people never notice."

We spent most of these moments in my car after work, stealing time together in the growing dusk. She would rest her head against my chest, and I would hold her, breathing in the scent of her hair, feeling the steady rhythm of her heartbeat against mine. Even in these peaceful moments, I could see that shadow of worry in her eyes - unspoken concerns about us, about everything we couldn't say aloud.

As the year-end approached, Elina called early one morning, her voice full of warmth. "I'll come over and spend time with you today," she said, and just those simple words made my heart leap.

"Sure, come over. I've made breakfast," I replied, already anticipating her presence.

She arrived early, coming through the main door this time. When she entered, I had prepared a special breakfast - wild vegetables, eggs, peppers, and spices melding into something that made her eyes light up.

"This smells delicious," she said, settling into what felt like her natural place at my table.

We spent the entire day together, lost in our own world. We watched movies, made silly dubsmash videos, laughed until our sides hurt. At one point, Elina leaned in and kissed my cheek with playful intensity.

"What are you doing?" I laughed, though my heart raced at her touch.

"I love you so much that I just want to bite you!" she declared, her joy uncontained and infectious.

"What kind of love is that? Who bites someone out of love?" I teased, though I understood perfectly - this overwhelming need to express feelings that went beyond words.

"You don't understand!" she said, eyes sparkling. "My husband is so irresistible, I can't help it. I have to bite him!"

"Then how should I love you back? Kick you?" Our laughter filled the space, making it feel like home in a way it hadn't in years.

That day was pure joy - every moment perfect in its simplicity. Being with her felt so natural that everything else faded away. The next morning, she surprised me again, arriving early to help clean my room - a gesture that spoke volumes about her care for me.

My room was a collection of my life: premium fountain pens, fly-fishing equipment, books, and memories. She transformed it all with loving attention to detail. When she carefully cleaned and repositioned Nadia's photo on my desk, the gesture moved me deeply - her respect for my past even as we built something new together.

After sharing pizza and our traditional "water-coffee," she prepared to leave, needing to clean her own room before the new year. The gratitude I felt went beyond words. In these simple moments together, I'd found something I hadn't known I was missing - a love that saw all of me, that cherished every detail of who I was.

"Thank you, Elina," I said softly, kissing her goodbye. "I really don't know how to express my gratitude." But we both knew it wasn't just gratitude I was trying to express - it was everything we'd become to each other, everything we hoped for in the year ahead.

After she left, I moved through my room, making final adjustments to her careful organization. Each object she had touched seemed to hold an echo of her presence - the perfectly aligned fountain pens, the meticulously arranged books, the carefully sorted papers. The space felt different now, transformed not just by her efficient cleaning but by the love she had poured into every detail.

As midnight approached, I sat at my desk, journal open before me. The blank page waited for my thoughts, but for once, words failed me. How could I capture the complexity of what I was feeling? The way this year had transformed everything I thought I knew about love and certainty?

Just as the clock struck midnight, my phone lit up with a message from Elina. Her words appeared on the screen, beginning with that tender repetition of my name that made my heart constrict: "Darian, my dearest Darian, dearer than my own life Darian, my lovable one..."

Before I could read further, Nadia's call came through. Her familiar voice, warm and full of love, reached across the distance between us. "Happy New Year, my love. I miss you too. Remember that you are the most precious thing I have in my life."

"Happy New Year to you too," I managed, keeping my voice steady despite the storm of emotions in my chest. When she mentioned visiting her in Shinar for the new year, I deflected, citing work commitments. The lie felt heavy on my tongue, but I couldn't face her now, not with Elina's unread message burning on my screen.

After completing the ritual of new year's calls - my mother, my brothers, close friends - I finally returned to Elina's message. Each word seemed to pulse with meaning, with a depth of feeling that both thrilled and terrified me. I read it again and again, letting her sentiments wash over me like waves.

"Darian, my dearest
Darian, dearer than my own life
Darian, my lovable one
Darian, my kind-hearted one

Happy New Year.
Your presence at the start of my new year is the most precious gift God has given me, and despite all the hardships I am going through, I am so, so happy to begin this year with you.

I hope in the new year, you achieve all the beautiful dreams that live in your pure and kind heart. Above all, I wish you health, and I hope that until the last moments of our lives, we stay by each other's side. Together, just like today and all the beautiful days we've spent, I hope our hearts remain happy. I hope we have many wonderful moments, great trips, amazing projects, and incredible teamwork like always.

I want you to know that, without exaggeration, you are the most delightful and soothing person I've ever had in my life. It's a bit tough to be together, but time with you is so sweet and enjoyable that in every moment, I am just waiting for the time to be with you again.

My message got really long, but I wanted to take this opportunity to tell you how much I love you and how valuable you are to me.

I'm certain we will shine in the new year. I'm sure whatever we start together will become the most extraordinary thing ever. I truly believe in us and the energy that flows between us, and we'll see its beautiful outcome in the new year.

Once again, Happy New Year, my lovable darling. "

Other messages continued to arrive - friends, colleagues, family - but they felt distant, unreal compared to the raw emotion in Elina's words. I found myself returning to her message repeatedly, each reading revealing new layers of meaning, new depths of feeling. Her hope for our future together, her belief in what we could build, her pure and unconditional love - it all resonated with something that had awakened in me, something I couldn't deny anymore.

As sleep finally claimed me, her words followed me into my dreams, painting visions of possibilities I had never dared to imagine before. The new year stretched ahead, full of promise and uncertainty, but one thing was clear - nothing would ever be the same again.

Happy New Year

The new year began steeped in tradition—a visit to my father's grave, where the morning air held the crispness of new beginnings. As I stood before the familiar stone, I felt Elina's presence through the gentle buzz of her messages. Even in these solemn moments, our connection hummed like a quiet symphony, our plans for the coming days already weaving through our thoughts.

On the second day, my heart raced with anticipation as I presented Elina with her gift: a portable Chemex coffee maker and matching thermos mug. Though she favored tea over coffee, her eyes lit up with understanding—this wasn't just about the drink, but about sharing a piece of myself with her. The way her fingers traced the elegant curves of the glass, the soft smile that played across her lips, told me she understood perfectly. Later, at the country's largest mall, she led me with barely contained excitement to choose my gift. The white and light blue zebra-striped shirt she selected spoke of how well she'd come to know me, her eyes shining as she imagined me wearing it. "This one," she said with certainty, "this is perfectly you."

The third day bloomed like a gift itself as we stepped into the national botanic garden. I'd chosen this place carefully for our day of birding and wildlife photography, but nothing could have prepared me for how magical it would feel. The garden came alive around us—fresh blooms opening to the winter sun, migratory birds calling from the trees as if singing just for us. Through my lens, I captured the dance of new life, but found myself increasingly drawn to Elina among the flowers. She moved with natural grace, her joy as pure as the morning light, and I couldn't help but preserve these moments despite the risk of being seen.

We had to be careful, of course, staying alert for other visitors, choosing less traveled paths. But even this need for caution added a bittersweet thrill to our day—each shared glance, each moment of connection, felt more precious for being stolen. The sunshine painted everything in gold, the mild weather wrapped around us like a blessing, and Elina's presence made every second feel like poetry.

When she paused beside a particularly beautiful flowering bush, the light catching her profile just so, I raised my camera almost without thinking. She turned to me with that smile that had become my new north star, and I knew with absolute certainty that no wildlife photo I'd ever taken could compare to capturing her in this moment of pure joy.

Everything aligned perfectly—nature itself seemed to conspire to create this perfect day. The fresh blooms, the birdsong, the gentle weather, but most of all, her company, made this feel like more than just a day in the garden. It was a celebration of what we'd become to each other, of the love that had grown between us as naturally as the flowers surrounding us.

Our only shadow was the need to remain vigilant, to keep our distance when others passed by, to pretend we were nothing more than casual acquaintances when we passed other photographers. But even this couldn't dim the radiance of what we shared. If anything, these moments of forced separation only made our connection feel stronger, more real, more precious.

As the day drew to a close, neither of us wanted to leave this paradise we'd found. We'd created our own world among the flowers and birds, and stepping back into reality felt like waking from the most beautiful dream. Yet we carried the magic of the day with us, preserved not just in my photographs but in our hearts, another perfect memory in our growing collection of shared moments.

The next morning started with breakfast, a ritual that had become the highlight of our days together. Sunlight streamed through the kitchen windows, catching the dust motes dancing in the air as Elina stood by the stove, whisking eggs with careful attention. I handed her the bowl while heating up my special frying pan—a prized possession I'd guarded zealously through years of cooking.

As she approached the stove, something protective stirred in me. "Just a reminder—don't use a metal spoon on this pan. It's my favorite. I've had it forever."

She paused, spatula hovering mid-air, and turned to me with that look that made my heart skip—half amusement, half adoration. Setting down the spatula, she stepped closer, pressing a soft kiss to my lips. "Your *favorite* frying pan? Why? Is it magical or something?"

"It's not magical. It's just… dependable," I replied, trying to maintain my dignity even as a smile tugged at my lips. She leaned in again, kissing me quickly before pulling back with a grin.

She raised an eyebrow, clearly savoring the moment. Then, with that mischievous smile I'd grown to love, she asked, "Darian, do you love me more than your frying pan?"

I froze, caught off guard by her playfulness, taking just a beat too long to respond.

Her face lit up with triumph, eyes dancing. "Oh my God, you're actually thinking about it! I can't believe this." She kissed me again, laughing against my lips.

I chuckled, shaking my head at her infectious joy. "No, of course not! It's just… it's a *really good* frying pan."

Her laughter, pure and unrestrained, filled every corner of the kitchen as she leaned against the counter, clutching her sides. "Wow, Darian.

That's the most romantic thing I've ever heard. 'It's a really good frying pan.' You're so smooth."

Unable to resist, I pulled her into a tight hug, breathing in the familiar scent of her shampoo as she peppered small kisses along my jaw. "Okay, okay, I get it. You're impossible."

"And yet, here I am," she teased, stealing one more kiss before turning back to the stove.

We moved around the kitchen in perfect synchronization, as if we'd been doing this dance forever. She'd pause occasionally to lean into me, stealing quick kisses between tasks. The kitchen soon filled with the comforting aroma of sizzling eggs, toasted bread, and fresh coffee—scents that would forever remind me of these precious mornings together. We sat close at the table, her legs tangled with mine beneath it, sharing bites and quiet conversations that meant everything and nothing at all.

After breakfast, the balcony beckoned. Elina had fallen in love with my plants from her first visit, and today she was determined to expand our little garden. She pulled me down for a lingering kiss before we headed out to a nearby flower garden, returning with an abundance of seeds, flowers, and planters.

I watched her work with natural grace, her hands moving skillfully through the soil, creating something beautiful from nothing. Occasionally, she'd look up and catch my eye, holding my gaze with such tenderness it made my chest ache. Each time she caught me watching, she'd smile and beckon me closer for a kiss, leaving traces of soil on my shirt that I couldn't bring myself to mind.

"Living with you is amazing," she said suddenly, her voice soft but filled with certainty, reaching for my hand and pressing her lips to my knuckles.

I couldn't help but smirk. "I know!" The teasing came naturally now.

She gave me that look—the one that could melt my defenses instantly—and pulled me down for another kiss. I softened. "Being with you is breathtaking. I wish time would just stop when we're together."

"Me too," she replied quietly, wrapping her arms around my neck, soil-covered hands and all. We let the moment pass without words, both understanding too well what remained unsaid.

As our balcony garden took shape under her careful attention, she looked around with satisfaction. "This feels like home now." She turned in my arms, kissing me deeply, tasting of coffee and morning sunshine.

"Good," I said simply, pulling her closer and feeling her smile against my lips.

That day, surrounded by fresh soil and new beginnings, we'd created our own sanctuary—a space where love could grow as naturally as the flowers we'd planted, sealed with countless kisses and tender touches that spoke of everything our words couldn't say.

As the new year holidays waned, reality began to seep back into our perfect bubble. Nadia's return loomed just a week away, and Elina's family had arranged a northern trip that would take her away from me. She paced my balcony when she told me about it, her reluctance evident in every movement.

"I don't want to go," she said softly, fingers trailing along the plants we'd tended together. "I can make an excuse, stay here..."

But I knew we needed this separation, however brief. "You should go," I insisted, though each word felt heavy. "Your family needs this time with you. Besides," I added, trying to keep my voice light, "Nadia will be home in three days."

She understood what I couldn't say: that we needed to maintain appearances, to protect what we'd built. Still, the way she held me before leaving spoke volumes about how difficult this separation would be.

Her absence left a void that work couldn't fill, despite my best efforts. My phone became a lifeline, lighting up throughout the day with her photos—snow-covered landscapes, family gatherings, quiet moments she wanted to share only with me. Each image was both comfort and torment: proof of our connection, yet reminders of the complexity of our situation.

That evening, looking at a photo she'd sent of the northern evening light dancing above her family's cabin, the weight of everything crashed over me. I needed space to think, to breathe, to understand what I'd started. Without really planning it, I found myself loading the Titanus with camping gear. Within an hour, I was driving toward the desert, leaving the city lights behind.

Sometimes the only way to face your truth is to sit with it in complete silence. And I knew exactly where to find that silence – in the vast emptiness where the desert meets the stars.

SIX

EMBERS AND ECHOES

The stars stretched endlessly above me as I sat beside my dying campfire, hundreds of miles from Tiraz and even further from answers. The desert night pressed in around me, bringing with it that profound silence that makes a person's thoughts sound like shouts. Out here, where the emptiness echoes like a heartbeat, I found myself wrestling with choices that seemed impossible just months ago.

Sparks danced upward into the darkness, each one carrying memories of recent months that had changed everything. Every time I checked my watch now, I thought of the 'E' hidden inside its case, a secret etched where only I would see it. The weight of that small mark seemed heavier than the timepiece itself – a constant reminder of how quickly certainty could dissolve into chaos.

The flames cast shifting shadows across the sand, reminding me of how perspectives could change in an instant. One moment, you're sure of your path, your future, your heart. The next, a single glance across a conference room can ignite something that threatens to burn everything down. Elina had entered my world like a desert storm – unexpected, powerful, transforming everything in its wake.

I watched another log collapse into embers, remembering the first time our hands had touched over coffee cups, the electricity that had jolted through me. Such a simple moment, yet it had started an avalanche in my heart. The warmth of the fire against my face recalled her fingertips brushing mine as she passed documents across my desk, each innocent touch adding fuel to something I couldn't control.

The desert wind whispered through the nearby rocks, carrying with it the scent of sage and stone. In the city, everything felt complicated – layers of obligations, expectations, and consequences tangled together like thorny vines. But out here, under stars that had witnessed countless human dramas, the truth felt starker: I had allowed my heart to split in two, and no amount of careful management could prevent the storm that was coming.

My father's words about the wilderness not caring for plans felt painfully relevant now. I had ignited something that would either consume everything in its path or burn itself out, leaving only ashes of what was. Each attempt to maintain control, to keep these two worlds separate, only seemed to make everything more combustible.

Tomorrow marked the end of Parin's New Year holidays, and with it, the end of this brief escape. I would have to return to the world I'd built, to face the choices that waited like wolves in the darkness. The board meetings, the investor negotiations, the careful dance of divided loyalties – it all loomed ahead, made more complex by the feelings I couldn't control. The new year had brought changes I never expected, turning every certainty into a question. But tonight, under this vast desert sky, I could at least be honest with myself: I had started something that would change everything, and there was no going back. The only question haunting me now was what happens next? How long could I maintain this delicate balance, this new life I'd created? The embers offered no answers, only the quiet hiss of time running out.

The end of the holidays brought both relief and renewed tension. Like water finding its level, Elina and I fell back into our careful routine of stolen moments and discrete messages. That first morning back at work, she was already waiting at our usual meeting spot, the dawn barely breaking over the city.

The moment she saw me, she crossed the distance between us in quick steps, pressing herself against my chest as if verifying I was real. The scent of her perfume, familiar yet intoxicating, made my heart race.

"I brought you something," she whispered, presenting a handmade basket and a box of cookies. "For your desk—for your pens and accessories."

"Thanks, darling," I smiled, brushing my lips against her cheek. The simple domesticity of the gesture made my chest ache.

But reality had a way of asserting itself. Nadia's return carried a weight I hadn't anticipated. Though I went through the motions of our usual reunion—the hug, the questions about her trip—something had shifted. She noticed immediately, her eyes catching what I couldn't hide.

The drive home began in silence, but her words, when they came, cut through the careful walls I'd built: "You weren't happy to see me. I could tell."

"It's not that," I deflected, the lie bitter on my tongue. "Work has been overwhelming lately."

The emotional chasm between us only widened. Following our counselor's advice, I tried to bridge it with shared activities—family visits, even a fly-fishing trip to revisit old passions. For brief moments, navigating challenging terrain together, I caught glimpses of what we'd once been. But like morning mist, these moments evaporated in the heat of what I'd become.

Then came the message that shattered everything:

"Darian, when I was away, did anyone come to our home?"

The words hit like physical blows. Across my desk, Elina saw my expression change. When I showed her the message, her face went pale.

"What will you tell her?" she whispered.

I squeezed her hand, projecting a certainty I didn't feel. "Don't worry. She'll never know about you."

But Nadia's pain, when it came, was devastating. Through tears, she confronted me: "Why, Darian? You were my god. I trusted you more than I trusted myself." Her sobs echoed through our home, each one a reminder of my betrayal. "I went to Shinar to work, not for pleasure. Everything I did was to build our life together."

I crafted more lies: a visiting friend from Germany, a one-time mistake, nothing more. Each falsehood added another layer to the wall I was building between us. When she finally fell into exhausted sleep, I slipped away to meet Elina at Jar, a hidden place for us.

She was already there, waiting. Her tears soaked through my shirt as she held me, her body shaking with silent sobs. In a desperate attempt to lighten the moment, I played an old breakup song, sharing a story about cheering up a heartbroken friend. Her laugh through tears only made my chest tighter.

"What are we going to do?" she asked, voice small against my chest.

"I'm still thinking it through," I replied, knowing the inadequacy of my words.

Our connection had grown beyond just passion—she was now my business partner, a cofounder with 10% of our company. I used this as justification, a logical shield protecting what we'd built. But as April approached—traditionally a time for travels with Nadia—the weight of deception grew heavier. My excuses about work commitments felt hollow, each lie another crack in the foundation of my marriage.

Then Nadia did something unprecedented—she read my journals.

The confrontation came on a night when the air itself seemed heavy with unspoken truths. Nadia had grown quieter in recent weeks, watching me with eyes that saw too much.

"There's someone else, isn't there?" Her voice was steady, but her hands trembled as she sat across from me at our kitchen table. The same table where we'd shared countless meals, planned adventures, built our life together.

My silence was answer enough. The world seemed to tilt on its axis as I watched tears gather in her eyes, though her voice remained controlled. "I see how you change when your phone lights up. How you smile at messages that aren't from me. How you've stopped looking at me the way you used to."

Each word felt like a physical blow. The guilt that had become my constant companion threatened to suffocate me. But beneath it was something else - a strange sense of relief that at least part of my truth was finally emerging.

"Who is she?" Nadia asked, her eyes searching my face. "Do I know her?"

I couldn't meet her gaze. "Nadia..."

"Just tell me who she is, Darian. I deserve that much."

But I couldn't. Not yet. Not when saying her name would make everything too real, too final. "I can't," I whispered.

She laughed then, a hollow sound that didn't reach her eyes. "Of course you can't. You're protecting her. Like you used to protect me."

We talked through the night, our voices growing hoarse as the truth of our crumbling marriage filled every corner of the room. The word "divorce" emerged gradually, first as a whisper, then as an inevitability. When Nadia finally asked for her ring back, her hands were steady but her voice cracked.

I slipped the band from my finger, feeling the weight of years lift away with it. Placing it beside hers on the table, I watched our shared dreams condense into two small circles of metal.

The next morning at the office, Elina noticed immediately. Her eyes found my bare hand - the hand that for six years had never been without that band of gold. Through every adventure, every storm, every quiet moment, that ring had been a part of me. I had slept with it, showered with it, climbed mountains with it. It had become so much a part of me that even in my deepest sleep, I would feel its presence. Now its absence felt like a phantom limb, a constant reminder of what I was leaving behind.

Elina reached for my hand, her fingers brushing the pale strip of skin where the ring had been - a marked difference from the tanned skin around it, telling its own story of years in the sun. Pure joy bloomed across her face, transforming her entire being.

"No ring," she whispered, her voice trembling with a mixture of disbelief and elation. The happiness radiating from her was almost tangible, filling the space between us. She knew what this meant - how this wasn't just removing jewelry, but removing a piece of myself that had been constant for so long.

For a brief moment, something dark and uncomfortable twisted in my chest. How could she smile at the ruins of my marriage? How could anyone find joy in the destruction of a decade of love? The thought hit me like a physical blow, making me pull back slightly. That ring had been more than metal - it had been a symbol of everything I'd built with Nadia, every promise I'd made, every adventure we'd shared.

But then I met Elina's eyes, and what I saw there stopped my breath. There was no triumph there, no cruel satisfaction. Instead, I saw a love so pure, so complete that it transformed everything it touched. Her joy wasn't about Nadia's pain - it was about the possibility of us, finally stepping into the light. The hope of no more hiding, no more stolen moments, no more guilt-laden happiness.

"I know it's complicated," she said softly, reading the conflict in my face. "But I can't help feeling like we're finally real. Like we're not just living in moments between other moments anymore."

Her words struck something deep within me. Yes, I had removed my ring - something I hadn't done in six years, something that felt like removing a part of myself. But looking at Elina now, seeing the depth of emotion in her eyes, I understood that this was also a beginning. The guilt was still there, heavy and real, but alongside it grew something else - a certainty that some loves, no matter how they begin, demand to be lived fully.

I reached for her hand, intertwining our fingers where my ring had been just hours before. Whatever came next, we would face it together. The pale line around my finger would fade with time, but what we were building - this consuming, impossible love - would only grow stronger.

The Willow's Dance

Spring arrived in Tiraz like a painter's masterpiece unfolding, the city transforming with blooming jacarandas and cherry blossoms. Their petals danced on warm breezes, creating a backdrop for a love story that grew more complex with each passing day.

Our relationship deepened through moments that seemed to exist outside of time. We had our secret places, each holding its own story. The "snake place" earned its name one afternoon when we encountered a serpent during a walk. While others might have fled, Elina's eyes lit up with fascination. She pulled out her phone, capturing photos and videos of the creature with the same fearless spirit I'd always admired in Nadia. That parallel struck me then - two women who faced life's surprises with such similar courage, yet so different in every other way.

But among all our special places, none held more significance than our willow - a magnificent tree on a quiet street in Baharvan where old houses whispered tales of generations past. Its trunk, gnarled and ancient, rose from the earth like a guardian of secrets, spreading upward into a cascade of sweeping branches that created our natural sanctuary.

We discovered it during an aimless drive through Baharvan's winding streets. Standing easily sixty feet tall, its canopy spread wide enough to create a perfect circle of shade beneath, like nature's own secret meeting place. The ground underneath was carpeted with soft grass, as if the tree had carefully tended its own little kingdom.

What drew me most to the willow was its extraordinary resilience - a quality I recognized from my years mentoring startups through their most challenging moments. Like the young entrepreneurs I guided at Nexara Labs, the willow knew how to bend without breaking, how to dance with adversity rather than fight against it. During storms, while other trees would crack and splinter, the willow's flexible branches would sway and bow, finding strength in their ability to yield.

We spent countless hours beneath its protective canopy, sometimes talking in hushed voices about our dreams and fears, other times sitting in comfortable silence, watching the play of light through its leaves. We gave names to specific branches - the "coffee branch" where we'd hang our thermos, the "sunset branch" that caught the last rays of day in the most spectacular way.

During one particularly fierce spring storm, we sat in my car watching the willow dance with the wind. "Look at how it moves," I explained to Elina, finding parallels with my work. "It's not fighting the wind - it's working with it. That's what I try to teach my startups. Resilience isn't about being rigid; it's about knowing how to adapt while staying true to your core."

Baharvan became our sanctuary, especially during Nadia's hospital shifts. I'd rented a discrete apartment there, a space that existed solely for us. The morning light would filter through gossamer curtains, painting patterns across the walls as we shared coffee and dreams. Elina brought life to every corner, her presence transforming the simple space into something magical.

Through it all, Clara Hale's "In This Moment We're Infinite" became our anthem. We'd often play it beneath the willow, letting the music mix with the rustle of leaves above us, creating a symphony that seemed to speak directly to our hearts. The lyrics captured everything we couldn't express - the joy, the guilt, the all-consuming nature of what we'd found together.

Our relationship had its storms too. When I discovered Elina's ongoing messages with an ex, jealousy flared unexpectedly. The thought of her connecting with anyone else created a physical ache in my chest.

During these moments of tension, we'd often find ourselves beneath the willow, its ancient presence offering silent wisdom about endurance and adaptation.

Living this double life wore on me. Each moment of joy with Elina came shadowed by thoughts of Nadia - her unwavering trust, her genuine love. The weight of betrayal sat heavy on my chest, yet I couldn't stop myself from falling deeper into this new love that had blindsided me completely.

Like the willow's branches in a storm, we bent but didn't break under the pressure of our complicated reality. Each challenge seemed to make our connection stronger, even as it added to the complexity of our situation. We were caught in love's most difficult paradox - knowing something is wrong yet being unable to walk away, feeling both trapped and more free than ever before.

The willow stood witness to it all - our laughter, our tears, our whispered promises and unspoken fears. Its resilience became a symbol of our own endurance, its ability to bend with life's winds while remaining rooted in what mattered most. Each day brought us closer to an inevitable choice, but for now, we existed in these perfect moments, suspended between reality and dreams, sheltered beneath branches that had weathered countless storms before us.

Mid-May

The wilderness called to me with an intensity I hadn't felt in years. Celestial Valley National Park was awakening into its most magnificent season - a time when life seemed to pulse through every branch and bloom. The valleys stretched before us like an artist's canvas, painted with carpets of alpine wildflowers that swayed in the mountain breeze. Ancient forests stirred with new life, their canopies sheltering secrets I longed to capture through my lens. Here, among these untamed spaces, leopards and brown bears moved like shadows through their domain, and the promise of photographing them pulled at something primal in my soul.

The trip materialized through a connection with an old friend whose father, a retired ranger, knew every hidden trail and secret grove in the park. He secured us a villa in a nearby village, along with the necessary permits that would allow us deep into the heart of the wilderness.

Initially, I yearned to go alone. The solitude of the wild had always been my refuge, a place where the noise of life fell away and I could hear my own thoughts clearly. But Elina's concern echoed in my mind - her insistence that I not venture out alone, especially given my recent health issues. Though I bristled at her protectiveness, there was something touching about her fierce care for my wellbeing.

Nadia joined me, though my heart wasn't fully in the invitation. Titanus, freshly serviced and ready for adventure, carried us north through changing landscapes. The seven-hour journey unfolded like a tapestry of the season - rocky outcrops giving way to lush valleys, mountain streams swollen with spring melt cutting through ancient forests.

We made three stops along the way, each one a chance to stretch our legs and take in the raw beauty around us. While Nadia explored nearby trails, I found myself reaching for my phone, composing messages to Elina through our secure company email. Each photo I sent felt like sharing a piece of my soul - the way morning light painted the mountains gold, how mist clung to valley floors like forgotten dreams.

The password on my phone had become a wall between Nadia and me - the first real barrier in our decade together. I didn't see her watching as I entered it, didn't know she had captured the moment on her own device. Her discovery of my correspondence with Elina lay ahead like a storm gathering on the horizon.

As we drove higher into the mountains, I felt the familiar thrill of approaching wilderness. But now it was tangled with something else - the constant pull of thoughts toward Elina, the guilt of my divided attention, the growing distance between Nadia and me. Even here, where I had always found clarity, my heart beat an unfamiliar rhythm, caught between the life I'd built and the path I found myself walking.

The first morning in Celestial Valley unfolded like a dream. Dawn light spilled over the mountains, painting everything in hues of gold and rose that made my fingers itch for my camera. Fresh tracks told stories in the damp earth - the careful padding of leopards, the heavy prints of bears. Though the great predators remained hidden, the forest was alive with other wonders. Through my lens, I captured the swift dance of mountain birds, the proud stance of mouflons against the sky, the clever eyes of foxes, and the majestic soar of vultures. For those precious hours, I felt whole again, as if the wild had the power to stitch together the fragments of who I used to be.

After four hours of hiking, we returned to Titanus. The ritual of brewing coffee in the wilderness had always been one of my sacred pleasures - the careful measuring of freshly ground beans, the meditative pour over the Chemex, steam rising like prayers into the mountain air. But today, even this familiar comfort felt different. As I poured a cup for Nadia, I caught myself wondering if Elina would appreciate this moment the way we once had.

The second day brought nature's challenge in full force. Overnight rain had transformed the mountain paths into treacherous slides, the kind that demanded absolute focus and respect. On a particularly narrow stretch, Titanus's wheels lost their grip, and for one heart-stopping moment, we hung suspended between control and chaos. The drop beside us seemed endless, a reminder of how quickly everything could change. Drawing on years of experience, I guided us through the crisis, but the adrenaline lingered in my veins long after we reached safety.

At the summit, the mundane task of deflating tires for better traction became an unexpected encounter with the wild. The hiss of escaping air echoed off the mountains, and suddenly, a leopard's powerful calls shattered the morning quiet. The sound vibrated through my chest, primordial and pure, before the great cat melted into the forest like mist. In that moment, I felt acutely alive, yet achingly aware of how far I'd drifted from the simple certainties that had once defined my life.

Our third dawn brought us face to face with a bear, its presence both magnificent and sobering. But panic gripped me when I realized Nadia wasn't beside me. As I searched for her, calling her name into the indifferent wilderness, I felt the weight of everything changing between us. When I found her, she was physically safe but emotionally distant - a metaphor for our marriage that wasn't lost on me. She moved through our day like a stranger, inserting herself into my photos with an almost desperate energy, seeking connection through her phone rather than the natural wonders around us. Even when we witnessed the raw drama of wolves taking down a mouflon lamb - the kind of moment that had once bound us together in shared awe - she remained unreachable, lost in her own thoughts.

That night, under a star-filled sky that had witnessed countless moments of our love, everything finally broke open. The argument felt inevitable, like watching storm clouds gather all day and finally release their rain. By morning, as we started our journey home, the word "divorce" hung between us like morning mist in the valleys. Nadia spoke of it with a composure that was more devastating than anger would have been. When she mentioned being invited to my wedding, her words carried no bitterness - only a sad acceptance that cut deeper than any accusation could have.

The drive home was heavy with unspoken words, each mile marking the distance not just between places, but between who we had been and who we were becoming. The wilderness had always been our sanctuary, the place where we found ourselves and each other. Now it had become the setting for the end of our story, as natural and inevitable as the changing of seasons.

Back to Tiraz

The moment we arrived home, I noticed Nadia's mother and sister waiting outside our apartment. For months, they had watched Nadia withdraw into herself, losing weight, sleeping less, her usual vibrancy dimming to a shadow. Today, they had come determined to understand what was destroying their daughter and sister.

"We need to talk," her mother began, concern etching deep lines around her eyes. "Nadia, you haven't been yourself. We can see you're suffering. Please, tell us what's wrong."

Something in their presence, their worried faces, their love - it broke something in Nadia. All the pain she'd carried alone for months, all the nights she'd lain awake knowing but not wanting to face the truth, everything she'd discovered during our trip - it all came crashing through the walls she'd built.

"Darian!" The scream that tore from her throat made us all jump. "I know about Elina! I know it's Elina!" She rushed past everyone to my desk, her hands sweeping across the surface with violent force. Ink bottles crashed to the floor, their contents spreading like dark rivers across the hardwood.

"I know she arranged these! I know she was here! I know everything!" Each word carried months of suppressed anguish, each crash of falling items punctuating her pain.

"Stop that! This can be solved," her mother pleaded, still trying to understand what was unfolding before her.

"He loves her, Mom!" Nadia collapsed then, her composure finally shattering as deep, wracking sobs shook her body. Her sister and mother screamed in shock as understanding dawned, their protective instincts surging as they moved to hold her.

The Third Day of the Trip

The morning of our third day in the mountains had started like so many before it. The crisp air held that special clarity we'd always loved, the kind that made photography perfect. We'd done this so many times over our decade together - chasing perfect shots, sharing in the thrill of wildlife sightings, moving in the synchronization that comes from years of shared adventures.

"Can I use your phone?" Nadia had asked casually as we paused at the viewpoint. "I want to try that new photo app you mentioned." It was such a normal request between us - we'd shared phones for photography hundreds of times before.

I handed it over without hesitation, my attention already caught by movement in the distance. "Bears!" I whispered excitedly, grabbing my camera with the long lens. Two magnificent brown bears had emerged from the tree line, their powerful forms silhouetted against the morning light.

Lost in the thrill of wildlife photography, I moved with practiced precision, adjusting settings and focusing on capturing the perfect shot.

Minutes passed as I worked, completely absorbed in my craft, the familiar excitement of documenting these magnificent creatures pushing everything else from my mind.

When I finally lowered my camera, the satisfaction of capturing the bears quickly turned to concern. Nadia was nowhere in sight. My heart began to race as I scanned the area. This region was known for its wildlife - not just bears, but wolves and leopards too. Attacks weren't uncommon, especially in the deeper parts of the wilderness where we'd ventured.

"Nadia!" I called out, my voice echoing across the mountainside. No response. "NADIA!" Louder now, panic beginning to edge into my voice. We'd been so careful all these years, always staying within sight of each other. This wasn't like her.

I started searching, moving in widening circles from our spot, calling her name every few steps. The silence that answered was deafening. Half an hour passed, each minute stretching endlessly as worst-case scenarios played through my mind. She still had my phone, so I couldn't even call her. The beautiful morning had turned menacing - every rustle in the undergrowth could be a predator, every shadow a potential threat.

What I didn't know then was that Nadia had found a secluded spot behind a large boulder, where she sat reading through months of messages between Elina and me. While I searched frantically for physical dangers, she was discovering a different kind of wound - each message, each photo, each intimate exchange between Elina and me cutting deeper than any predator's claws could. Her hands trembled as she scrolled through conversation after conversation, piecing together the story of how her marriage had slowly unraveled while she wasn't looking.

Finally, after what felt like hours, I spotted her. She stood at the edge of a small clearing, still clutching my phone, her back to me and shoulders rigid. Something about her posture made me pause - there was a tension there I'd never seen before.

"Nadia! Thank god!" I rushed toward her. "I was worried sick! There are bears and leopards out here - you can't just disappear like that!"

She turned slowly, and for a moment, I caught an expression on her face that I couldn't quite read before she masked it. She handed me back my phone without a word, her movements mechanical. I had no idea that in those thirty minutes of searching for her, she had uncovered every secret I'd been trying to hide.

****

Standing in our destroyed living room, watching Nadia finally share her burden with her family, everything became terrifyingly clear. That moment by the bears had changed everything - though I hadn't realized it until now. The truth had been there in my phone, in messages and photos I thought were safely hidden, in the evidence of a love that had grown alongside our marriage until it threatened to destroy everything we'd built together.

I grabbed my laptop and a few essentials, my movements automatic as Nadia's mother tried to block my path. "I can't live here anymore," I said quietly but firmly, the words feeling final as they left my mouth.

The familiar rumble of Titanus's engine offered no comfort as I drove away into the gathering darkness. In my rearview mirror, I caught one last glimpse of our apartment building - the home where Nadia and I had built our life together, now the scene of its destruction. Behind me, three women bound by love and now by shared grief supported each other through the aftermath of my choices. And somewhere in the city, Elina waited, unaware that everything had changed.

After leaving the ruins of my apartment, with the echo of Nadia's sobs still ringing in my ears, I called Elina as I drove.

"Hi, my life," she answered, her voice trembling with worry. "Welcome back."

"Elina, there's a problem. Nadia knows everything and knows it's you. I just left the house. I'm coming to you so we can figure out what to do."

When I arrived, she climbed into my car, her face pale and etched with stress. As we talked, Nadia called her. The moment Elina saw the name on her screen, her hand shook so badly she nearly dropped the phone.

"Didn't you see those pictures when you came to our house?" Nadia spat venomously. "I just hope you build a house, a family with love and passion, and someone comes and destroys it for you."

"I wish Nadia were a bad person," I said after the call ended, watching Elina try to compose herself. "She has a kind heart, and that makes this so much harder."

Elina was terrified that Nadia would confront her family. I assured her no one knew where she lived and suggested she lie if necessary, claiming I had tricked her into the relationship. It was the only way to protect her, though the thought of putting her in such a position made my chest tighten with guilt.

Then my phone buzzed - my mother's name appearing on the screen. My stomach tightened as I hesitated, but I knew I had to answer.

"Darian, what is going on?" she asked, her voice tight with worry and frustration. "Nadia called me. She's devastated. She says you've been talking to... to some girl."

I gripped the steering wheel harder. "Mom, it's not that simple," I began, but she interrupted me.

"Not that simple? What's not simple about this, Darian? You're married! To Nadia! You built a life together. How could you do this to her?" Her words were laced with a mix of disappointment and disbelief.

"I didn't plan for this to happen, Mom," I said, my voice faltering. "It just... it happened."

"Don't you dare tell me it just happened," she snapped. "Who is this girl? What has she done to you?"

"She hasn't done anything, Mom," I said, trying to stay calm. "This is my fault."

"Darian," she continued, her tone now more pleading than angry, "Nadia is a good woman. She's loved you, supported you, and been there for you through everything. And now you're throwing her away for... what? For someone who has no place in your life?"

Her words cut deep, and for a moment, I couldn't respond.

"I'm not throwing anyone away, Mom. Things just aren't working anymore," I tried to explain, but she didn't want to hear it.

"What's not working, Darian? You've been together for years. And now, because of some girl, you're ready to destroy everything?"

"It's more complicated than that," I said, my voice barely above a whisper.

"Complicated?" she repeated bitterly. "The only thing complicated here is how you can justify breaking Nadia's heart—and mine. I thought I raised you better."

Her words hit me like a punch to the gut. "I didn't mean for any of this to happen," I said, my voice breaking. "I'm trying to figure things out."

"Well, figure it out fast," she snapped. "You're losing everything that matters, Darian."

And then, without another word, she hung up on me. The silence that followed was deafening, the weight of her words settling heavily on my chest. Beside me, Elina sat motionless, her eyes fixed on the dashboard, tears silently rolling down her cheeks. In that moment, the full weight of what we'd done - of the lives we'd upended - pressed down on both of us like a physical thing.

I continued with the evening after everything exploded. That night, despite the chaos we'd unleashed, Elina snuck out to bring me a pillow and blanket. She moved like a shadow through the darkness, her concern for my comfort a sharp contrast to the pain we'd caused others. An hour later, she returned with a sandwich, accidentally letting her dog escape in the process. I watched, finding an unexpected moment of lightness as she chased the dog down the street in her pajamas. She handed me the sandwich, her face flushed from the chase, and disappeared back inside without a word.

Exhausted from the seven-hour drive, the fight, and the emotional turmoil, I fell asleep in the car. The confined space felt fitting somehow - a self-imposed exile from the life I'd destroyed. At dawn, I refreshed myself at a gas station and headed to work, my mind a chaotic swirl of thoughts. When Elina arrived later, her face mirrored the stress I felt.

During the day, Nadia's mother called me and requested to meet at a coffee shop. Her voice carried the weight of desperation, and I agreed, knowing this conversation was inevitable. She was here to save her daughter's life—or at least, what was left of it.

"This morning, I went into her room," she began, her voice heavy with sorrow. "She was hugging your T-shirt, clutching it to her chest as if it was the last piece of you she could hold on to."

I felt my chest tighten. The image hit me hard - Nadia had taken one of my T-shirts with her to Shinar after she discovered the betrayal. She had always said my scent comforted her, made her feel close to me. Now, in the depths of her pain, she was doing the same thing again— trying to hold on to something tangible when everything else felt like it was slipping away.

"I'm sorry for what happened," I said finally, though the words felt hollow. "I have no idea how it got to this point."

Her eyes searched mine, sharp and piercing, as though trying to extract the truth from me. "What is your plan, Darian? Be honest with me."

I hesitated. The truth? The truth was chaos. "I'm sorry… I don't know what to say," I replied.

"Are you going to fix this, or are you going to leave her?" she pressed, her voice firm but pleading.

"I… I need to talk to Nadia about this," I muttered.

"She doesn't want to talk to you right now," she said flatly. "If you truly want to get back to your life and correct this, you have to stop lying. No more lies. She gave you a second chance, and even then, you didn't stop seeing that girl."

"I know," I said softly, looking down at my hands. "It's so complicated."

Her voice cracked with emotion. "Let me make it simple for you. If this was just some mistake, if you can be honest and stay honest, I will help you. But if you're not going to try, if you've made up your mind to leave her… just leave her alone. Don't drag her through this pain any longer."

She leaned forward, her voice trembling as she continued. "Do you realize what you've done? You haven't just hurt Nadia. You've destroyed three families. I love your mother and brothers—they've become my family, too. But you've torn all of us apart."

I sat there, silent, feeling the weight of her words pressing down on me. I wanted to speak, to defend myself, but I had no defense. Not really.

Later that evening, she came by with a bundle of my shirts. She handed them to me without a word, her expression a mix of sadness and resolve. I took them, unable to meet her gaze. Each shirt seemed to carry the weight of memories - moments with Nadia, the life we'd built, everything I'd thrown away for a love I hadn't seen coming.

That night, my mother called. "Come home," she said sharply, her tone leaving no room for argument. She suspected I was staying at Elina's house in the western village, and her mistrust only amplified the tension. When I arrived at my parents' home, my mother's questions came like arrows, each one finding its mark.

"Why, Darian? How could you do this to Nadia?" she demanded. "What could possibly make you throw away ten years of marriage?"

I had no answers that would satisfy her - no way to explain how I'd found myself falling in love with someone else while still loving my wife. How do you tell your mother that your heart had betrayed not just your marriage, but everything she'd taught you about loyalty and commitment?

Throughout this, Elina and I maintained constant contact. Each message felt like a lifeline - but also like evidence of my inability to make a clean break in either direction. I was living two lives: one surrounded by family who reminded me of my betrayal with every look, and another with Elina, where love and guilt twisted together until I could hardly tell them apart.

The next day, I met Elina in Arj. She looked small and fragile in the corner of the café, her usual confidence dimmed by the weight of our situation. We sat holding hands across the table, the warmth of her fingers contrasting with the cold knot in my stomach.

"The whole world is against us, Elina," I said finally, breaking the heavy silence between us.

"I know," she replied, her eyes brimming with tears. "But you're my life, Darian. I can't imagine living without you."

Her words both warmed and wounded me. The depth of her love was clear, but so was the impossibility of our situation. How could I promise her anything when my entire life was unraveling?

"I need to get away for a while," I said, avoiding her gaze. "I want to go out this weekend, be with nature, clear my head."

She nodded silently, her grip on my hand tightening slightly. Even her silence spoke volumes about the fear she couldn't voice - fear that I might not come back, that the pressure would prove too much.

I left my mother's house the next day, unable to bear her constant reminders of what I'd done to Nadia. The weight of disapproval and disappointment followed me as I drove to a quiet village, seeking refuge in solitude. Elina's messages came steadily, each one a mix of love and worry, support and fear.

Meanwhile, Nadia's presence in my life had transformed into something unrecognizable. She came once to bring some of my clothes, but the woman who'd shared my adventures for a decade might as well have been a stranger. Her eyes, once warm with love, now held only cold distance. Her family had taken possession of my belongings - my pens, cameras, everything that made up my daily life - hoping the pressure would force me to choose.

I found myself adrift between the wreckage of my marriage and the uncertain promise of a new love, weighted down by guilt yet unable to let go of either path. Each day brought new complications, new pain, new evidence of how thoroughly I'd destroyed not just my own life, but the lives of everyone who loved me.

Early June

The weight of our wedding anniversary pressed heavily in the June air. In years past, this date had been marked with adventures and celebration - now it stood as a monument to everything we'd lost. Nadia had retreated deep into her work at the hospital, building walls not just against me, but against everyone who tried to reach her. Her silence felt like an accusation.

During these days, my meetings with Elina became both refuge and reminder of what I'd done. In our rented apartment, we could pretend the world outside didn't exist, that our love hadn't left such destruction in its wake. But reality had a way of intruding, usually through my constantly buzzing phone.

One evening, as I was finishing work, Marjan called - one of Nadia's closest friends from the hospital. Her voice carried the weight of someone who had witnessed too much pain.

"You have no idea how much she loves you," Marjan began, frustration and sorrow threading through her words. "I haven't seen anything like this in my entire life."

I sighed, guilt and defensiveness warring in my chest. "Do you know what she's done to me, Marjan? She involved my mom, my family, her family... everyone. She didn't just hurt herself; she dragged everyone into this."

"I know," Marjan admitted. "She made mistakes, but you have to understand—she's not in a normal state of mind. You should talk to her."

"She won't even answer my calls," I replied, the futility of it all weighing on me.

"She's devastated, Darian. She's not eating, not sleeping properly, and she was seriously considering ending her life. You're the only one who can pull her out of this."

Her words hit me like physical blows. Despite everything, the thought of Nadia in such pain made my chest constrict.

"Everyone in the hospital knows about you, by the way," Marjan continued softly. "Nadia talked so much about you before. She made sure they all knew how much she loved you."

Later, when Nadia finally agreed to meet, we found ourselves at a sushi restaurant with Marjan and her husband - a place that held countless memories of happier times. When a familiar song began playing - one that had accompanied so many of our Titanus adventures - Nadia's eyes filled with tears. She fled to the bathroom, leaving behind a silence heavy with shared understanding.

On the drive home that evening, I noticed something strange. Nadia was deliberately avoiding contact with her family, hiding the fact that she was with me.

"Why are you hiding this?" I asked, puzzled by this secrecy from someone who had initially involved everyone in our drama.

"My mom keeps intruding," she admitted quietly. "They're pressuring me to get a divorce."

The irony wasn't lost on me - here I was, planning to end our marriage, while she hid from those pushing her toward the same conclusion. The complexity of our situation seemed to deepen with each passing day. Even as I told myself this was just about helping her through the transition, about easing her pain before making the final break, something in her vulnerability kept pulling at threads I thought I'd severed.

The city lights blurred past us as we drove in silence, each lost in thoughts of what had been and what could never be again. Somewhere across town, Elina waited, representing a future I both yearned for and feared. And beside me sat the woman who had shared my life for a decade, now more stranger than wife, yet still capable of stirring emotions I couldn't quite name.

The Day Everything Changed

Summer heat pressed against the windows of Titanus as I drove toward the mall, my thoughts on the coffee meeting planned with Elina. These meetings had become our sanctuary—moments stolen from an increasingly complicated life. But today would shatter everything we thought we knew.

My phone's harsh ring cut through the quiet. Nadia's name flashed on the screen, and something in my chest tightened. When I answered, her voice carried an edge I'd never heard before.

"Where are you, Darian?" The sharpness in her tone made me grip the steering wheel tighter. "You should come to me now—and bring Elina with you."

"I'm out," I snapped, defensive walls rising instantly. "Where do you think I am?"

"You and Elina need to meet me in half an hour, or I'll come to your office and wait for you both there!" The threat in her voice was unmistakable.

I tried to maintain control, keep my voice steady. "Ask Elina yourself. I have no idea where she is." The lie felt bitter on my tongue as I hung up.

Minutes later, Elina called. We quickly agreed to meet Nadia separately, though neither of us fully understood what awaited us. As I pulled up to the address Nadia had provided, I watched them approach my car through the rearview mirror—Nadia, her movements sharp with purpose, heading for the passenger seat, and Elina, hesitant but determined, sliding into the back.

The tension in the car was suffocating. Nadia turned in her seat, her eyes blazing with a fury I'd never seen. "When you came to our house," she directed at Elina, her voice trembling with barely contained rage, "didn't you see the pictures on the wall? Didn't you notice the ring on his hand?"

Elina's reflection in my mirror showed tears beginning to form. "I'm sorry," she whispered, the words seeming to catch in her throat.

I couldn't bear to watch her pain. "Elina, please wait in your car," I said softly, though my heart hammered in my chest.

Alone with Nadia, the façade crumbled completely.

"You went to the therapist together. I know everything," she spat, each word a bullet aimed at my conscience.

Something in me snapped. "What do you want, Nadia? Get out of my life. We're over." The words came out harsher than I'd intended, but I couldn't stop. "When someone doesn't want you, why do you insist on staying?"

Her response was explosive. In one fluid motion, she grabbed my glasses and smashed them into my face. Pain bloomed above my eye as the frames cut into my skin. Blood trickled down as she reached for my phone, and in that moment of chaos and pain, I did the unthinkable— I slapped her.

The sound seemed to echo in the confined space of the car. We both froze, the reality of what had just happened settling over us like a heavy blanket. In ten years of marriage, through all our struggles and disagreements, I had never raised a hand to her. The look of shock and betrayal on her face would haunt me forever.

From her car, Elina had witnessed everything. She approached quickly, sliding into the passenger seat, her face a mask of disbelief and anger. Without warning, she began hitting me, her fists connecting with my shoulders and chest.

"You slapped Nadia because of me?" she cried, tears streaming down her face. Before I could respond, she was gone, the car door slamming behind her.

In the aftermath of the confrontation, Elina took Nadia to her meeting. Hours stretched like years until Nadia called again, asking for a ride home. When I picked her up, the tension between us was different now—no longer explosive, but heavy with the weight of what we'd broken.

"Just drive," she said softly. "Anywhere."

I drove aimlessly through the city streets as she requested, each familiar turn now feeling somehow foreign. Eventually, she asked for a cigarette. Without thinking, I headed to our spot—the hill overlooking the city where we'd spent countless evenings together.

She held the unlit cigarette between her fingers, turning it over and over. We both knew I wouldn't let her light it. She'd given up smoking when we first got together, one of many changes she'd made for our relationship. Now that sacrifice felt like another accusation in the growing list between us.

"Take me to my mother's," she finally said, her voice barely above a whisper. The cigarette disappeared into her bag, unlit.

Before we reached her parents' house, she asked to get out early. The reason hung unspoken between us—her father would be waiting, and we both knew what would come next. I watched her walk away, her figure growing smaller in my rearview mirror.

I drove to my mother's house, seeking refuge in the only place that still made sense. As I lay in bed, emotionally drained from the day's events, her father's messages began flooding my phone. Each word was a bullet of rage and accusation, the fury of a father watching his daughter's heart break. I blocked his number, letting my phone fall beside me on the bed.

Minutes later, another message appeared—this time from Elina. She told me she'd been to the doctor because of leg pain caused by the overwhelming stress of the day. Though she tried to reassure me she was fine, her words couldn't hide the weight of everything that had happened.

The darkness pressed in around me as I stared at the ceiling, the day's events playing on an endless loop in my mind. Between Nadia's quiet despair and Elina's distress, the web of love, betrayal, and broken trust seemed impossible to untangle. My life, once so full of clarity and purpose, had become a storm of unwritten futures, each path more uncertain than the last.

The Morning After

The morning after the confrontation, I found myself driving toward Baharvan, unable to face the sterile confines of the office. Yesterday's events played through my mind like a fever dream—the violence with Nadia, Elina's tearful rage, the barrage of messages from Nadia's father. Each memory felt like a fresh wound.

When I picked up Elina, the difference was immediately apparent. Usually, she would eagerly slide behind Titanus's wheel, her joy in driving my cherished vehicle a quiet symbol of our connection. Today, she settled silently into the passenger seat, her usual vibrancy dimmed by exhaustion and unspoken words.

The drive to our usual coffee shop passed in heavy silence. Inside, surrounded by the familiar warmth and aroma of coffee, I reached for her hand across the table, seeking some connection through the tension that stretched between us.

"Your crazy therapist was the cause of all these problems," I said, unable to keep the frustration from my voice. The words felt like stones dropping into still water.

Her eyes narrowed as she studied my face. "How so?"

"When we sent Nadia to that stupid therapist, it seems like she intentionally dropped hints about us," I explained, the words tumbling out. "Nadia somehow pieced everything together. That therapist probably wanted to stir the pot and send her to us, knowing she'd unleash her anger."

"I'm going to call their clinic today," Elina said firmly, her fingers tightening around her coffee cup until her knuckles whitened.

"Ok, but I honestly have no energy left for another fight," I sighed, meeting her gaze. "Especially with you after what happened yesterday."

Her expression shifted, a mixture of pain and accusation crossing her face. "You slapped Nadia for me."

"No," I said firmly, needing her to understand. "It wasn't about you. She took my phone, broke my glasses right into my face, and was about to walk away with my phone. Everything I have is in that phone, Elina. I didn't have a choice."

I rubbed my arm unconsciously, remembering her own fury. "But you have a heavy hand. You slapped me and hit me pretty hard."

"I am sorry," she said after a long pause, her voice smaller than I'd ever heard it. "You have no idea what kind of night I had."

"I know. I was on the phone with you most of the time," I reminded her gently. "But I also had to deal with Nadia's dad. It wasn't just you."

We let the conversation fade into silence, each sip of coffee an attempt to return to normalcy. But work waited for no one, especially with the looming deadline for our Netherlands startup visa application. The prospect of leaving Parin—our home—felt increasingly real, a strange mixture of escape and exile.

The weight of other changes pressed in as well. This would be our final month at Nexara Labs, the company that had been the backdrop to our evolving relationship. The new CEO's decision not to retain Elina, given her position as my assistant, meant our last days would align. Two weeks remained to say goodbye to the place where everything had begun.

As we sat there, processing yesterday's chaos while planning tomorrow's escape, I realized how completely our lives had become entangled. Every decision, every plan, every future step now involved us both—a fact that both thrilled and terrified me. The bruises from yesterday's confrontations were still fresh, but here we were, already planning our next chapter together.

Echoes of Dreams

Standing in my emptying office at Nexara Labs, my hand traced the smooth glass desk where I'd sketched countless ideas over the years. As I packed away the last remnants of my time here, memories washed over me like waves, pulling me back to where it all began.

Five years earlier, I stood in an abandoned factory hall, dust motes dancing in the weak sunlight that filtered through grimy windows. The space was vast, empty, and full of possibility. My footsteps echoed as I walked through the cavernous room, my mind already transforming the decay into something vibrant and alive.

We started in a tiny room off the main hall - just five of us crammed into a space barely big enough for our dreams. The paint was peeling, the heating unreliable, but the energy was electric. I can still see Maya's face when she presented her first prototype, her hands trembling with excitement as she explained how her solar purification system could change lives. Tom hunched over his laptop in the corner, coding until dawn, fueled by cheap coffee and pure determination. Sarah's laughter bouncing off the walls as she celebrated landing our first major investor.

That first winter tested everything we had. The insulation was practically non-existing, making the vast factory hall feel like an ice cave. We could see our breath hanging in the air during morning meetings, and the tiny space heaters we'd brought in would trip the ancient electrical system if we dared to run more than two at once. I remember Maya wearing fingerless gloves while soldering circuit boards, her determination stronger than the cold that crept through every crack and crevice.

Then came the rain. None of us will ever forget that first major storm - the sound of water hitting the metal roof was like a thousand drums, making it almost impossible to hear each other speak. At first, we thought we could weather it, huddled in our small office space with cups of steaming coffee. Then Tom noticed the puddle forming in the corner.

Within hours, our innovative hub had transformed into an indoor lake. Water poured through hidden gaps in the roof, creating streams that snaked across our newly installed flooring. We scrambled to save equipment, forming a human chain to move computers and prototypes to higher ground. Sarah's laptop got caught in the flood - three months of market research floating away in the deluge. But instead of crying over it, she laughed, took off her shoes, and started wading through the water to rescue what she could.

I remember standing in ankle-deep water at 2 AM, watching our dreams quite literally drowning around us. The team had gone home hours ago, but I couldn't leave. This factory, this space - it wasn't just a building. It was everything we believed in, everything we hoped to create. As I moved through the flooded hall with a flashlight, checking for any salvageable equipment, I made a silent promise to these walls that we would rebuild, stronger than before.

The next morning, instead of giving up, our small team showed up with mops, buckets, and an unshakeable determination. We spent days drying out the space, replacing damaged materials, and reinforcing the roof. Each setback only seemed to strengthen our resolve. We weren't just building a business incubator - we were building a testament to resilience.

I remember our first demo day at Tiraz University like it was yesterday. The auditorium was too big for our small group, making us look almost comically ambitious. I had paced backstage, adjusting my tie for the hundredth time, while our first batch of startups rehearsed their pitches until their voices were hoarse. The projector had malfunctioned ten minutes before we were set to begin, and I'd found myself on my knees under the podium, frantically rewiring connections while trying to maintain a calm facade.

But when the lights dimmed and our first founder took the stage, something magical happened. The room filled with an energy I'd never felt before - the pure, raw potential of ideas taking flight. I watched from the wings as each team presented, my heart swelling with a pride that felt almost paternal. Even now, I can close my eyes and hear the applause that erupted when Maya demonstrated her prototype, the excited murmurs that rippled through the crowd as investors reached for their phones.

From there, everything seemed to accelerate. The abandoned factory transformed into a buzzing hub of innovation, its walls now gleaming with fresh paint and new ideas. Our tiny room expanded into an entire floor, then two, then the whole building. Each success story added another layer to our legacy - the AI startup that revolutionized farming, the sustainable energy project that caught international attention, the medical device that saved countless lives.

We became more than just an incubator; we became a family. Every failure was shared, every victory celebrated together. Late-night strategy sessions turned into early morning breakthroughs. The coffee machine became our gathering spot, where billion-dollar ideas were born between sips of espresso.

Now, standing in my office one last time, these memories feel so vivid they're almost tangible. The glass walls I'd insisted on - my statement about transparency and openness - reflect the afternoon light, creating patterns that seem to dance with ghosts of past conversations. Every scratch on my desk tells a story, every worn spot in the carpet marks a path I've paced while solving problems.

This was where I first met Elina, her quiet confidence and sharp intelligence immediately catching my attention. Here, in this very room, I'd watched her grow from an efficient assistant into someone who understood the heartbeat of what we'd built. Someone who saw not just what Nexara Labs was, but what it could become.

The irony doesn't escape me - that this place which represented my greatest professional achievement would also be where everything in my personal life began to shift. These walls have witnessed both my triumphs and my struggles, the slow unraveling of one life as another began to take shape.

As I pack the last box, my fingers brush against the marker I used for sketching ideas on glass - a simple tool that helped shape so many dreams. Everything we built here started with just an idea, scribbled hastily on these transparent surfaces. Now those same surfaces would hold someone else's visions, someone else's dreams.

The sun is setting as I take one final walk through the halls, each step echoing with memories. From that dusty, abandoned factory to this thriving center of innovation - what a journey it has been. I pause at the main entrance, remembering all the times I'd walked through these doors burning with purpose and possibility. Now, walking out for the last time, I carry with me not just memories, but the weight of knowing that endings and beginnings are often the same thing.

This chapter of my life was closing, but another was already being written. As I turned the key in the lock one final time, I couldn't help but wonder - what dreams would these walls hold next? What stories would they tell after I'm gone? The answers weren't mine to know anymore, and perhaps that was the hardest part of all.

Choices and Consequences

After those final moments at Nexara Labs, the world seemed to shift on its axis. The company I'd built from a flooded factory floor into a thriving innovation hub now belonged to someone else. The halls that had witnessed countless breakthroughs, failures, and triumphs would now hold different dreams. As I drove away that last time, the rearview mirror showed more than just a building growing smaller - it showed a chapter of my life closing irrevocably.

The days that followed blurred together, filled with stolen moments with Elina and guilt-laden messages with Nadia. Each morning brought both anticipation and remorse - the thrill of planning a future with Elina warring with the knowledge of what it was costing others. Nadia's messages remained unfailingly kind, each one a reminder of the grace I didn't deserve.

When my mother's heart problems sent her to the hospital, these carefully separated worlds collided with the force of a thunderclap. I arrived to find Nadia already there, every inch the skilled doctor, conferring with colleagues about treatment options. The sight of her in her element - competent, caring, completely focused on helping others - made my chest ache with a familiar pride that I no longer had the right to feel.

My brothers' reaction to her presence cut deep. They embraced her without hesitation, their faces lighting up as if nothing had changed, as if she was still their sister in every way that mattered. But it was my mother's response that nearly broke me. The moment she saw Nadia, tears spilled down her weathered cheeks. "My daughter," she whispered, reaching for her with trembling hands. The way Nadia held her, gentle yet sure, speaking soft words of medical reassurance mixed with daughter-like love, showed everything she'd been to our family - everything I was throwing away.

After my mother's recovery, when Nadia tentatively suggested rebuilding our life together, her voice carried both hope and fear. The pain that flashed across her face at my refusal haunted me for days. But the truth was inescapable - I couldn't imagine my life without Elina anymore. What we shared had become as essential as breathing, even as it destroyed the foundations of everything I'd built before.

Her call about watering the flowers felt like another twist of the knife. Walking into what had been our home felt like entering a museum of memories - each room, each corner holding echoes of the life we'd built together. The space felt both achingly familiar and somehow foreign, as if the house itself knew I no longer belonged there.

Among the flowers on the balcony, my eyes were drawn to Hope, thriving in its ceramic box. The memory of how it came to be there flooded back with startling clarity. It had been one of those perfect mornings with Elina, sunlight streaming through the leaves as we worked on the balcony garden together. She had pulled out a small paper envelope, handling it with such care that I knew immediately it held something precious.

"These seeds," she had said softly, her fingers trembling slightly as she opened the envelope, "they're from my grandmother's garden. She collected them herself from her favorite flowers." Her voice had carried such tenderness, such reverence for this connection to her past. "I've been saving them, waiting for the right moment, the right place."

Then she had placed them in my palm, her fingers lingering against my skin. The trust in that gesture, sharing something so personally valuable, had taken my breath away. We had planted those seeds together in this very box, both of us watching in anticipation as they slowly sprouted and grew into something beautiful.

Now, seeing Hope's box among Nadia's carefully tended garden felt like both a blessing and a betrayal. Without hesitation, I lifted the ceramic container, knowing this piece of our story needed to come with me. This wasn't just a plant in a box - it was a living testament to the trust Elina had placed in me, to the future we were building together.

When I brought it to Elina later, her eyes welled with emotion as she recognized what I held. "You kept it alive," she whispered, reaching out to touch the leaves with gentle fingers. "My grandmother's flowers..."

"This is Hope," I said softly, watching as she looked at the plant that carried so much meaning for both of us. In that moment, the name felt more significant than ever - not just a plant grown from cherished seeds, but a symbol of everything we were risking, everything we were building together.

Early July

Early July The mountain air carried a crisp sweetness as I drove up to the skiing resort, seeking solitude in its off-season quiet. Summer had transformed the winter playground into a sanctuary of stillness, perfect for the escape I desperately needed. For four nights, I immersed myself in the rhythm of archery practice, the familiar tension and release of my bow grounding me as I worked on finalizing plans for our Netherlands venture.

Without my camera - now with Nadia's family along with other personal items - I felt somehow incomplete. Yet the mountains held their own medicine, offering a different kind of clarity through their ancient silence. Each arrow I released seemed to carry with it some of the confusion that had been clouding my mind.

The discovery that I'd left my earpods at the hotel seemed trivial at first. It was the other loss that weighed more heavily - one of three special arrows Elina had given me. Each arrow carried profound meaning: one for her, one for me, and one for our imagined future child we'd named Arlen. The arrow I'd lost during practice was Arlen's, and its absence felt oddly prophetic.

Our relationship had been strained lately. Trust issues surfaced when I discovered she'd hidden the true nature of her relationship with someone she'd claimed was "just a friend." The revelation that he was an ex created fissures in our connection that ran deeper than either of us wanted to admit. When she learned about the lost arrow, it became another point of tension, another reason to make the drive back to the resort together.

The two-hour journey to retrieve both the earpods and arrow marked our first longer road trip together. The silence in the car felt heavy with unspoken words, the distance between us measured not in kilometers but in the space between our hearts. When we reached the resort, Elina immediately began searching for the arrow with an intensity that spoke of deeper meanings.

"Elina, stop searching," I called out, watching her comb through the grass with increasing desperation.

The sadness in her eyes when she looked up struck something in me. Here we were, searching for a symbol of a future that seemed increasingly uncertain. The reality of our situation pressed in - the complexity of our age difference, our fundamentally different approaches to life, the weight of my ongoing divorce. Yet every time we were together, these obstacles seemed to dissolve in the magnetic pull between us.

Our problems crystallized in a moment of frustration when words escaped me that I knew I couldn't take back: "I had a happy life and you came in the middle of my marriage and ruined it." The moment the words left my mouth, I watched them land like physical blows. The silence that followed was deafening, filled with the kind of hurt that changes things forever.

Trying to salvage something from the wreckage of my outburst, I pulled over near a river. The water flowed with an indifferent serenity, a stark contrast to the turbulence between us. We took photos by the riverside, each click of the camera capturing forced smiles that couldn't quite mask the pain underneath. These moments felt like desperate attempts to hold onto something that was slowly slipping through our fingers.

Further down the road, fate offered a small chance at redemption. A farmer's honey stall caught my eye, set back about 500 meters from the main road. I pulled the Titanus over, the gravel crunching under its tires.

"I want to buy honey for my mom. Do you want some too?" I offered, trying to bridge the chasm between us.

"No!" Her response came sharp and quick, laden with lingering hurt.

While she wandered toward the water, I bought two jars anyway. Without a word, I slipped one into her bag - a silent gesture of care that felt insufficient against the weight of my earlier words. When I returned to her, the dam finally broke. She turned to me, tears streaming down her face, and collapsed into my arms. The honey jar pressed between us, a small token of sweetness in our bitter moment.

"This place is beautiful," she whispered through tears.

"I know somewhere even better," I offered, grasping at any chance to extend our time together, to maybe find our way back to each other. "We've got time. We can always return here later."

The drive led us to a narrow valley where mountains pressed close on either side, the river running alongside us like a silver thread. The scene that greeted us seemed almost staged - two cars stranded mid-river, their occupants waving frantically for help. Without hesitation, I turned the Titanus toward the water.

"Ready for some adrenaline?" I asked, watching her expression shift from sadness to curiosity.

But the river had other plans. Soon, the Titanus too sat mired in mud, the front differential failing to engage. What started as a rescue attempt had turned into shared predicament, forcing us to work together despite our earlier conflict. As we dug at the mud surrounding the wheels, I caught glimpses of the woman I'd fallen for - determined, resilient, willing to get her hands dirty alongside me.

With determination, I grabbed the shovel from Titanus and began attacking the mud around our wheels, sweat mixing with river water as I worked. The task felt impossible - each shovelful of mud seemed to be replaced by more sliding down from the riverbank. I was so focused on my work that I almost missed Elina joining me.

She had quietly picked up another shovel and, without a word, began digging alongside me. The sight of her - still dressed for a casual outing but now ankle-deep in river mud, working with fierce determination - caught me off guard. Despite our earlier argument, despite my cruel words, here she was, refusing to let me face this challenge alone.

"Stop, Elina," I said finally, watching her struggle against the relentless mud. "It's no use. We need to call for help."

She paused, leaning on her shovel, mud splattered across her clothes but a stubborn set to her jaw that spoke of her unwillingness to give up. In that moment, watching her stand there determined despite everything, I felt that familiar pull toward her - that inexplicable connection that seemed to defy all logic and circumstance.

Our shared predicament had drawn a small crowd of onlookers and fellow stranded travelers. Among them was a man with striking red hair who took charge of rallying help. From across the river, where some girls were having a picnic, someone called out "Hey, Donald Trump!" referring to his distinctive hair color. The nickname spread instantly, and soon we were all calling out "Trump, help us!" The absurdity of it broke through our tension, and I heard Elina laugh - a genuine sound that seemed to wash away some of the day's heaviness.

In the midst of our shared laughter, Elina disappeared briefly to her bag. When she returned, her expression had softened completely, the earlier strain replaced by something tender and vulnerable. She stood before me, holding the jar of honey I'd secretly slipped into her bag.

"How can you be so sweet and lovable?" she asked, her voice catching slightly. The question hung between us, heavy with implications neither of us was ready to face - how I could be both the source of her pain and her joy, how we could move from conflict to connection so seamlessly, how something as simple as a jar of honey could bridge the gap between hurt and healing.

As evening fell and a tractor finally pulled us free, I let Elina drive us home, too exhausted to maintain the walls we'd built between us. In the quiet of the car, with the day's drama behind us, I felt that familiar pull - the inexplicable rightness of being together that made everything else fade away. It was the paradox of us: apart, we were a mess of doubts and complications, but together, even covered in river mud, everything somehow made sense.

The drive back to Baharvan ended at a small coffee shop, where we sat recounting the day's adventures, finding humor in what had felt like disasters hours before. The warmth between us had returned, as it always did, but now carried a new understanding - that love, even at its strongest, sometimes needs more than just chemistry to survive. Yet as I watched her laugh over her coffee, I couldn't help but wonder if that "more" was something we could find together, or if we were just prolonging the inevitable.

***

The night at my mom's house was restless. Thoughts swirled in my mind like a storm—memories of the river, Elina's laughter as she found the honey, and the way everything seemed to fall apart when we were apart. I lay in bed staring at the ceiling, feeling the weight of two worlds pulling me in opposite directions. The Titanus sat in the driveway, caked in mud, a silent witness to my turmoil.

The next morning, I woke up early, unable to sleep any longer. I texted Elina a simple "Good morning" and stared at the screen, waiting for her reply. It came almost immediately.

"Good morning, my life. How are you feeling after yesterday? Are you okay?" she wrote.

"I'm okay. Tired, though. Yesterday was... something else," I replied.

"Let's take it easy today. No adventures, just us. Meet me at our place?" she suggested.

When we met at our usual café, Elina's eyes lit up with that special warmth she reserved just for me. She was wearing the same shoes from yesterday, now cleaned but still bearing faint traces of mud.

"My brave shovel warrior," I teased, pulling her close for a kiss.

She laughed against my lips. "Says the man who got us stuck in a river trying to play hero."

"Hey, at least we met the US president," I countered, referring to our red-haired friend from yesterday.

"Trump!" we said in unison, dissolving into laughter.

We settled into our favorite corner, hands intertwined across the table. The morning light caught in her hair, and I found myself memorizing every detail of her face - the way her eyes crinkled when she smiled, how she bit her lip when trying not to laugh.

"You know what I keep thinking about?" she asked, tracing patterns on my palm with her finger. "How you just slipped that honey into my bag, even after I said no. You knew exactly what I needed, even when I was too stubborn to admit it."

"Well, I've learned that sometimes you say no when you mean yes," I said softly, bringing her hand to my lips.

"Only with you," she whispered, her eyes meeting mine with an intensity that made my heart race. "Only ever with you."

We spent the morning trading gentle touches and soft words, the world beyond our corner fading away. Every now and then, one of us would mention something from yesterday - the mud, the tractor, our impromptu president - and we'd collapse into laughter again. But beneath the humor lay something deeper - the recognition that even in chaos, even in conflict, we somehow found our way back to each other.

The simplicity of just being together, no adventures or drama, felt like a gift. Each shared smile, each casual touch, each moment of comfortable silence reminded me why being with her felt so right, even when everything else felt wrong. In these quiet moments, the complexity of our situation seemed to dissolve, leaving only the pure, undeniable connection between us.

A Week Later

The morning light filtered through the windows of our rented apartment as I arrived, fresh from breakfast with my mom. This space had become our sanctuary, a world apart where time seemed to move differently. The familiar scent of jasmine tea greeted me as I entered - Elina was already there, curled on the couch with her favorite cup, the one she'd brought from home to make this place feel more ours.

When she saw me, her entire face transformed. The smile that bloomed across her features wasn't just happiness - it was recognition, as if some essential part of her had been waiting for this moment. She rose and came to me, and as her arms wrapped around me, I felt that now-familiar shift in my universe, the way everything else seemed to fade into soft focus when she was near.

"Did you sleep well?" The question carried more weight than its simple words, her eyes searching my face with the kind of attention that made me feel both seen and exposed.

"Not really," I admitted, my fingers almost unconsciously finding their way to the small of her back. "Too much on my mind."

"Me too." She pulled back just enough to meet my eyes, her hands still resting on my chest. "But we'll figure it out together, won't we?"

I nodded, though uncertainty churned beneath the surface. The past weeks had been a storm of emotions - moments of pure joy shattered by reality, dreams of future happiness clouded by practical concerns. Yet here we were, drawn together again and again, like magnets finding their natural alignment.

We spent the day in our bubble of shared space and quiet understanding. She teased me about my obsession with finding the perfect honey for my morning coffee, and I joked about her determined but graceless attempts at river fishing during our last trip. Our laughter felt like a shield against the world outside, if only temporarily.

As daylight began to fade, reality crept back in through the lengthening shadows. The Netherlands loomed in our future - a dream and a challenge wrapped into one. Visa applications waited on my laptop, lists of things to arrange grew longer each day, and the weight of all we'd have to leave behind pressed against my chest.

And then there was Nadia. Even here, in this space that belonged only to Elina and me, I couldn't completely silence the echo of ten years of shared life. The guilt was a constant companion, made sharper by the knowledge that I couldn't regret the path I'd chosen, even as it hurt someone I'd once promised to protect.

That evening, Elina's head rested on my chest, her breath warm through my shirt. The familiar weight of her body against mine felt like an anchor in a storm of uncertainty.

"Do you think we'll be happy there?" Her whispered question hung in the air between us, heavy with hope and fear.

"I don't know," I said honestly, my fingers threading through her hair. "But I think we have to try. It's our chance to write our own story."

She shifted slightly, her hand finding mine in the growing darkness. "I just want to be with you, Darian. The rest... we'll figure it out as we go."

Her words warmed something in my chest, but couldn't quite silence the questions that haunted my quiet moments. What if distance wasn't enough? What if our love, burning so bright now, couldn't survive the weight of everything we were leaving behind?

As night settled around us, we remained intertwined on the couch, neither willing to break the spell of the moment. Her head rose and fell with my breaths, her hair spread across my chest like silk, her hand resting over my heart as if keeping time with its beats.

"I love listening to your heartbeat," she murmured into the darkness.

I looked down at her, brushing a strand of hair from her face. The simple intimacy of the gesture caught in my throat. "Why?"

Her answer came soft but certain, like a truth she'd known all along: "Because it makes me feel safe. When I'm here, listening to your heart, it feels like home."

The future stretched before us, full of unknowns and possibilities. But in that moment, with Elina's warmth against me and the night wrapping around us like a blanket, I let myself believe that maybe love - this wild, unexpected, all-consuming love - could be enough.

Yet even as that thought settled over me, I found myself overwhelmed by the depth of her devotion. Her words about feeling safe with me still echoed in the quiet room, and something shifted in my chest - a tightening that had nothing to do with her weight against me and everything to do with the raw honesty in her voice. I found myself needing to understand more, to grasp how she could love so completely despite everything.

"What is it about me, Elina?" The question came out softer than I intended, almost vulnerable. "What is it that makes you love me so much?"

She lifted her head slightly, her eyes finding mine in the dim light. The intensity of her gaze made my breath catch - there was something almost luminous in the way she looked at me, as if she could see straight through to my core.

"Everything," she said simply, but then her words began to flow like a river breaking through a dam. "Your smell, your warm hands, your kind heart. The way you carry yourself in meetings, somehow both powerful and gentle. It's how you focus completely on whatever captures your attention - whether it's a rare bird or someone sharing their dreams. The way you look at me when you think I'm not noticing..." She paused, her fingers tracing patterns on my chest. "There are so many little things, tiny moments that add up to something I can barely explain. They just make me love you in ways that sometimes overwhelm me."

The raw honesty in her voice made something catch in my throat. Her love reflected back a version of myself I couldn't always recognize - someone worthy of such complete devotion. The weight of it pressed against my chest, not as a burden but as a truth I was still learning to carry.

I pulled her closer, needing the physical connection to anchor me as I asked, "Do you ever regret loving me?" The question emerged before I could stop it, carrying all my doubts and fears.

"Never." The word came instantly, filled with such certainty it made my heart ache. "Even with everything, I wouldn't trade a single moment of us for anything else."

Her conviction was both beautiful and terrifying. Looking down at her, I felt a sudden urge to lighten the intensity between us. A playful smirk tugged at my lips as I said, "And I love you so much too. Even more than..."

I let the words hang, watching as understanding dawned in her eyes.

"Your frying pan!" she exclaimed, her whole face lighting up with laughter.

"Exactly," I admitted, grinning as our shared joke broke through the heavy moment.

Our laughter filled the room, pushing back against the weight of reality. When it faded, she settled back against my chest, her breath warm against my skin. The steady rhythm of my heartbeat filled the silence between us, keeping time like a metronome marking moments we wished would never end.

For a precious while, the world outside ceased to exist. There were no complications, no impossible choices, no consequences waiting to catch up with us. There was just this - her warmth against me, the scent of her hair, the way her body fitted perfectly against mine as if we'd been designed to hold each other this way.

As I held her, feeling the profound weight of her love and the lingering lightness of our laughter, one truth crystallized with stunning clarity: no matter what storms lay ahead, no matter what price we might have to pay, I couldn't imagine letting her go. The realization should have frightened me, but instead it felt like coming home - as if my heart had finally found its true north, even if the path there had broken other promises along the way.

SEVEN

CIRCLES BREAKING

August descended on the city like a heavy blanket, the heat pressing against windows and seeping through walls. I found myself seeking refuge in a coworking space, far from the polished office I'd built over years of success. The anonymity of the shared desks offered something my old life couldn't - a space where I could exist without the weight of expectations, of memories, of the life I was slowly leaving behind.

For those who recognized me, it must have seemed strange - the founder of Nexara Labs hunched over a laptop at a communal table. But here, among the gentle hum of keyboards and distant conversations, I found a different kind of peace. The simplicity of the space matched the clarity I was desperately seeking in my complicated life.

Elina would join me sometimes, her presence transforming the mundane workspace into something electric. The air seemed to change when she walked in, as if the very molecules around us responded to our connection. We worked side by side, our shoulders occasionally brushing, each point of contact sending ripples of awareness through me. Even in silence, we communicated in a language of shared glances and subtle smiles, building our own world within the public space.

During the days Nadia was home, I felt the full weight of my divided heart. Our apartment, once filled with adventure stories and shared dreams, now echoed with unspoken words. Each morning brought another performance of normalcy - coffee made, pleasantries exchanged - while beneath the surface, everything crumbled. The guilt of my growing feelings for Elina twisted inside me, even as I couldn't stop myself from falling deeper.

The marriage counseling sessions laid bare the truth I'd been avoiding. "Darian wants to get divorced," they said, "but he wants Nadia to make that decision." The words cut through my carefully constructed justifications, exposing the cowardice at my core. I wanted freedom without having to be the one to break what we'd built, wanted absolution without having to face the full weight of my choices.

Nadia, ever perceptive, saw through it all. Her pain was evident in the way she moved through our home, in the careful distance she maintained even as she refused to let go. She'd always been the stronger one between us, and even now, facing the dissolution of our marriage, she showed a dignity that made my heart ache.

Each night, lying awake in our separate spaces, I felt the loop tightening around us. The woman I'd built a life with slipped further away, while thoughts of Elina consumed me. The heat of August pressed against the windows, but it was nothing compared to the burning in my chest - the desperate need to move forward colliding with the guilt of destroying something precious.

We were caught in a dance none of us knew how to end - Nadia holding onto the last threads of our marriage, me unable to fully step away yet unable to stay, and Elina waiting in the wings, her love offering both salvation and complication. The coworking space became my confessional, each day spent there another acknowledgment of how far I'd strayed from the life I'd once thought would last forever.

As summer deepened, the weight of indecision became unbearable. The loop tightened around us - every conversation with Nadia loaded with unspoken pain, every moment with Elina tinged with both joy and guilt. Days stretched into weeks, and I found myself increasingly unable to inhabit either world fully. The passionate connection I shared with Elina made returning home to Nadia feel like betrayal, while memories of my marriage haunted every stolen moment of new love.

Desperate for escape from this emotional maze, I found sanctuary in the rhythmic dance of archery. The familiar weight of my bow became an anchor in the storm of my emotions. Each evening, after leaving the coworking space where Elina and I had spent the day in our careful dance of professional distance and hidden intimacy, I would stand at the shooting line. There, my world narrowed to the perfect alignment of arrow and target. The precise movements - drawing, anchoring, releasing - offered a clarity that eluded me everywhere else.

I stayed at the club until late, often the last person to leave. Under the harsh fluorescent lights, I could pretend that my only challenge was hitting the bullseye, that my life wasn't splintering into pieces I couldn't quite hold together. But even as each arrow found its mark, my thoughts would drift to Elina - how her smile lit up our shared workspace, how her presence made everything else fade away. Then guilt would follow, sharp as an arrowhead, as I remembered Nadia's quiet dignity in the face of our crumbling marriage.

The drive home became a nightly meditation on choices and consequences. Sometimes I'd head to my mother's house, seeking the uncomplicated comfort of childhood memories. Other nights, drawn by a mix of habit and unresolved feelings, I'd return to the apartment I shared with Nadia. These visits were like ghost stories - unspoken, heavy with meaning, filled with the echoes of what we'd once been to each other.

Only Elina knew about these returns to my married home. Her understanding both comforted and confused me - how could she accept this complicated dance I was performing between past and present, between loyalty and desire? Yet she did, offering a love that seemed to expand to hold all my contradictions.

The rest of my world remained unaware of these nocturnal wanderings. To them, I had made a clean break, chosen a new path. The truth was messier, more human. Each night at the archery club, each arrow released, carried the weight of this duality - the man I had been with Nadia, the man I was becoming with Elina, and the stranger I sometimes saw in the mirror, caught between these versions of myself.

In the quiet moments between arrows, when only the soft whisper of the bowstring broke the silence, I would feel the full weight of my situation. The intensity of my feelings for Elina burned bright and undeniable, while the embers of my life with Nadia still glowed, refusing to fade completely. Each perfect shot brought momentary peace, but no amount of practice could resolve the fundamental tension of loving two women in such different ways.

The nights blended together, marked by the steady thud of arrows finding their targets, the solitary drives through sleeping streets, and the constant presence of Elina in my thoughts. Even in my moments of greatest focus, she was there - her encouragement a whisper in my mind, her love both salvation and complication. Yet alongside this new passion, the ghost of my marriage lingered, refusing to be exorcised by either time or distance.

That Virus

Mid-August brought a revelation that shattered what remained of my careful balancing act. Nadia, with the clinical precision that made her an excellent doctor, decided to get tested for sexually transmitted diseases. When she called me, her voice carried a weight I'd never heard before.

"I'm HPV positive, Darian," she said, each word falling like stones between us. "This is what you've brought into my life."

The accusation struck deep, cracking the already fragile foundation of trust between us. For ten years, our marriage had been built on absolute faith in each other. Now, standing in my office with the phone pressed to my ear, I felt the full impact of how far we'd fallen. Her tears, even through the phone line, cut through my defenses like glass.

"I've never been with anyone else before Elina," I said, the words sounding hollow even to my own ears. But it was true - despite our current situation, I had been faithful until Elina awakened something in me I couldn't control.

When I told Elina about Nadia's diagnosis, her reaction came swift and fierce. "I'll take the test," she declared, her chin lifting with determination. "But why am I automatically to blame? She works in a hospital, surrounded by patients. How can she be so sure it came from me?"

The defensive edge in her voice created a new tension between us. I found myself in an impossible position - trying to support Nadia through her health crisis while also protecting my relationship with Elina. The waiting period for Elina's test results stretched like an eternity, each day adding another layer of strain to our already complicated situation.

When Elina's results came back negative, her relief was palpable. "See?" she said, pushing the paper across the table toward me. "I told you it wasn't me." But something had shifted between us. The accusation, even proven false, had cast a shadow over our passionate connection.

During this time, I found myself drawn back to Nadia more frequently. Her vulnerability, her need for support, awakened the protector in me - the man who had promised to stand by her through sickness and health. Our shared history, the depth of our connection, pulled me back into her orbit even as my heart still yearned for Elina.

The distance this created with Elina was subtle but undeniable. Her smile, usually bright enough to light up any room, dimmed slightly. Her touch, once confident and claiming, became hesitant, questioning. We still worked side by side at the coworking space, still shared intimate moments and passionate kisses, but there was a new undertone to our interactions - a fear, perhaps, that what we had built might be more fragile than we'd imagined.

The situation forced me to confront the reality of my choices in a way I hadn't before. It wasn't just about love anymore - it was about responsibility, consequences, and the very real pain my actions had caused. Each night, as I drove home from the archery club, my thoughts would swing between them like a pendulum - Nadia's tears on one side, Elina's fading smile on the other.

The Competition

It was late August when something shifted in my life - a subtle change that would grow into something transformative. One night, after an intense session at the archery club, I posted a photo of my shooting in the dimly lit range. The image captured an arrow mid-flight, a stark silhouette against the glowing target. Within minutes, comments began to pour in, but one stood out.

A club mate had commented: "Why don't you take part in a competition? You've got the skills for it."

I stared at the message, letting the possibility sink in. Compete? Archery had always been my sanctuary, a space where I could find peace and focus. The thought of stepping onto a competitive stage felt foreign, yet somehow right. Maybe this was exactly what I needed - a challenge to channel my energy into.

The next day, I registered for an upcoming competition in Arvan, set to take place in three weeks. As I prepared, my evenings at the club took on new meaning. Each arrow I released carried purpose, each adjustment to my stance felt significant. Arvan became more than a destination - it became a beacon, something to focus on beyond the growing complexity of my daily life.

Throughout my preparation, Elina's presence became a constant source of warmth and encouragement. Her genuine interest in my practice, her thoughtful questions about technique, and her unwavering belief in my abilities touched something in me I hadn't expected. Each evening after practice, she'd ask about my progress, her voice carrying an enthusiasm that made my own excitement grow.

The drive to Arvan took about four hours, though with Titanus, I managed it in three. The solitude of the journey gave me time to think, to focus. I checked into an old, traditional hotel next to the venue, its wooden beams and stone walls creating an atmosphere that felt timeless.

That evening, watching other archers practice, I felt a familiar buzz from my phone. Elina's messages came steadily, each one carrying care and encouragement. Her attention to detail - asking if I'd eaten, if I was resting enough, if I needed anything - created a cocoon of support around me. Meanwhile, Nadia sent brief replies from her hospital shift, our connection feeling increasingly distant despite her genuine care.

The competition day arrived with crisp morning air and nervous energy. Competing in three barebow categories demanded every bit of focus I possessed. The familiar weight of my bow grounded me as I stepped onto the shooting line for the first round. Each arrow felt like an extension of my being, finding its mark with satisfying precision. Between rounds, I found myself reaching for my phone, drawing strength from Elina's steady stream of encouraging messages. Her presence, even from afar, anchored me.

By midday, I was leading in my categories, the morning's success building my confidence. During the lunch break, I headed to Titanus to prepare for the afternoon rounds, planning to switch out some arrows. The familiar click of the door closing behind me sent a jolt of panic through my system. In that split second, I saw my keys sitting on the driver's seat where I'd absently tossed them while grabbing my gear. My heart sank as I tried the handle, confirming my fear: the door had locked automatically, trapping not just my equipment but also my only means of getting back in. Only three arrows remained in my quiver, the rest locked away with my keys.

Time seemed to compress as I stood there, staring at my reflection in Titanus's window. Inside lay my carefully selected arrows, each one balanced and tested for optimal performance. The afternoon rounds would begin soon, and I had only three arrows to work with. My phone buzzed - another message from Elina: "You've got this, my hero. I believe in you."

Taking a deep breath, I focused on the problem at hand. Breaking the window wasn't an option - Titanus had been through too much with me to deserve that. I could see my keys sitting there on the seat, mocking me, just inches away yet unreachable. Years of off-road adventures had taught me to stay calm in crisis. I channeled that same composure now, methodically examining the door frame, looking for any weakness in the locking mechanism. After several tense minutes of careful manipulation, using techniques I'd learned from years of handling mechanical challenges in remote locations, I managed to trigger the lock release. The door swung open with a triumphant click, and I grabbed my keys with a mixture of relief and frustration at my own carelessness.

But the delay had cost me. The afternoon rounds began before I could properly warm up, and my rhythm felt off. Those first few ends with my remaining arrows showed in my scores - each shot carrying the residual tension from the lockout incident. I could feel my lead slipping away.

As the day stretched on, an unexpected challenge emerged. Technical difficulties with the field lighting pushed the final round into dusk. While others grumbled about the failing light, I felt a spark of anticipation. This was my element. Years of traditional archery had taught me to trust my instincts, to feel the shot rather than rely solely on sight.

The targets stood like ghostly circles in the growing darkness, but my hands knew the way. Each release became pure instinct - the culmination of countless hours of practice, of learning to trust my body's wisdom over my eyes. In these conditions, my traditional training became my greatest advantage.

My phone lit up again - Elina: "Remember what you told me about shooting in the dark? This is your moment." Her words brought a smile to my face. She had listened, really listened, when I'd explained my love for traditional archery, understanding that what others saw as a disadvantage could be a strength.

The final arrows flew true, finding their marks in the dimming light as if guided by something beyond mere sight. When the last arrow struck home, I knew before the scoring that I had done it. The gold medal in traditional barebow was mine, a victory made sweeter by the challenges overcome to achieve it.

The award ceremony felt surreal, the medal heavy around my neck reflecting the last rays of daylight. As I stood on the podium, I thought of how this day had embodied so much of what archery had taught me - patience, persistence, and the ability to find calm in chaos. The gold medal for traditional barebow and silver in the standard category caught the fading light, their weight a testament to the day's challenges overcome.

The moment I stepped down from the podium, my hands were already reaching for my phone. My first instinct, stronger than the urge to photograph the medals or text anyone else, was to share this moment with Elina. The screen lit up with her messages - a stream of encouragement and anticipation that had flowed steadily throughout the day.

Her scream of joy through the phone wrapped around me like an embrace, drowning out the noise of the dispersing crowd. "You're my hero!" she exclaimed, her pride in me amplifying my own sense of achievement. The warmth in her voice made my heart race in a way I hadn't expected, her excitement more intoxicating than the victory itself. Standing there in the gathering dusk, medal around my neck and Elina's voice in my ear, I felt something shift inside me - a realization that her belief in me had become as essential as the bow in my hands.

I called Nadia afterward, and though her congratulations were sincere, our conversation was brief due to her work schedule. "That's amazing," she said. "You're my hero." The same words as Elina's, yet somehow different.

The next day, driving to Baharvan, anticipation built in my chest with each mile. As I reached Elina's street, I slid into the passenger seat - our ritual, where she would always take the wheel of Titanus. It had become our thing, this small act of trust and intimacy.

When I saw her walking toward me, carrying colored papers decorated with "Welcome back, hero," something shifted inside me. Her eyes sparkled with joy, and as she reached me, she threw herself into my arms. The way she held me - tight, close, as if trying to eliminate any space between us - awakened something I'd been trying to ignore.

"Elina..." I started, but she silenced me with her embrace. Her warmth, her scent, her presence - everything about her felt right in a way I couldn't explain. Her passion was overwhelming, her affection undeniable, and in that moment, every complication in my life seemed to fade away.

We drove to our special place - our willow tree that had become witness to our growing connection. Standing beneath its sweeping branches, Elina's hand found mine naturally, our fingers intertwining. The setting sun painted everything in gold, and as she rested her head on my shoulder, I felt a peace I hadn't known I was missing.

Later at the coffee shop, the evening had settled into that perfect moment between day and night, when the world seems to hold its breath. A cool autumn breeze carried the scent of coffee and distant rain, rustling through the leaves of nearby trees. We sat at our usual corner table, the familiar hum of conversation around us creating a cocoon of privacy.

When the lights suddenly went out, a collective gasp rippled through the café. But in that instant, as darkness fell, the world transformed. Moonlight poured through the large windows like liquid silver, painting everything in ethereal shades of blue and white. The full moon hung low and impossibly large in the sky, as if it had drawn closer just to witness this moment.

The cool evening breeze whispered through the open door, carrying with it the fresh scent of autumn leaves and possibility. Elina's hand found mine under the table, her fingers intertwining with mine with a certainty that made my heart race. I held on tightly, afraid to let go, feeling the warmth of her skin against mine in contrast to the cool air swirling around us.

The silver moonlight caught in her hair, creating a soft halo that took my breath away. Her face was illuminated in the gentle glow, and I found myself memorizing every detail - the subtle curve of her smile, the way her eyes caught the moonlight and held it, the soft shadow her eyelashes cast on her cheeks. She looked at me as if I was the only person in the world, her gaze holding something that made my chest tighten with emotion.

Time seemed to slow, marked only by the gentle flutter of napkins in the breeze and the steady rhythm of our synchronized breathing. Other patrons' voices faded to a distant murmur, and in that moment, our world narrowed to just us - two people finding each other in the darkness, guided by moonlight and the magnetic pull of something deeper than words could express.

Her thumb traced gentle circles on my palm, each touch sending electricity through my veins. When she spoke, her voice was barely above a whisper, yet it carried clearly through the darkness. "This feels like magic," she said softly, and I couldn't help but agree. The moonlight painted her smile in silver, and I found myself drawing closer, drawn by an invisible force as natural as gravity.

A gust of wind swept through the café, stronger this time, making the candles that staff had begun to light dance wildly. It carried the promise of rain and change, matching the turbulent emotions in my chest. Elina shivered slightly, and without thinking, I shifted closer, our shoulders touching, sharing warmth in the cool evening air.

Everything felt heightened in the darkness - the soft brush of her arm against mine, the way her perfume mingled with the scent of rain in the air, the gentle sound of her breath. The moon continued its vigil above us, casting long shadows that seemed to dance with each gust of wind, nature itself conspiring to create this perfect moment between us.

That night, driving her home, the quiet between us felt electric. Every glance, every shared smile, every moment of connection spoke of something deeper growing between us - something that both thrilled and terrified me. As I returned to my mom's house late that night, my heart was heavy with the complexity of what was developing, yet lighter because of the pure joy I'd found in Elina's presence.

The realization was beginning to dawn - I had fallen in love with her, completely and irrevocably, and there was nothing I could do to stop it.

Early Autumn

In early autumn, life spiraled into a whirlwind of decisions, plans, and overwhelming emotions. Elina and I had taken the first step toward a shared future by beginning our visa application process for the Netherlands—a move that carried with it both exhilarating promise and crushing weight. Each form we filled out, each document we gathered, felt like both a step toward freedom and a betrayal of the life I'd built with Nadia.

The reality of loving two women tore at me daily. With Elina, every shared moment felt electric—her touch, her laugh, the way her eyes lit up when she spoke of our future together. Our connection had grown into something profound and undeniable. Yet my history with Nadia couldn't be erased so easily. Ten years of shared adventures, quiet mornings, and absolute trust had woven themselves into the fabric of who I was. Each time I saw Nadia, memories of our life together would crash over me like waves—making me question everything, even as my heart pulled me inexorably toward Elina.

In an attempt to manage this impossible situation, I made what felt like the only choice I could. While Elina and I proceeded with our visa applications, I delayed applying for Nadia's, trying to create a clean break. I told myself it was kinder this way, but the guilt ate at me. To Nadia, I explained that Elina's role was purely professional—a necessary part of my business expansion. The lie felt bitter on my tongue, but I convinced myself it would hurt her less than the truth.

Only two of Elina's closest friends knew about us, and even they had been told I was already divorced—a story Elina had crafted to protect our secret. They saw our relationship as something pure and promising, unaware of the complex web of emotions and commitments that truly defined our situation. Their innocent belief in our love story only added to the weight of guilt I carried, knowing how many lives were being shaped by our carefully constructed deceptions.

The pressure of our situation began taking its toll on both of us. Elina started seeing a therapist, recommended by a friend—seeking clarity in the storm of emotions we'd created. The sessions were intense, raw, laying bare the complexities of our relationship. When her therapist requested my presence, I agreed, though something in me knew it would only complicate things further.

Each therapy session seemed to trigger a cascade of doubt and pain. The therapist's well-meaning advice—to separate until my marriage situation was resolved—would send us into spiraling arguments. These weren't just disagreements; they were battles between what we knew we should do and what our hearts demanded. After each session, Elina would call, her voice trembling with determination, saying we needed to end things. But by the next morning, the magnetic pull between us would prove too strong, and we'd find ourselves back in each other's orbit, as inevitable as gravity.

One evening, after a particularly devastating phone call where we'd promised to let each other go, we met at our usual coffee shop for what we convinced ourselves would be our final goodbye. The autumn evening pressed against the windows, and Elina sat across from me, tears streaming down her face. My chest ached watching her—every tear felt like it was being torn from my own heart. We were trying to do the right thing, but it felt like trying to stop breathing.

Then, as if the universe itself couldn't bear to see us part, our song began playing through the café's speakers. The familiar melody wrapped around us like a embrace, and we both froze. Every shared moment, every stolen kiss, every whispered promise seemed to pulse through the air between us. Elina's tears fell faster now, and I reached across the table without thinking, taking her hand in mine. The touch sent electricity through my veins—how could something that felt so right be wrong?

Words weren't necessary in that moment. We both knew, with bone-deep certainty, that we couldn't walk away from each other. The love we shared, complicated and messy as it was, had become as essential as air. Though we made hollow promises to limit our contact, we both recognized the futility of it. Our connection had grown beyond our control, beyond reason, beyond the boundaries we tried to set.

That night in the coffee shop became another chapter in our story— not an ending, but a confirmation of something we'd known all along:

some loves are too powerful to deny, even when they come at an impossible price. As we left, the echo of our song following us into the night, we understood that we were bound together now, for better or worse, our hearts beating in a rhythm that only we could hear.

The Second Archery Competition

The familiar weight of my bow settled into my hands as I prepared for the nationwide 3D competition in the north. Fresh from my recent gold and silver victories, I felt that unique combination of confidence and nerves that preceded important competitions. The stakes were higher this time, with archers from across the country gathering to test their skills.

When Nadia expressed her desire to join me, something flickered in my chest - a mixture of warmth and guilt that had become all too familiar lately. With Titanus at the mechanic's, we had no choice but to take a taxi. The suggestion brought an unexpected smile to her face, reminiscent of our early days together.

The taxi ride unfolded like a journey through time. As buildings gave way to open countryside, I found myself stealing glances at Nadia beside me. She sat with that quiet grace I'd always admired, her presence both comforting and unsettling. The gentle sway of the car triggered memories of our younger selves - two dreamers sharing taxi rides across the city, planning adventures and building castles in the air. Back then, our love had felt as vast and certain as the sky above us.

She caught me watching her and smiled - that same smile that had once been my anchor through every storm. "Remember our first competition together?" she asked, her voice soft with memory. "You were so nervous you forgot your lucky charm."

"And you made me a new one from a blade of grass," I finished, the memory rising unbidden. She had twisted it into a tiny ring, declaring it would bring me more luck than any store-bought charm. I had won gold that day.

The competition venue hummed with energy. As I took my position, I felt the familiar focus descend - each breath measured, each movement precise. The target seemed to pulse in my vision, everything else fading away. When my final arrow found its mark, securing second place, the crowd's applause felt distant, muffled by the storm of emotions in my chest.

Afterward, we walked along the shore, the sea stretching endless before us. Nadia's footprints in the sand beside mine felt like a metaphor for our marriage - parallel lines being slowly erased by the incoming tide.

"We can rebuild, Darian," she said, her voice carrying above the waves. "Everything we had - everything we were - it's still here." She placed her hand over her heart, and the gesture nearly broke me. "We just need to choose it again."

I looked at her then, really looked at her - this woman who had weathered every storm with me, who still believed in us even as I was letting go. The setting sun painted her in gold, and for a moment, I saw every version of her I'd ever loved - the adventurous girl who'd stolen my heart, the steady partner who'd built a life with me, the woman now fighting for our future.

"Sometimes," I said carefully, "things break in ways that can't be fixed." The words felt hollow, inadequate against the depth of what we were losing.

"Nothing breaks beyond repair unless we choose to stop trying," she countered, her eyes meeting mine with unwavering certainty. "That's what you taught me, remember? On every mountain, every trail - we never gave up. Why start now?"

The drive home was quiet, heavy with words unsaid. As city lights replaced stars, I felt the weight of my choices pressing down. Nadia's quiet strength beside me, her continued faith in us, made my heart ache. Yet even as I recognized the beauty of what we had built together, I couldn't deny the magnetic pull toward a different future - one that both thrilled and terrified me.

Early October

October painted the world in amber and gold, a season of change that mirrored the transitions in my heart. I planned what would likely be my last fly fishing trip before winter's approach - a ritual that had always brought me peace, though now it carried the weight of complicated emotions.

When Nadia expressed her desire to join me, something in her voice - a mixture of hope and determination - made it impossible to refuse. Our shared love for these outdoor adventures had been a cornerstone of our relationship, and even now, with everything falling apart, that connection remained.

The days leading up to the trip were filled with a strange tension. Each moment with Elina felt electric, charged with both passion and secrecy. We had mastered the art of stolen moments - quick meetings beneath the old willow tree in Baharvan, shared meals from carefully packed containers, hushed conversations in the sanctuary of Titanus. Her mother's cooking, always lovingly prepared, became another thread in the tapestry of our hidden romance.

Life had become a careful dance of timing and discretion. Once, while Elina was driving Titanus, we encountered her brother on a narrow street. The moment crystallized the delicate nature of our situation - her quick thinking as she pulled down her cap, the practiced ease with which she reversed the car, the shadow of a tree providing just enough cover to maintain our secret. Afterward, we laughed about it, but the laughter carried an edge of awareness about the precarious nature of our happiness.

The fishing trip with Nadia began under clear autumn skies. On the water, muscle memory took over - the rhythmic casting of lines, the patient wait, the shared excitement of a catch. For brief, shining moments, it felt like nothing had changed. Nadia's laugh still carried across the water, her movements still synchronized perfectly with mine, a decade of shared adventures evident in every gesture.

You're right - let me add that crucial element about the physical distance, as it's an important aspect of showing the growing separation between Darian and Nadia during the fishing trip:

[Previous section remains the same until the hotel scene, then continues:]

In the hotel room, the physical distance between us spoke volumes. Where once we would have naturally gravitated together, now an invisible barrier seemed to exist. I deliberately maintained space between us - choosing to sit in the chair rather than on the bed, keeping my movements measured and distant. It wasn't just emotional walls we were building; the physical separation had become a tangible representation of our fracturing relationship.

During the night, I stayed firmly on my side of the bed, rigid and conscious of every inch between us. This deliberate distance was my unspoken loyalty to Elina, even in her absence. Each time Nadia moved closer in her sleep, I would carefully edge away, my heart heavy with the knowledge that this small act of distance was causing her pain.

The contrast was stark to our earlier trips, where we'd naturally sought each other's warmth, where physical closeness had been as natural as breathing. Now, every avoided touch, every careful movement to maintain separation, felt like another brick in the wall growing between us.

These moments of physical distance seemed to hurt Nadia more than our arguments. In the darkness, her quiet sobs broke the silence.

"Why won't you even hold me anymore?" she whispered, her voice raw with pain. "Have I become that repulsive to you?"

"It's not that," I replied, my voice tight with the complexity of emotions I couldn't express. "I just... I can't."

The truth was, physical intimacy with Nadia now felt like a betrayal of my feelings for Elina. Every maintained distance, every avoided touch, was my way of remaining faithful to the new love that had captured my heart, even as it meant watching Nadia's heart break piece by piece.

During the day, on the water, the distance was easier to maintain. The focus on fishing, the natural spacing required by the sport, gave us both a respite from the conscious awareness of our growing separation. But in the confined space of the hotel room, the deliberate maintenance of physical space between us became impossible to ignore - a glaring symbol of everything that had changed.

Days blurred into weeks until a moment of clarity arrived - our visas for the Netherlands. The document felt like a key to a new life, but it also carried the weight of finality. Riverton, the coastal city we'd chosen, represented both promise and farewell. Elina and I had received our approvals, bringing our shared future into sharper focus.

The situation with Nadia took an unexpected turn when we discovered she had misplaced her passport. Whether conscious or unconscious, this meant she would need to apply for a new one - a process that would take weeks, effectively ensuring she wouldn't be able to travel with me immediately. The timing felt somehow symbolic, another sign of our diverging paths.

My therapist, during our private sessions, continued pushing me toward decisive action. "You can't keep one foot in each world," she would say, her words cutting through my hesitation. "It's not fair to anyone - not to you, not to Nadia, and not to Elina." But endings are rarely clean, and hearts don't follow logical timelines. Each day brought new complications, new emotions, new challenges to navigate.

In these autumn days, I found myself standing at a crossroads. Behind me lay a decade of love and trust with Nadia, ahead stretched an unknown future with Elina. The weight of choice pressed down on me, even as the season's changes reminded me that nothing, not even the deepest love, stays the same forever.

Meanwhile, our therapist - the one Elina and I had independently chosen to see in separate sessions - continued pushing me toward decisive action. During my appointments, she urged me to finalize things with Nadia, to stop prolonging the inevitable. I knew from occasional mentions that in Elina's separate sessions, they worked through her own perspectives on our situation. The therapist never shared details between us, maintaining strict professional boundaries, but her message to both of us was clear: we needed to be honest about where this was heading.

One evening after Elina's therapy session, I drove to Baharvan to meet her. The usual warmth in her voice carried an unfamiliar weight when she greeted me. As we sat in our familiar spot beneath the willow tree, she seemed distant, her fingers tracing absent patterns on the wooden table, her gaze lost somewhere I couldn't follow.

"I need to tell you something," she began, her voice uncharacteristically hesitant. She shared a story from her past—about her parents' marriage, about betrayal and blame, about how she had come to view relationships through a lens colored by early experiences. As she spoke, the existing cracks in our trust seemed to widen.

The way she had processed her parents' situation—placing blame on her mother rather than her father for his choices—amplified my existing concerns. Our trust had always been complicated by small things—her continued contact with her ex, her sometimes unclear boundaries with other men, moments of jealousy that seemed to come from nowhere. But now these pieces began forming a clearer pattern.

I found myself revisiting past moments that had given me pause—times when her stories didn't quite align, instances where her behavior with other married men had made me uncomfortable. These weren't new doubts, but her revelation about her parents gave them new context, new weight.

These thoughts followed me into my next therapy session, though I kept them unspoken. The complexity of our relationship—built on secrecy and complicated by our own histories—made it difficult to address these issues directly, even in the safety of therapy.

Even as we planned our future together, these doubts cast longer shadows. I loved her deeply, but our foundation had always been uncertain. Her confession about her parents didn't create new problems—it simply illuminated the fault lines that had been there all along.

As October deepened into autumn, the promise of Riverton loomed larger in my thoughts. The picturesque coastal city in the Netherlands had become more than just a destination—it was the physical embodiment of the future Elina and I were trying to build. With its historic canals and wind-swept dunes touching the North Sea, the city seemed to offer everything we were seeking: a fresh start, new opportunities, and most importantly, freedom from the complicated web we'd woven in Parin.

During our late-night planning sessions, Elina and I would pore over maps and business proposals, our fingers tracing the paths of possibility along Riverton's cobblestone streets. The city's blend of historic charm and modern innovation mirrored what we hoped to create—something new built on the foundation of what came before. The entrepreneurial community there promised connections and opportunities, but it was the distance from our current lives that drew us most strongly.

Yet even as we planned, doubts whispered at the edges of my mind. Each time I looked at apartment listings or researched business locations, I felt the weight of what I would be leaving behind. Nadia's absence from these plans felt like a physical presence—a shadow that lengthened as our departure drew closer. How could I build a new life while the foundations of my current one were still crumbling?

The business aspects gave us something concrete to focus on, a way to channel our emotions into practical action. We spent hours developing our strategy, reaching out to contacts, laying the groundwork for what we hoped to build. But beneath the spreadsheets and market analyses lay deeper questions that no amount of planning could answer.

Riverton represented more than just a fresh start—it was a test of everything I believed about love, commitment, and redemption. Could I truly honor my growing feelings for Elina while respectfully ending my life with Nadia? Would the distance help heal the wounds we were creating, or would it only deepen them?

My dream of creating something significant had always been part of who I was, but now it was inexorably linked with this move. The innovation hubs of Riverton offered the perfect stage for the impact I hoped to make. Yet even this professional ambition felt complicated by the personal choices driving it.

As autumn leaves fell around us in Parin, Elina and I clung to our vision of Riverton like a lifeline. We filled our conversations with plans and possibilities, using the future to avoid facing the present. But in quiet moments, when the planning gave way to reflection, I couldn't help wondering if any city, no matter how perfect, could provide the clarity I was seeking.

Early November

As October's leaves turned to November frost, our focus shifted entirely to the Netherlands. The visas in our hands felt both liberating and heavy with responsibility - tangible proof that our future in Riverton was more than just a shared dream. But like everything in our relationship, even this step forward was complicated by the lives we were trying to leave behind.

One crisp autumn morning, I drove to Baharvan to pick up Elina. We made our way to our usual coffee shop, where the familiar scent of freshly ground beans and the quiet hum of conversation created a bubble of normalcy around us. Over steaming cups, we began untangling the complexities of our departure.

"My family wants to see me off," Elina said, her fingers tightening around her cup. "They can't see us together at the airport. We can't risk it."

"I know," I replied, thinking of Nadia and the unfinished business between us. "My situation isn't settled either. We need to be careful."

The irony wasn't lost on me - here we were, planning our escape to build an honest life together, yet having to orchestrate it through layers of deception. Elina had crafted a careful narrative for her family about pursuing independent business opportunities in the Netherlands. I had maintained a strategic distance in my conversations with Nadia, speaking of Elina as a past business connection, nothing more.

"What if we took different flights?" I suggested, the idea forming as I spoke. "We could meet during the layover in Greece."

Elina's eyes lit up with that spark I'd come to love. "That could work," she said, already pulling out her phone to check flight schedules.

We crafted our plan with the precision of people accustomed to hiding. Elina would take the first flight, departing two hours before me. We'd reunite during the transit in Greece, continuing to Riverton together. December 6th became our target - a date that felt both too distant and terrifyingly close.

"We'll need somewhere quiet when we first arrive," Elina said softly. "Just us, away from everything."

I found us a cottage in Rosdijk, a small village outside Riverton. The photos showed a peaceful retreat surrounded by rolling countryside - the perfect place to begin writing our new chapter together.

As we finalized the details, I felt the familiar mix of excitement and guilt that had become the backdrop of our relationship. Every step toward our future together was also a step away from the lives we'd built, the promises we'd made to others. But sitting there in our coffee shop sanctuary, watching Elina's face glow with hope as we planned our escape, I knew there was no turning back.

EIGHT

FAREWELL TO PARIN

Mid-November arrived like a storm gathering on the horizon, bringing with it a convergence of events that would change everything. My life felt suspended between two realities - the comfortable world I'd built with Nadia over a decade, and the magnetic pull of what Elina and I had discovered in each other. As I packed for our upcoming journey to the Netherlands, every item I touched seemed weighted with meaning, with choices I wasn't sure I was ready to make.

The timing felt cruel - selling my beloved Titanus, hiring developers for our new venture, preparing for my third archery competition. Each task carried its own emotional weight, but none compared to the storm brewing in my heart. The life I'd known, the certainties I'd built my world around, were crumbling beneath my feet.

After a particularly intense therapy session, where the counselor had pushed relentlessly for decisive action, I returned home to find Nadia waiting. The air between us crackled with unspoken words, with pain too deep for casual conversation. Her eyes, once filled with unconditional love, now held a mixture of hurt and resignation that made my chest ache.

"You weren't even happy about getting the visa for me," she said, her voice barely above a whisper. "I don't want it if your heart is somewhere else." The tremor in her words betrayed the strength she was trying to maintain.

"You know this isn't working, Nadia. I've done everything to fix it," I replied, though even as I spoke the words, I knew they weren't entirely true. Had I really tried everything? Or had I already given up, drawn inexorably toward the future Elina represented?

"No, you haven't," she countered, her eyes suddenly blazing with an intensity that stripped away my defenses. "Why, Darian? What did I do wrong? What didn't I give you? I've done everything for you, and you still won't try. Be honest with me—for once, be a man and tell me what you really want. You don't want this, do you?"

Her words struck like arrows, each one finding its mark with devastating accuracy. I felt cornered, not by her questions, but by the truth they exposed. "With everything that's happened, how can this work?" I gestured helplessly at the space between us. "Your family intervening, talking to my colleagues at Nexara Labs... How can we build a life on this mess? How can I be a father with this history? It's all broken." Even as I spoke, I knew I was deflecting, using circumstances to justify what my heart had already decided.

"I made mistakes, I know," she admitted, tears now flowing freely down her cheeks. The sight of them made my chest constrict - this was Nadia, my partner of ten years, the woman who had stood beside me through everything. "But you don't know what I've endured. I kept it all inside, hoping you'd stop seeing her." The raw honesty in her voice made me look away.

"I don't think this can be repaired," I said quietly, the words feeling like stones in my mouth.

She stared at me, and in her eyes I saw a decade of shared dreams crumbling. "So that's it? After everything, you're leaving me?" Her voice broke. "After you've destroyed me, you're walking away? How am I supposed to live without you? Everywhere I go, I see you. You're in everything. You've left me with nothing." Her words weren't just accusations - they were the sound of a heart breaking in real time.

"You're trying to guilt me because you know that's my Achilles' heel," I said, my voice tight with frustration. But wasn't that just another deflection? Another way to avoid facing what I was doing to her?

"Do what you want," she said finally, her voice hollow. "If your heart isn't with me, give it to her." The resignation in her tone felt worse than anger would have.

"I'll pack and leave," I managed, trying to steady myself against the wave of emotions threatening to overwhelm me.

The next morning arrived with cruel clarity. As I packed my things, each item I touched seemed to hold a memory - adventures shared, quiet moments, the life we'd built together. Nadia had left the house, unable to watch as I dismantled our shared world piece by piece. When she returned in the evening, she wasn't alone. Her uncle Zemir, the voice of reason in her family, stood beside her like a quiet guardian.

"I'm here because Nadia needed me," Zemir said simply, his calm voice a stark contrast to the emotional storm swirling around us. "She's been feeling awful." His presence made everything feel more final, more real.

"I don't know what to say," I replied, my voice thick. "It just didn't work." The words felt inadequate, a pale reflection of the complexity tearing us apart.

As I moved toward the door with my last bag, Nadia suddenly broke. She ran to me, throwing herself against my chest with such force it nearly knocked me back. Her body shook with sobs as she clung to me, her fingers gripping my shirt as if she could somehow keep our life together through sheer force of will. I held her, my own tears falling freely now, breathing in the familiar scent of her hair one last time. Each sob that wracked her body felt like an accusation, a reminder of the pain I was causing.

With trembling hands, I gently unwound her fingers from my shirt. The physical act of separating from her felt like tearing something vital inside me. Walking out that door was the hardest thing I'd ever done.

In the car, I caught a glimpse of her in the rearview mirror - a silhouette in the window, tears streaming down her face. I had to stop the car, my vision blurring. My phone buzzed: Elina. As I told her what had happened, her voice shifted from joy to concern, reflecting the complexity of our situation.

"Are you sure about this, Darian?" she asked softly.

"I don't know. Nothing feels right anymore," I admitted, gripping the steering wheel until my knuckles turned white. How could something feel so right and so wrong at the same time?

"If you're happy, Darian, I'll support you no matter what. You're my life," Elina said, her voice full of love yet tinged with the weight of what we were doing.

That night, I arrived at my mother's house, Titanus loaded with the boxes containing my married life. I couldn't bring myself to unload them - each box felt like it held not just possessions, but pieces of the life I was leaving behind. My mother offered me a room and quiet solace, but even in the stillness of her home, with Titanus sitting heavy with my packed life in the driveway, I couldn't stop myself from reaching out to Nadia.

"Are you okay?" I texted, knowing it was a foolish question.

Her response came quickly: "I don't have hope to live anymore."

The words hit me like a physical blow. "I feel terrible too," I wrote back, my chest so tight I could barely breathe.

I sat in my childhood room, staring at my phone, typing and deleting the next message multiple times before finally sending it: "I want to come home. We shouldn't give up." The words felt both right and terrifying as they left my screen.

Even as I waited for her response, I found myself messaging Elina, confessing my weakness. "I couldn't do it. I told her I'll come back," I wrote, feeling the full weight of what that meant.

"Thank God," Elina replied. "The guilt has been eating me alive."

The next morning, I drove back home, Titanus still heavy with my unpacked life. Seeing our apartment building, where just hours ago I'd been certain of leaving, now filled me with a confused mix of relief and uncertainty. When I walked in, Nadia was there, her eyes red but holding a cautious hope that made my heart ache.

Without words, we began unpacking the bags and boxes I'd packed the day before. Each item we returned to its place felt like both a promise and a question. The silence between us was heavy with everything we weren't saying - the hurt still fresh, the trust damaged, but something still worth fighting for pulling us forward.

The Last Trip

As we finished unpacking, we quietly began preparing for our upcoming trip to Safarun - what would be my final journey with Titanus. There was something painfully symbolic about it all - this last adventure with the vehicle that had carried us through so many chapters of our life together. Our hundredth "last trip," as we'd sometimes joked, though this time it really was the end of an era.

The trip itself carried a bittersweet weight. We found ourselves falling into familiar patterns - stopping to photograph autumn leaves in a quaint village, walking together by the river, sharing memories of past adventures. These moments felt precious yet fragile, like holding something beautiful that might shatter at any moment. The underlying current of unresolved pain hummed beneath every interaction, every shared glance.

At the hotel, fate seemed determined to test us further. As Nadia handed me a cup of tea, it slipped, scalding my bow hand severely. Despite everything between us, her doctor's instincts took over immediately. She rushed to Titanus, retrieved her medical supplies, and tended to my injury with the same gentle care she'd always shown. Even in our brokenness, some things remained unchanged - her instinct to heal, to help, to care for me.

That night, sleep evaded me. The pain in my hand pulsed with each heartbeat, but it was nothing compared to the ache in my chest. Lying in the dark hotel room, listening to Nadia's quiet breathing, I felt the weight of every decision, every moment that had led us here. The competition looming ahead seemed trivial compared to the larger contest happening in my heart.

The archery competition the next day was a blur of missed shots and distracted attempts. My burned hand throbbed with each draw of the bow, but the physical pain felt almost welcome - something tangible to focus on instead of the emotional storm raging inside. I tried to lose myself in the familiar rhythm of nock, draw, release, but my thoughts kept drifting between the woman who had stood beside me through countless competitions and the one whose messages I could feel waiting on my phone.

I caught Nadia watching me from the sidelines, her face a complex mixture of concern and something deeper - perhaps remembering all the times she'd been there to celebrate my victories, to console me in defeat. The distance between us now felt greater than any target I'd ever aimed at.

When we finally returned to Tiraz, exhausted and quiet in Titanus's familiar cabin, my phone lit up with a message from Elina. Her grandmother had passed away. The news hit me with unexpected force - another reminder of how life could change in an instant, of how the choices we make ripple out beyond just ourselves.

In that moment, sitting in the vehicle that had carried me through so many chapters of my life, about to be sold, I felt the full weight of the crossroads I was facing. Every turn ahead seemed to lead to someone's heart breaking - perhaps my own included. The certainty I'd felt about my future with Elina wavered as I looked at Nadia's profile against the gathering dusk, yet the pull toward what Elina and I shared remained undeniable.

The road home had never felt longer, each mile marker a reminder of the journey still ahead - not just the physical distance, but the emotional landscape I would have to navigate. The future I'd once seen so clearly now seemed to shift like sand beneath my feet, leaving me uncertain of where solid ground could be found.

Nadia's Visa

The morning we went to the embassy, the weight of what we were doing pressed against my chest like a physical thing. Nadia's hand in mine felt both familiar and strange as we walked through the grand entrance. Ten years of marriage had taught me every nuance of her touch, yet now each point of contact seemed to burn with the complexity of what I was hiding.

As we sat in the waiting area, I watched her fill out the paperwork with that careful precision I'd always admired - the same attention to detail she brought to everything in our life together. Her dark hair fell forward as she wrote, and for a moment, I saw her as I had that first morning by the Velan Gulf, camera in hand, waiting to capture the perfect sunrise. The memory made my chest ache.

The decision to apply for her visa as my partner had come after nights of sleepless deliberation. Each signature on those forms felt like both a promise and a betrayal. Here I was, planning a future with Nadia on paper while my heart pulled me in another direction entirely. The guilt of it all twisted in my stomach as I watched her carefully document our shared life, our plans, our supposed future together.

Later that evening, alone in my study, I shared the day's events with Elina through carefully typed messages. Her responses carried both understanding and an undercurrent of pain that I felt echoed in my own heart. She knew I couldn't fully let go of Nadia yet - whether from loyalty, guilt, or some deeper attachment I couldn't quite name. The complexity of loving two women so differently yet completely had become my daily reality.

The therapy sessions Nadia insisted on were another layer of this elaborate dance I was performing. I sat in the therapist's office, sharing selective truths while the biggest one remained unspoken. Yes, there was anger - at feeling trapped, at the expectations that had slowly built walls around me. But there was also love, deep and enduring, for the woman who had been my partner in every adventure for the past decade. The therapist noted my resistance, my carefully constructed answers, but couldn't see the full picture I was so desperately trying to hide.

Each session felt like walking a tightrope - balancing between honesty and protection, between the man I had been and the one I was becoming. The therapist spoke of communication and healing, while I sat there holding the knowledge that every step toward reconciliation was also a step deeper into deception.

Whispers to the Willow

December 1st arrived with the weight of significance I hadn't anticipated. Elina's birthday. Even amid the whirlwind of preparations for the Netherlands, I knew I needed to see her. The envelope of euros in my pocket felt inadequate somehow - how do you quantify love in currency? But it was practical, necessary for our future, and somehow that made it more intimate than any traditional gift could have been.

When I arrived in Baharvan, she didn't hesitate. The moment she slipped into Titanus's driver's seat, her arms were around me, her presence filling every space that had felt empty. "I missed you so much, my life," she whispered against my neck, and the simple truth of those words made my heart race.

I held her close, breathing in the familiar scent of her perfume, letting myself sink into the comfort of her embrace. These moments of connection had become my anchor in the storm of changes ahead. "Happy birthday, darling," I murmured, reaching for the envelope.

Her reaction to the money was pure Elina - surprise, protest, and then that deep understanding that had drawn me to her in the first place. "This is too much, my love!" she exclaimed, but I could see in her eyes that she understood what it really meant - not just cash, but a promise of our future together.

"No, it's not," I said firmly, watching her face. "I want you to have something you truly want when we're in the Netherlands. This is just the beginning." The words carried weight beyond their surface meaning - a pledge of sorts, a commitment to the life we were choosing to build together.

She tucked the envelope away carefully before pulling me close again. Her kiss held everything we couldn't say aloud - gratitude, love, anticipation, fear. The complexity of our situation seemed to dissolve in these moments of pure connection.

As she drove through the familiar streets of Baharvan, her hand found mine on the gearshift. The simple intimacy of our intertwined fingers spoke volumes - how natural we felt together, how right this all seemed despite the circumstances. Every turn through these streets felt meaningful now, knowing we were counting down our last moments here.

"I can't believe we're really going," she said softly, her voice carrying both excitement and trepidation.

"You will soon," I replied, squeezing her hand. "We have so much ahead of us - finding a home, building our business, creating our life together." The future stretched before us, full of possibilities and challenges we would face as one.

When she steered us toward the willow tree - our special place - the significance wasn't lost on me. We sat there in silence for a moment, watching its branches dance in the autumn wind. This tree had witnessed so many of our moments together, had sheltered our growing love when we needed to hide from the world.

"Dear willow," she spoke softly, "we're leaving. We came to say goodbye to you forever."

I couldn't resist lightening the moment, falling into our familiar pattern of playful banter. "Dear willow," I added with a mischievous grin, "Elina didn't kiss me enough today."

Her response was immediate - that playful bite on my cheek that had become her signature show of affection, followed by her teasing threat: "If it wouldn't leave a mark, I'd bite you harder."

Our last dinner together that evening felt both eternal and fleeting. Every glance, every touch, every shared smile seemed to carry the weight of what lay ahead. When it came time to part, she said goodbye not just to me but to Titanus as well, her hand gentle on the dashboard - acknowledging how this vehicle had been part of our story from the beginning.

The drive home that night was the hardest - the silence in the car deafening without her presence. My chest felt tight with emotions I couldn't quite name. Everything was changing, and while I knew I was choosing this path, the weight of what we were leaving behind pressed heavy on my heart.

The Final Drive

The morning I had to sell Titanus dawned with a cruel clarity. Every detail seemed sharper, more significant - the way early sunlight caught the curves of its frame, how dew had settled on the windshield like tears. I stood in my driveway, keys heavy in my palm, each breath feeling like it might shatter something inside me.

Six years of memories were carved into every inch of this vehicle. That dent in the rear quarter panel from the time we'd pushed through an unmarked trail in the northern forests, where pine branches had reached out like desperate hands. The slight scrape along the driver's door from a narrow mountain pass, where Nadia had held her breath as we'd inched past a sheer drop. The worn spot on the steering wheel where my hands had gripped through countless adventures, through storms and sunsets and stars.

I ran my fingers along Titanus's hood, feeling the familiar warmth of metal that had cooled under countless desert nights. The engine still held traces of heat from my early morning drive - one last journey through empty streets, one final communion between machine and driver. Each touch brought back another flood of memories: the purr of the engine echoing off canyon walls, the way it had never once failed me on treacherous mountain switchbacks, how its headlights had cut through the darkest nights like faithful stars.

Inside, the leather seats held the imprints of countless journeys. Here was where Nadia had fallen asleep on long night drives, trusting me completely to guide us home. Here was where Elina had first held my hand over the gearshift, changing everything. Every surface told a story - the dashboard where I'd traced routes on unfolded maps, the back seats that had carried camping gear through every season, the roof rack that had born the weight of dreams and equipment across thousands of miles.

The familiar scent of leather and adventure filled my lungs as I sat in the driver's seat one last time. My hands found their places on the wheel automatically, muscle memory carved by years of companionship. I could still hear the echo of laughter from past trips, still feel the ghost of every hand that had rested on my shoulder from the back seat, still taste the coffee from countless sunrise stops in remote places.

When Rayan arrived, the sound of his footsteps on the driveway felt like a countdown. I started Titanus one final time, and the engine's rumble resonated in my chest like a living thing. How many times had this sound been my welcome home? How many mornings had it been my call to adventure? The deep, steady purr spoke of power and reliability, of promises kept and paths taken.

"You're sure about this?" Rayan asked softly, understanding in his eyes as he watched me run my hand along the steering wheel one last time.

I couldn't speak for a moment. Every journey flashed through my mind: the desert trails where sand had stretched endless under vast skies, the forest paths where trees had parted like ancient guardians, the mountain passes where clouds had wrapped around us like dreams. Titanus had been more than transportation - it had been freedom, sanctuary, companion.

The keys felt impossibly heavy as I placed them in Rayan's palm. The metal clinked with a finality that made my chest tight. "Take care of it," I managed, my voice rougher than I'd intended. "Get it there safely."

Rayan nodded, knowing better than to say more. As he adjusted the seat and mirrors, each movement felt like another goodbye. When he started the engine, the familiar rumble hit me like a physical thing - the voice of a friend saying farewell.

I stood in my driveway, watching as Titanus pulled away. The sun caught its silver paint one last time, a flash of brilliance that burned in my vision. The engine's sound lingered in the air, growing fainter with each second, carrying away years of memories with it. Every meter of distance felt like something tearing loose inside my chest.

When the sound finally faded completely, the silence pressed against my ears like a weight. In that moment, I understood I wasn't just losing a vehicle - I was watching a vital part of my life disappear around the corner, carrying with it the man I had been, leaving behind someone I wasn't sure I recognized yet.

Echoes of Goodbye

The days after Titanus's departure unfolded like scenes from a dream, each moment sharp with the knowledge that it would soon be memory. Time seemed to move differently now - both too fast and agonizingly slow, every hour weighted with the significance of lasts: last sunset over the city skyline, last coffee at my favorite café, last walk through familiar streets.

The goodbye party at our friend's house felt like watching a play where I had forgotten my lines. Nadia moved through the evening with grace, her smile never faltering even as I caught the shadows in her eyes. Our friends maintained a careful dance of conversation, their words skating around the edges of what everyone seemed to sense but nobody dared to name. I watched her across the room, the way she laughed at a friend's joke, how she unconsciously touched her wedding ring when she was deep in thought - habits I had memorized over ten years of marriage. Each gesture now felt like something precious slipping through my fingers.

Between moments, my phone would buzz with messages from Elina - her words both anchor and storm, pulling me toward a future I could barely imagine while tethering me to a present that grew more complex with each passing hour. The guilt of these secret communications mixed with an undeniable anticipation, creating a cocktail of emotions that left me dizzy.

Our last dinner at Café Lumière, the restaurant where Nadia and I had celebrated every milestone of our marriage, was an exercise in exquisite torture. The maître d' greeted us by name, leading us to "our" table by the window. Ten years of memories lived in these walls - our first anniversary, the night Nadia got her residency acceptance, countless quiet evenings when the world beyond these windows ceased to exist. Now each familiar detail felt like a witness to what I was leaving behind.

"Remember when we came here after that disaster camping trip?" Nadia asked, her eyes soft with memory. "When it rained for three days straight and we ended up sleeping in Titanus?"

I nodded, my throat tight. We had been soaked to the bone but laughing, seeking refuge in this very spot. She had looked beautiful then, rain-damp hair curling around her face, eyes bright with adventure. She looked beautiful now, the soft restaurant lighting catching the silver threads that had begun to appear in her dark hair - threads I had contributed to, no doubt.

The night my family gathered hit me with unexpected force. My mother's cooking filled the house with the scents of childhood - cardamom and saffron, cumin and rose water. She moved through the kitchen with practiced grace, but I caught how her hands trembled slightly as she served my favorite dishes. My brothers maintained a steady stream of conversation about practical matters - flight times, shipping arrangements, power adapters for European outlets - their words a thin veneer over deeper emotions.

"You'll call when you land?" my mother asked, her voice steady though her eyes glistened. "The time difference... I've looked it up."

"Of course, Maman," I promised, watching as she nodded and turned quickly back to her cooking. The weight of her unspoken questions pressed against my chest like physical things.

Later that night, alone in my increasingly empty apartment, I stood at the window watching the city lights blur through unshed tears. Parin spread out before me, a tapestry of memories woven into every street and building. This land had shaped me, from its harshest deserts to its most forgiving valleys. The specific quality of light at dawn, the way clouds cast moving shadows across mountain faces, the song of birds I had known since childhood - all of it was written into my bones.

My phone lit up with a message from Elina, waiting in Greece. Her words glowed in the darkness: "I miss you. Our future is waiting." Something lurched in my chest - guilt, excitement, fear, love, all tangled together in a knot I couldn't unravel. Behind me, the apartment held the ghostly echoes of the life I had built with Nadia. Ahead lay something unknown, terrifying in its newness yet pulling me forward with magnetic force.

I pressed my forehead against the cool glass, watching my breath fog the window. Below, the city continued its nighttime rhythm, unaware that one of its sons was preparing to leave. The stars above were the same ones that had witnessed every crucial moment of my life - my father's death, meeting Nadia, falling in love with Elina. Now they would witness this too - this ending, this beginning, this moment of standing between two lives, two loves, two versions of myself.

NINE

THE DUTCH DAWN

The moment my plane touched down in Amsterdam, everything felt surreal. The weight of what I'd left behind - my life with Nadia, our shared dreams, the comfortable certainty of familiar routines - pressed against my chest even as anticipation coursed through my veins. My fingers trembled slightly as I dialed Elina's number.

"I've landed," I said, my voice betraying more emotion than I'd intended.

"I'm here," she replied, those two words carrying all the promise of our future together.

The transition hall stretched endlessly before me, but then I saw her. Standing there, her eyes found mine across the crowd, and suddenly everything else fell away. The automatic stairs brought me closer, and when I reached her, she threw herself into my arms with such complete abandon that my heart nearly burst.

"Hi, darling," I managed, breathing in her familiar scent.

"Hi, my life!" she whispered against my neck, her voice trembling with emotion that matched my own.

She pulled back slightly, her eyes bright. "I want to buy you a coffee."

"Let's save it for another time," I said softly, unable to take my eyes off her. "Right now, I just want to be with you."

On the flight to Amsterdam, the attendants noticed something in how we looked at each other and arranged for us to sit together. As Elina claimed the window seat with a triumphant smile, I felt a surge of tenderness that took me by surprise. Halfway through the flight, she fell asleep against my shoulder, her complete trust in me evident in her peaceful expression. I watched her breathe, each rise and fall of her chest a reminder of the magnitude of what we were undertaking together.

The Netherlands welcomed us with typical Dutch weather - cold rain and howling wind that seemed to mirror the turbulence of our journey here. Our cottage in Rosdijk felt tiny but perfect, a space that would become our first real home together. As I plugged in the electric heater to ward off the chill, Elina's relief was palpable.

"Thank God you're here," she said, moving closer to me. "This wind and silence would terrify me if I were alone."

"You're not alone," I assured her, pulling her into my arms. "You have me."

She looked up at me then, her eyes holding a mixture of trust and uncertainty that made my heart ache. "This is the first time I'm going to spend the whole night with a man."

Something about her candor, her complete openness with me, made me fall in love with her all over again. I kissed her forehead gently, wondering how I'd gotten so lucky to find this kind of love twice in one lifetime - even as guilt tugged at the edges of my consciousness.

That first night, exhaustion claimed us quickly. But as I drifted off with Elina curled against me, I couldn't help but think about how different this felt from my nights with Nadia. Not better or worse - just profoundly different. Where Nadia and I had built our love on shared adventures and quiet understanding, what Elina and I had was like a force of nature - intense, all-consuming, impossible to resist even when I'd tried.

The next morning brought reality into sharper focus as we ventured out into our new neighborhood. The cold air bit at our cheeks as we walked to the nearest supermarket, Elina's hand warm in mine. Every step felt like we were writing the first pages of our story together, even as I carried the weight of the story I'd left behind.

Back at the cottage, we began the delicate process of merging two lives into one space. Suitcases sprawled across every corner, their contents spilling out like physical manifestations of our shared dreams. Each item we unpacked felt weighted with meaning - not just belongings, but pieces of the life we were choosing to build together. My fly-fishing gear leaned against one wall, a testament to the parts of myself I couldn't leave behind, though my bow remained in Parin. I made a mental note to buy a new one soon, not just as a replacement, but as a symbol of putting down roots in this new life.

A sudden shriek broke the quiet as I leaped backward, my heart racing. Elina's laughter filled the room as I stared down at the plastic cockroach she'd planted at my feet. Her eyes danced with mischief as she watched my reaction, clearly pleased with her prank.

"I can't believe you remembered," I said, trying to maintain my dignity while my pulse slowly returned to normal. She'd discovered this particular fear months ago in Tiraz, when a falling leaf in Titanus had sent me jumping in my seat, mistaking it for a cockroach.

"They're terrible creatures!" I defended myself, which only made her laugh harder. "They're literally the only thing in the world that scares me."

"Not even wolves?" she asked, eyebrows raised in playful challenge.

"Not at all," I replied with complete certainty, reaching for her. She danced away, still giggling, and the sound of her joy made everything - every risk, every sacrifice - feel worth it.

As evening approached, hunger finally interrupted our unpacking. "It's cooking time," I announced, surveying our limited supplies.

"And as you know," Elina said with that smile that never failed to make my heart skip, "the only thing I can cook is scrambled eggs."

"Then let me teach you something simple," I offered, pulling her close to the counter. The tiny kitchen barely had room for both of us, but somehow that made it better, more intimate. "Onion, garlic, bread, minced beef, mushrooms - we'll create something together."

What followed was less a cooking lesson and more an intimate dance. Every brush of her hand against mine as we chopped vegetables, every shared taste test, every small correction in technique became an excuse for touch, for closeness. When she accidentally burned the edges of the meat, her disappointed pout drew me in for a kiss that tasted of garlic and promises.

After our imperfect but perfect meal, inspiration struck. I slipped out to the supermarket, returning with a red velvet cake and "Happy Birthday" candles. The surprise in her eyes when I presented it made my chest tight with emotion.

"We didn't celebrate your birthday properly," I said softly. "We didn't have time."

In the warm glow of candlelight, watching her make a wish, I found myself making one too - that this feeling, this perfect sense of rightness, would last forever. We captured the moment with her phone, though no photo could truly capture the way her eyes shone with happiness, or how my heart felt full enough to burst.

The evening deepened into night as she produced a deck of cards with a challenging smirk. "I brought these so we can play."

"Are you sure?" I teased, settling across from her. "You're about to get addicted to losing."

Hours melted away as we played court pieces, the electric heater casting dancing shadows on the walls. Every shuffle of the cards, every playful accusation of cheating, every victory celebration became another thread in the tapestry of our new life together. Her competitive spirit matched mine, and though I won every round, her determination never wavered.

Watching her in these unguarded moments - the way she bit her lip in concentration, how her eyes lit up with each good hand, the small victory dance she did when she thought she had me beat - I felt myself falling even deeper. This tiny cottage, with its cramped kitchen and temperamental heater, had become more than just a temporary stop. It was becoming our first real home together, filled with laughter and love and the kind of happiness that makes your chest ache.

That night, as I watched her smile and plot her strategy for the next game, I realized we were more than just two people who had fallen in love. We were partners, adventurers, dreamers - building something extraordinary one small moment at a time. And there, surrounded by half-unpacked suitcases and the warmth of new beginnings, our journey truly began.

***

The streets of Riverton stretched before us, each cobblestone seeming to echo with the complications of our choices. While Elina photographed the canals with enthusiasm, I felt the weight of uncertainty pressing against my chest. My feelings for her remained intense, but doubt had crept in, casting shadows over what once felt certain.

"We'll live here for a long time," I said, my tone sharper than necessary. "Can you stop taking pictures and come with me?"

"It's my first time here. Why don't you let me enjoy this?" The hurt in her voice still affected me, though not as deeply as before.

"Because you don't understand why we're here!" I snapped, frustration bleeding through. "We're here to run a business, Elina, and every second counts. These beautiful buildings aren't going anywhere!"

She strode ahead, and I matched her pace automatically. Even with my growing doubts, our bodies maintained their familiar rhythm - a reminder of everything we'd shared, everything I now questioned.

That night, in our cottage, the tension finally broke.

"You don't love me anymore. I know you don't. You love Nadia!" Her words carried an accusation I couldn't fully deny. "You don't even talk about our future anymore. You don't mention our kids or their names like you used to."

The truth clawed at my chest, more complicated than simple accusations. Recent revelations about her past had shaken something in me, yet my heart refused to follow my mind's logical path. I tried to force myself into numbness, deliberately ignoring her messages with male friends, fighting against the jealousy that had once consumed me. But even as I attempted this emotional distance, every glance from her sent electricity through my veins, every touch broke down the walls I desperately tried to build.

I found myself in an impossible battle with my own heart. Part of me strived to create distance, hoping her feelings would fade naturally, even as my own burned brighter with each passing day. The depth of her love showed in every gesture, every look, and though I tried to pull back, my body betrayed me - leaning into her touch, seeking her presence even as my mind screamed for space. Here in this foreign country, I told myself I stayed close out of obligation, out of responsibility. But that was a lie I couldn't even convince myself of. The truth was simpler and more devastating: I loved her with an intensity that frightened me, that defied every attempt at distance. Each step back only showed me how helplessly drawn to her I remained, how completely she had captured my heart despite every reason to guard it.

"It's not that, Elina," I said carefully. "I love you, and you know that. But we're here for something bigger. We have dreams to chase, a company to start. We have to focus."

She threw herself into my arms, and I held her, feeling the familiar comfort of her presence even as questions churned inside me. My jokes came easily, making her laugh through tears, but underneath lay a growing uncertainty about our future. The intensity of what we'd built together remained, but now it felt shadowed by doubt, complicated by revelations I couldn't unlearn.

Those days strained us both. The pressure of finding our footing in a new country weighed heavily, and it became clear we needed separate spaces - she would rent her own place, and I would rent mine. The decision felt right, giving us room to navigate this shifting landscape between us, where love remained but trust had begun to waver.

Each day brought new questions I couldn't answer, new doubts I couldn't shake. The future I'd once imagined so clearly with her had become hazy, uncertain. Yet even as I tried to create distance, I found myself drawn back to her, caught in the gravity of what we'd built together, even as it seemed to be slowly unraveling.

Let me help edit this section while maintaining emotional depth and consistency with the rest of the story. I'll keep the core events but enhance the emotional resonance and human connection:

The Rain-Soaked Evening

"Tomorrow, I have to go to Amsterdam to get the money I arranged from Iran," I told her one evening, watching how the lamplight caught the worry that immediately flickered across her face.

"Let me come with you," she said softly, reaching for my hand across the small space between us. Her fingers were warm against mine, grounding me in the moment.

"No, my love. The amount is too significant - I need to be careful. The Netherlands may be safe, but money can make people unpredictable." I squeezed her hand gently, trying to ease the concern in her eyes.

"That's exactly why I should come," she insisted, her grip tightening on mine. The protectiveness in her voice made my chest tighten with emotion.

"Elina," I said, drawing her closer, "I need to know you're safe. Let me handle this alone."

She studied my face for a long moment, her eyes holding mine with an intensity that made my heart race. Finally, she nodded, though reluctance lingered in every line of her body. "Promise you'll call the moment you're finished?"

"Of course," I replied, pressing a kiss to her forehead.

The rain fell in heavy sheets as I made my way through Amsterdam later that day. Each train change, each metro stop, felt like another step away from her warmth. The exchange person was late, caught in traffic they claimed, leaving me standing in the cold rain, thoughts drifting back to the cottage where Elina waited.

By the time I finally returned, night had fallen and I was drenched to the bone. I'd forgotten to message her about being close - lost in thoughts of what this money meant for our future together.

The door opened before I could reach for it, and there she stood, her face a mixture of relief and loving reproach. "Oh my God, come in, my love!" The warmth of her voice wrapped around me like a blanket.

"Is there anything to eat?" I asked, exhaustion making my voice rough. She was already helping me out of my wet jacket, her movements full of tender efficiency.

"Why didn't you call?" she asked softly, pressing dry clothes into my hands. "I made dinner - I wanted to have it warm for you."

Looking at her then - the genuine care in her eyes, the way she anticipated my needs - something shifted in my chest. "I'm starving," I admitted, letting her see my vulnerability.

"I know," she said, her voice carrying a warmth that seemed to thaw the cold from my bones. "You barely touched lunch."

The smell hit me then - something rich and promising that made my mouth water. "You made my favorite?" I asked, amazement coloring my voice.

"With my own special touch," she replied, a hint of pride in her smile.

"Will you marry me?" The words came out playful, but carried an undercurrent of truth that made my heart race.

"I married you last year," she countered with that smile that never failed to captivate me. "Now sit down and let your wife show you her cooking skills."

The dish she placed before me was a masterpiece - chicken and rice prepared with what she said was her mother's recipe. The first bite was a revelation - flavors melding perfectly, speaking of home and comfort and love.

"This is incredible," I said, watching joy bloom across her face at my words.

We sat together while I ate, her presence as nourishing as the food itself. In that moment - rain pattering against the windows, warmth surrounding us, her eyes soft with love - everything felt right. The complications of our situation, the challenges ahead, all seemed to fade against the simple perfection of being together, sharing this quiet moment in our own private world.

The meal became more than just dinner - it was another thread in the tapestry of intimacy we were weaving together, another moment that bound us closer despite the obstacles in our path. Every bite reminded me of how deeply she had woven herself into my life, how natural it felt to share these simple pleasures with her, how impossible it seemed now to imagine a future without her in it.

Let me enhance this section while maintaining the emotional depth and consistency of the narrative:

After The Storm

The evening settled around us like a warm blanket as we played cards, the steady drumming of rain against the windows creating our own private symphony. Each shuffle of the deck, each shared smile, each moment of comfortable silence felt precious - another memory being woven into the tapestry of our hidden life together.

Later, as we lay in bed, reality crept back in with the weight of decisions yet to be made. "We need to start looking for apartments tomorrow," I said, staring at the ceiling, my voice carrying all the complexity of our situation. "It's time to get serious about everything we need to do."

Elina's head rested on my bicep, her fingers tracing delicate patterns through the hair on my chest - a gesture that had become as familiar as breathing. The simple intimacy of it made my heart ache with both joy and sadness. These quiet moments felt simultaneously perfect and precarious, like holding something infinitely precious that could shatter at any moment.

"Yes, my husband," she whispered, the words carrying that mixture of playfulness and profound truth that always moved me. Her hand stilled on my chest, right above my heart, as if trying to memorize its rhythm.

"And you know..." I began carefully, my free hand finding hers, "we'll need to get separate apartments." The words felt heavy, weighted with everything we couldn't change.

"I know," she replied, her voice barely above a whisper. She pressed closer to me, as if trying to deny the inevitable distance that would come. "I wish you hadn't gotten it into your head to get married." There was no accusation in her voice, only a tender sadness that squeezed my heart.

I tightened my arm around her, drawing her impossibly closer. Her hair tickled my chin, carrying that familiar scent that had become synonymous with home. "I can't imagine being without you," she confessed into the quiet between us, each word carrying the weight of everything we'd built together.

I stroked her hair gently, trying to offer comfort even as my own heart twisted with the complexity of our situation. "Let's see what happens," I said softly, though we both knew the road ahead would be far from simple. "We need to focus on the business right now, honey. We're still finding our feet."

The darkness wrapped around us like a cocoon as we lay there, neither sleeping nor speaking, just existing in this moment together. Each breath, each heartbeat seemed to whisper of both possibility and limitation - of love found and choices made, of dreams shared and sacrifices demanded. In these quiet hours, our love felt both infinite and fragile, a paradox we were learning to live with, one tender moment at a time.

The weight of everything - our hidden love, the separate apartments we'd need to maintain appearances, the delicate balance we'd have to strike - settled over us like a familiar blanket. Yet underneath it all ran that current of connection that had drawn us together, that made every complicated step worth taking. We held each other in the darkness, saying everything and nothing, letting the night cradle our dreams and fears alike.

A Temporary Haven

The search for our own space led us down multiple paths - two separate apartments for appearances and a temporary solution for the immediate future. The cottage had become our sanctuary, a place where we could simply be together without pretense or hiding.

"I have an idea," I said one evening, watching how the lamplight played across Elina's face. "The cottage owners return tomorrow. We could ask about extending our stay."

"That would be perfect," she replied, her eyes lighting up with that spark that never failed to catch my breath.

Martha and Johan's home radiated warmth when we arrived to discuss the possibility. Their two young children, ages two and four, filled the space with innocent laughter and movement. I watched, captivated, as Elina immediately connected with little Mina, lifting the child into her arms with natural grace.

The way she held the little girl, her eyes occasionally finding mine across the room, stirred something deep in my chest. Each glance carried dreams neither of us dared voice - possibilities that hung in the air between us like delicate soap bubbles, beautiful but fragile. Martha noticed these exchanges, though she kept her observations to herself.

"Starting a business in a new country - that's quite courageous!" Martha remarked, her tone warm with genuine interest.

"Yes," I replied, focusing on the practical matters at hand. "We were hoping to discuss extending our stay in the cottage. And perhaps," I added carefully, "the possibility of using this address temporarily for bank accounts and paperwork - just until we find our own place."

Martha explained that she and Johan had already discussed our situation. "We can extend the rental for a month," she offered. "The cottage was meant for family visits, so we can't go beyond that."

"That means more to us than you know," I said, relief coloring my voice.

Back at the cottage, our private world enveloped us once again. Elina's laughter filled the space as she shared Martha's warning about mice and their cat's hunting prowess.

"Martha mentioned their cat catches mice. Do you think we have any here?" she asked, a hint of concern in her voice.

"Don't worry," I assured her with a smile, already forming plans to make our temporary home more comfortable. "We're safe from any unwanted visitors."

The energy between us remained magnetic - every shared glance, every casual touch charged with meaning. In her presence, the rest of the world seemed to fade to watercolor, leaving only us in vivid focus. I made a decision then, watching her move through our borrowed space with such natural belonging - I would stop fighting this connection, stop talking about separation. Some things were meant to be, and fighting destiny only led to more pain.

The weight of our choices hung in the air like evening mist - not heavy enough to suffocate, but impossible to ignore. Like the cottage itself, our time together felt borrowed, yet precious. We were building something real in a temporary space, creating permanence in impermanence. Each moment together added another brushstroke to the masterpiece of what we were becoming, even as we both sensed the storm of consequences gathering on the horizon.

In the quiet moments between decisions and plans, we found our own rhythm, our own truth. The future might be uncertain, but here, now, in this space we'd carved out for ourselves, everything made perfect sense. Each shared smile, each tender touch, each moment of quiet understanding reinforced what I already knew in my heart - some choices, once made, become your destiny.

Patterns of the Heart

The December chill had settled into our temporary home, but there was warmth in the simple rhythm we'd developed together. Our newly purchased bicycles leaned against the wall - a small step toward building our life here. Each morning, we'd ride to the library or local cafes, searching for apartments between sips of coffee and shared glances.

That Christmas Eve morning felt different somehow. The holiday season, usually filled with joy and celebration, carried a weight of uncertainty this year. No permanent home, a fledgling company to nurture, engineers waiting for payment - our dreams felt both thrillingly close and terrifyingly precarious.

After a quiet breakfast, as sunlight filtered through the cottage windows, Elina disappeared into the bedroom. When she returned, she held something wrapped in tissue paper, her steps measured as if carrying something precious.

"Darian," she said softly, my name on her lips still sending subtle shivers through me. "I have something for you." She stood before me, a mix of pride and nervousness playing across her features.

As she handed me the package, her fingers brushed mine, lingering for just a moment. "I made this myself," she continued, watching intently as I began unwrapping it. "Not because of... everything between us, but as a thank you. For being who you are, for everything you've done."

The tissue paper fell away to reveal a seal-grey scarf, each stitch speaking of hours of patient dedication. The pattern was intricate, waves of texture flowing through the soft wool. I ran my fingers over it, remembering a conversation weeks ago about my mother's knitting, amazed that she had captured this piece of my history in such a tangible way.

"This is..." I began, words failing as I took in the craftsmanship. "Elina, this is beautiful."

"Those times I seemed distant," she explained, moving closer, "when you thought I was pulling away - I was working on this. I started over so many times, wanting it to be perfect." Her voice carried a hint of apology mixed with determination.

The realization hit me then - all those moments I'd questioned her dedication, she had been pouring her heart into every stitch, creating something that bridged our worlds. My fingers traced the pattern again, feeling the warmth of her effort, her care, her... love.

"I remember telling you about my mother's knitting," I said softly, looking up to meet her eyes. "How did you manage to capture exactly what I love about handmade things?"

She smiled, that special smile that seemed reserved just for me. "I pay attention to everything about you, Darian. Everything."

The morning light caught her face just so, and something shifted in my chest - a recognition of how deeply she understood me, how carefully she had woven herself into my life, stitch by stitch, moment by moment.

I pulled her close, breathing in the familiar scent of her hair, the scarf pressed between us. "Thank you," I whispered against her temple. "Not just for the scarf, but for understanding what it means."

Her arms tightened around me, and we stood there in the winter sunlight, the scarf a tangible testament to something growing between us that was becoming impossible to deny. In that moment, the uncertain future, the complicated present - none of it mattered. There was only this: her warmth against me, the soft wool in my hands, and the undeniable recognition that what we shared was transforming into something profound and irreversible.

Let me enhance this scene with more emotional depth while maintaining its playful essence. I'll title it:

Laughter in the Last Light

The cottage had become our sanctuary over these weeks, every corner filled with memories of shared moments. That evening, as we organized our belongings, the familiar comfort of our routine wrapped around us like a warm blanket. I watched Elina sorting through papers, her movements graceful and focused, when mischief struck.

"MICE!" I shouted suddenly, fighting to keep a straight face.

Elina's reaction was spectacular - in one fluid movement that would have impressed any Olympic athlete, she launched herself across the room, her face a perfect picture of horror. Her hair flew around her as she spun, eyes wide with panic, only to find me doubled over with laughter.

"You!" Understanding dawned on her face as she caught her breath. "After I bought you that plastic cockroach?"

Our laughter filled the small space, echoing off the walls that had witnessed so much of our journey together. I crossed the room in two strides, pulling her into my arms, feeling her mock resistance dissolve as I pressed kisses to her temple, her cheek, finally finding her lips.

The cottage glowed with evening light, casting long shadows across the floor as we held each other, our laughter softening into something more tender. With New Year's approaching, we both knew our time here was drawing to a close. The practical concerns - the expensive rent, our desperate search for permanent housing - seemed distant in this moment, overshadowed by the simple joy of being together.

Finding a new place had been challenging. Landlords looked at us skeptically - no jobs, no credit history, just dreams and determination. It took until after Christmas, just before the new year, to finally secure an apartment, and only then by offering nine months' rent upfront. It felt like buying our future with both hands.

Elina found her own small studio in a family home, moving in first. The kind landlady who picked her up eased my worried heart - at least she would be safe, cared for. But watching her go stirred something deep in my chest, a reminder that our cocoon of shared days was transforming into something new.

My last night alone in the cottage felt surreal. The space seemed to echo with phantom laughter, with whispered conversations and stolen kisses. Every corner held memories - our morning coffees, our late-night discussions, our moments of pure joy and quiet understanding. The walls that had sheltered our beginning now stood witness to its evolution.

As I packed up the next morning, preparing to inspect my new apartment, I touched the walls one last time. This place had been more than just temporary shelter - it had been the cradle of something profound, something that would follow us far beyond these humble walls. In the morning light, I could almost see the ghosts of our laughter dancing in the dust motes, a reminder that sometimes the simplest moments become our most precious memories.

Separate Spaces

When I arrived at the new apartment, disappointment washed over me. The space that had promised a fresh start was instead filled with dust and neglect. My frustration mounted as I took in the uncleaned surfaces and general disarray - this wasn't the beginning I had imagined. The call to the agency was terse, their apologies hollow against my vision of what this place could be.

That evening, talking to Elina, I found myself sharing more than just complaints about the apartment's condition. Each word seemed to carry the weight of everything we weren't saying - about the future, about what this move really meant.

"It's nothing like they promised," I said, my voice softer than intended.

"Tell me everything," she replied, and I could hear the smile in her voice, the one that had begun to feel like home.

We had agreed she would never visit her apartment - the risks were too high, the future too uncertain. But when she offered to help me move the next morning, I couldn't refuse. We orchestrated our arrivals carefully - me in the first Uber, her following with the remaining luggage, maintaining the careful dance of discretion we'd perfected.

The neighborhood was beautiful - historic buildings with high ceilings and character-filled corners. As we began unpacking together, every movement felt charged with meaning. The makeshift bed we created from sheets became a symbol of our temporary paradise, even as exhaustion pulled us into sleep.

The next day, while the cleaning service worked, Elina took charge of the kitchen. I watched her hands move through soapy water, cleaning dishes with careful attention. Every few minutes, she would find her way back to me, pressing soft kisses against my lips before returning to her task. Each kiss felt like a promise, like a small act of defiance against the temporary nature of our situation.

Standing in the kitchen doorway, watching her work, something caught in my chest. She moved through the space with such natural grace, as if she belonged here. Yet we both knew this wasn't meant to be her home. The quiet dignity with which she cleaned and organized a space that would eventually welcome another woman struck me deeply.

Her hands moved methodically through each task, but her presence filled every corner of the apartment with warmth. When she spoke, her voice carried no trace of bitterness, only genuine care. It was this selfless attention to my comfort that made my heart ache the most.

The guilt sat heavy in my chest - not just for her, but for everyone caught in this web of emotions we'd created. For Nadia, who had no idea another woman was making her future home livable. For Elina, who gave so freely knowing she might never truly belong here. For myself, watching someone I was growing to love deeply care for a space she could never claim as her own.

The afternoon light streamed through the windows, catching dust motes in its beam, as we continued our work in companionable silence. Each moment felt precious and painful at once - a perfect snapshot of what we had and what we couldn't keep.

That night, Elina returned to her place to settle in, unpacking the last of her things and trying to make her small studio feel like home. As soon as she left, the silence of my apartment pressed in around me. I found myself reaching for my phone, instinctively dialing Nadia. Her voice came through familiar yet somehow distant, as if we were speaking across more than just miles. Our conversation flowed with practiced ease, but underneath ran currents of things unsaid, of changes neither of us were ready to name.

After hanging up, I lay in bed, watching shadows dance across the high ceiling. The apartment still carried the sharp scent of cleaning products - a sterile reminder that this space hadn't yet become anyone's home. In the quiet, every thought seemed to echo: the uncertainty of this new country, the complexity of what I was building with Elina, the steady unraveling of everything I'd known with Nadia. Sleep finally came, but it brought little peace.

Morning Blooms

Morning arrived with soft winter light and a gentle knock that pulled me from restless dreams. Making my way to the door, still wrapped in sleep's haze, I found Elina standing there. The early light caught in her hair, her cheeks flushed from the cold, and in her hands she held an Anthurium plant - its deep red blooms like hearts against the grey morning.

"Good morning, my life," she said, her voice carrying warmth that seemed to chase away the apartment's lingering chill.

She stepped inside, bringing with her the crisp scent of winter air and something else - a sense of possibility that made my heart race. The Anthurium's leaves glistened with tiny droplets, catching the morning light like scattered diamonds. Each drop seemed to hold a fragment of our shared future, precarious but brilliant.

"I woke up early," she explained, setting the plant down carefully on the windowsill. "I wanted to be the first one to bring life to your new home." Her fingers lingered on the leaves, arranging them with tender attention.

Looking at her there, silhouetted against the growing dawn, I felt something shift inside me. This wasn't just about a plant - it was about roots, about growth, about the courage to nurture something new even when the future seemed uncertain.

"The flower shop owner told me Anthuriums need special care," she continued, turning to face me. "They're particular about light and water, about the soil they grow in. But if you care for them properly..." She paused, her eyes meeting mine with an intensity that made my breath catch. "They can bloom for years."

I crossed the room to her, drawn by something deeper than just physical attraction. This woman, who thought to bring me not just beauty but life itself, who understood that new beginnings need tender care - she had somehow wound herself around my heart when I wasn't looking.

"Show me," I said softly, standing close enough to feel the warmth radiating from her. "Show me how to care for it."

She smiled, taking my hand and guiding it to one of the heart-shaped blooms. "Feel how strong it is," she murmured. "How resilient. But also how delicate." Her fingers intertwined with mine as we touched the waxy surface together. "It's like love that way - needs the right balance of strength and gentleness to flourish."

The morning light strengthened around us, painting everything in shades of gold. Outside, the city was waking up, but in here, time seemed to pause. We stood together, our joined hands still resting on the Anthurium's bloom, as if by touching this living thing together we could somehow ensure our own growth, our own flourishing.

"Thank you," I whispered, turning to pull her into my arms. She came willingly, fitting against me as if she'd always belonged there. "Not just for the plant..."

"I know," she breathed against my neck, her arms tightening around me. "I know."

The apartment still smelled of cleaning products, still felt new and uncertain, but now there was something else too - the subtle fragrance of soil and green things, the promise of growth, the possibility of making something beautiful take root even in uncertain ground. As I held her there in the strengthening morning light, I realized that maybe home wasn't a place at all - maybe it was this feeling, this moment, this shared understanding of what it means to nurture something precious into bloom.

New Year's Eve

The city hummed with anticipation as dusk settled over Riverton. Lights twinkled through a gentle mist, transforming ordinary streets into something magical. In my apartment, Elina moved with natural grace, helping arrange the last details of our private celebration. Every glance we shared carried the weight of unspoken promises, of a future we dared to imagine despite everything.

The evening unfolded slowly, precious in its simplicity. We cooked together, our movements synchronized as if we'd done this a thousand times before. The kitchen filled with warmth and laughter as I attempted to teach her my special recipe, her playful attempts to steal tastes of everything making my heart swell. When she dabbed sauce on my nose, her eyes dancing with mischief, I couldn't help but pull her close, both of us forgetting about dinner for a moment.

As midnight approached, we made our way to the famous lake where the city's grand fireworks display would paint the sky. The streets of Riverton had transformed, buzzing with an electric energy that matched the anticipation in my chest. Droplets of rain caught the streetlights, turning the world into a shimmering dreamscape. We walked close, our shoulders brushing, each point of contact sending sparks through my skin.

The crowd around the lake grew denser, but somehow we found our perfect spot - a quiet corner where the water met the shore. Elina shivered slightly in the cool air, and without thinking, I wrapped my arm around her. She leaned into me naturally, fitting against my side as if she'd been designed for exactly this moment.

The countdown began, voices rising in unified anticipation.

"Ten!" The crowd shouted, but I was lost in the way the lights reflected in Elina's eyes.

"Nine!" Her hand found mine, fingers intertwining.

"Eight!" My heart thundered against my ribs.

"Seven!" She turned to face me, and the world seemed to slow.

"Six!" The crowd faded away until there was only us.

"Five!" Her lips parted slightly, drawing my gaze.

"Four!" Rain began to fall more steadily, but neither of us moved.

"Three!" Droplets caught in her eyelashes like diamonds.

"Two!" She squeezed my hand tighter.

"One!"

The world erupted in light and sound, but I barely noticed. Our lips met in a kiss that felt like coming home and setting sail all at once. Fireworks exploded overhead, their colors painting us in fleeting shades of gold and red and blue, but the real fireworks were in my chest, in the way my heart seemed to expand beyond its bounds.

We stayed by the lake long after the official display ended, watching the last sparks fade from the sky. The rain had soaked through our clothes, but neither of us cared. There was something perfect about this moment - standing together in the gentle rain, the city lights reflecting off the wet pavement, creating halos around us.

The walk home felt dreamlike. Water dripped from our hair, our clothes clung to our skin, but we couldn't stop smiling. Every few steps, one of us would pull the other close for another kiss, making the journey take twice as long as it should have.

Back at the apartment, we shed our wet coats and I turned up the heat. Elina's hair curled damply around her face as she moved to stand by the window, watching the city celebrate below. I wrapped my arms around her from behind, and she leaned back into me with a contented sigh.

"Happy New Year," she whispered, turning in my embrace.

"Happy New Year," I replied, my voice rough with emotion.

As we stood there, holding each other in the warm darkness of my apartment, I knew this moment would be forever etched in my memory - this perfect beginning to what promised to be the most complicated year of our lives. Outside, the city continued its celebrations, but in here, we had created our own world, one where nothing existed except us and the love that had grown between us, as unstoppable as the rain that still fell softly outside.

Fresh Days

Those first days of the holiday wrapped around us like a cocoon. Outside, rain painted abstract patterns on the windows, its gentle rhythm becoming the soundtrack to our stolen paradise. Inside, the warm glow of lamp light created shadows that danced across the walls as Elina and I lost ourselves in endless games of cards, cooking adventures, and conversations that seemed to flow like wine.

The card games started as simple entertainment but evolved into something more intimate - a dance of minds, a way to learn each other's tells and quirks. Elina's competitive spirit emerged immediately, her frustration at losing making her scrunch her nose in a way that made my heart flutter.

"This is impossible," she declared after her fifth straight loss, throwing her cards down with dramatic flair. "You must be cheating." Her eyes narrowed playfully, but I could see the genuine determination beneath her teasing.

I couldn't help but smile, my hands automatically shuffling the deck with practiced ease. "Not cheating," I explained, dealing the cards with flourish. "Just strategy. You're playing with your heart instead of your head."

She leaned forward, elbows on the table, her face close enough that I could see flecks of gold in her eyes. "Then teach me," she challenged, her voice soft but intense. "Show me how you see the game."

I found myself mesmerized by her eagerness to learn, the way she absorbed every detail I shared. Teaching her became an exercise in intimacy - explaining how to read opponents' patterns, how to anticipate moves, how to maintain composure even when victory seemed certain. Our hands would brush as I demonstrated card placement, and each touch sent electricity through my skin.

"See here," I'd say, my voice dropping lower as I leaned closer, "when I play this card, I'm not just thinking about now. I'm thinking three moves ahead." The scent of her perfume would distract me momentarily, making me lose my train of thought.

As the evening progressed, I began making subtle mistakes - not obvious enough to be detected, but just enough to give her an edge. Watching her confidence grow with each successful play filled me with a warmth I hadn't expected. Her victories became mine in a different way.

When she finally won a game outright, her joy was luminous. She jumped up from her chair with a squeal of delight, her eyes sparkling with triumph. "I did it!" she exclaimed, doing a little victory dance that made my chest tight with affection.

"I have no idea," she said, leaning down to kiss my cheek, her lips lingering just a moment too long, "what an amazing teacher I had." Her words carried a warmth that had nothing to do with the game.

Between rounds, our conversation meandered like a lazy river, touching on memories and dreams. The soft lamplight created an intimate atmosphere that made sharing stories feel natural, necessary even.

"Remember that impossible parking situation with Titanus?" I asked, watching her deliberate over her next move. "When that car had us blocked in at the coffee shop?"

Her face lit up with recognition, and the smile she gave me made my heart skip. "Oh my God, yes! I was certain you'd never get out of that spot without at least a scratch. But you handled it like some kind of driving wizard."

I chuckled, though my chest tightened at the memory of Titanus. "He never let me down, that car. We went through everything together."

"You miss him," she said softly, reaching across the table to take my hand. Her touch was gentle, understanding. She didn't just mean the car - she meant everything it represented: freedom, adventure, a life I'd built that was now changing in ways I never expected.

"Yeah," I admitted, turning my hand to intertwine our fingers. "Titanus wasn't just transportation. He was..." I trailed off, searching for words.

"Part of your soul," she finished, her thumb tracing patterns on my palm. The simple gesture carried more comfort than any words could have.

We sat there for a moment, connected by touch and understanding, while the rain continued its gentle percussion against the windows. Then Elina straightened, her competitive spark returning as she reached for the cards.

"Enough nostalgia," she declared, shuffling with newfound confidence. "Time for me to show you what I've learned."

I laughed, settling back in my chair. "Let's see if the student is ready to become the master."

This time, I played with everything I had, no held punches, no subtle mistakes. She matched me move for move, her strategic mind now working in concert with her natural intuition. Watching her play, seeing how quickly she'd absorbed every lesson, filled me with a pride that went beyond the game.

In that moment, surrounded by the warm light and gentle rain, I realized we'd created something precious in these quiet hours - a space where we could just be ourselves, where the complications of our situation faded into the background, where love could grow as naturally as breathing.

Post Holiday

After the holidays, life accelerated into a whirlwind of moments both tender and tense. During the days, I immersed myself in work—coordinating with the tech team, refining strategies, writing chapters of my book. But the evenings... the evenings belonged to a different world entirely. A world where Elina and I created our own sanctuary of shared glances and quiet understanding.

We'd settle into what had become our ritual—cards spread across my desk, coffee cups leaving rings on scattered papers, laughter echoing off glass walls. The way she'd bite her lip when contemplating her next move, how her eyes would catch mine across the table, carrying messages only we could read. These moments felt stolen from time itself, precious in their simplicity.

In these evening hours, I found myself noticing things I'd never paid attention to before—the graceful arc of her wrist as she dealt cards, the soft cadence of her voice when she spoke about her dreams, the way she'd absently twist a strand of hair around her finger when deep in thought. Each detail seemed to etch itself into my memory, building a picture of something I wasn't ready to name.

But love, even as it blossoms, brings its own kind of storm.

We fought. Not constantly, but with an intensity that matched everything else between us. The weight of our situation—the complexity of what we were building, the uncertainty that shadowed every stolen moment—would sometimes crash over us like waves. Words would turn sharp, silences would stretch too long, and the space between us would fill with all the things we couldn't say.

Yet somehow, we always found our way back to each other. It never took more than ten minutes before one of us would break—a touch, a whispered apology, a look that could dissolve every wall we'd tried to build. In those moments of reconciliation, everything else would fade away, leaving only the undeniable pull between us.

The fear lived there too, constant as a heartbeat—the fear of losing what we'd found, of watching this precious, dangerous thing slip through our fingers. So we held on tighter, each touch a promise, each shared smile a secret rebellion against the world that seemed determined to keep us apart.

These evening hours became our truth, even as they complicated everything I thought I knew about love. In Elina's presence, I found myself becoming someone new—someone who could feel this deeply, want this completely, risk this recklessly. And even as guilt shadowed every moment, I couldn't stop myself from falling deeper into whatever this was becoming.

That Virus

Martha from the cottage had messaged our shared group chat about letters arriving at their address. While we were settling into our new places, Johan and Martha had graciously allowed us to use their address for important documents, even letting us register the company there. Their kindness made our transition much smoother.

The next day, Elina and I headed to the cottage together. The sky hung low and grey, winter's chill still clinging to the air despite spring's approach. We took the bus, sitting close enough that our shoulders touched, the silence between us comfortable yet charged with unspoken thoughts. When we arrived, Johan and Martha weren't home, so we collected our mail and began sorting through it at the bus stop.

I watched Elina's hands move through the envelopes, noting how gracefully her fingers handled each one. She paused at a particular letter, her movements becoming more deliberate. A medical clinic's logo was visible in the corner. Without a word, she opened it, her eyes moving across the page with increasing intensity.

I noticed the change in her expression immediately - the way her face fell, how her shoulders tensed. The letter trembled slightly in her hands.

"What's wrong?" I asked, already moving closer to her.

She didn't answer immediately. Instead, she looked up at me, her eyes carrying a weight that made my heart clench. "It's positive," she whispered.

The words hung between us as understanding dawned. The HPV test she'd taken here in the Netherlands, after testing negative in Parin, had come back positive.

I reached for her hand instinctively, our fingers intertwining. The touch felt both natural and electric, as it always did between us. The realization hit hard - Nadia had been right. Elina had unknowingly carried the virus, passing it first to me, then to Nadia.

Standing there at the bus stop, holding each other in the grey afternoon light, we faced this new reality together. Our choices, our love, our future - everything seemed to shift and realign in that moment, adding another layer to the complex tapestry of our relationship.

In that moment, nothing else mattered. I pulled her into my arms, feeling her collapse against me, her warmth familiar yet somehow more precious in her distress. The world continued moving around us - passersby, traffic, the distant sound of another bus arriving - but we remained in our bubble of shared pain and comfort.

The journey home felt endless. On the bus, she stayed close to me, her fingers intertwined with mine, drawing strength from our connection. Each tear that fell seemed to carry the weight of everything we'd built together, everything we stood to lose. I wanted to shield her from this pain, to take it all away, but all I could do was be there, my thumb tracing gentle circles on her hand.

When we finally reached my apartment, the silence between us shifted, crystallizing into something sharper. Elina turned to me, her eyes bright with unshed tears and a new intensity that made my chest tighten.

"You gave this to me," she said, her voice carrying an edge I'd never heard before.

I exhaled slowly, feeling the delicate balance between us begin to tip. "Elina—"

"No," she cut me off, stepping away from my attempted embrace. "You transferred it to me. My previous tests were negative. I was clean before you."

I tried to keep my voice steady, to be the anchor we both needed. "It's not important who the source is. We need to focus on what we can do now."

The moment the words left my mouth, I knew they were wrong. Her expression shifted, hurt and anger warring across her features. The space between us seemed to grow wider with each passing second.

"Not important?" She laughed, but it was hollow, nothing like the joyful sound I'd grown to love. "How can you say that? I need to know how this happened!"

I ran a hand through my hair, the weight of months of suppressed thoughts and suspicions pressing against my chest. The truth hung between us, undeniable now. Elina had been the source, though neither of us wanted to face what that meant.

"I doubt your previous tests were even correct," I said quietly, the words falling like stones into still water.

The fragile tension shattered. Elina's eyes flashed with a mixture of hurt and fury that made my heart ache. This wasn't just about the diagnosis anymore - it was about everything. Every choice we'd made, every lie we'd told, every moment of happiness we'd stolen at others' expense. The fight that erupted wasn't about finding solutions; it was about finally facing the consequences of our love.

As accusations flew between us, I realized we were both drowning in the same ocean of pain, unable to save each other because we were the source of each other's storm.

That night, as the anger ebbed away, exhaustion took its place. Elina moved to me instinctively, her hand finding its familiar place over my heart. We lay in silence, the steady rhythm beneath her palm saying everything words couldn't. The comfort of our closeness spoke of a love that persisted even through pain, even through anger. We drifted to sleep like that, connected despite the storm we'd weathered.

The next morning, watching her gather her things to leave, I felt something protective stir in my chest. She looked fragile in the morning light, but there was still that quiet strength about her that had first drawn me in. I couldn't let her face this alone.

"Stay here tonight," I said softly but firmly, reaching for her hand.

She paused, her fingers intertwining with mine naturally, as if they belonged there. "Okay."

That evening settled around us like a gentle blanket. We didn't need many words - our connection had always run deeper than that. She curled against me on the couch, her body fitting perfectly against mine as it always did. I held her close, breathing in the familiar scent of her hair, feeling the slight tremor in her breathing that betrayed her anxiety.

Running my fingers through her hair, I pressed a kiss to her forehead, letting my lips linger there. "We'll figure this out," I whispered against her skin.

She looked up at me, her eyes carrying that trust that never failed to humble me. "Promise?"

"I promise." The words felt like a vow.

Morning brought a different kind of intimacy - the quiet determination of facing challenges together. Over breakfast, which neither of us really ate, we began calling doctors. Each rejection seemed to dim the light in Elina's eyes a little more, her voice growing tighter with each "no."

"Another rejection," she sighed, setting down her phone. "It feels endless."

I reached across the table, taking both her phone and her hand. "Let me try for a while."

She attempted a smile, though exhaustion lined her face. "You think they'll magically say yes to a man?"

"No," I said, bringing her hand to my lips. "I just think you need a moment to breathe."

She leaned back, watching me make calls with those eyes that seemed to see straight through to my soul. When she finally got through to a doctor in her neighborhood, the relief in her voice made my heart ache.

"Two days," she said after hanging up, reaching for me again. "They can see me in two days."

I pulled her close, feeling her melt against me. "That's good. We'll get answers."

"Thank you," she whispered against my chest. "For everything."

"You never have to thank me," I replied, holding her tighter. "We're in this together."

She squeezed my hand, and though worry still shadowed her eyes, there was also love there - steady and unwavering, like the connection we'd built between us.

Two days later, I could hear the tension in Elina's voice over the phone. She'd spent the night at her place, but morning brought back all her fears.

"I can go alone," she said, though her voice wavered slightly.

"I'm coming with you," I replied without hesitation, already reaching for my keys.

"Are you sure? You have work—"

"I don't care. You're not doing this alone. Send me the location and I'll meet you there."

When I arrived, she was waiting outside, a solitary figure against the grey morning. The moment she slipped into my car, her presence filled the space with a familiar warmth, though today it was tinged with anxiety. I reached for her hand instinctively, finding her fingers cold against mine. The drive was quiet, but our joined hands spoke volumes. That shared intimacy, so natural between us, would soon feel like a distant memory in the sterile environment of the clinic.

At the clinic, Elina dropped my hand and introduced me simply as "a friend who came to support." The shift in her demeanor was subtle but unmistakable - gone was the woman who had sought comfort in my touch minutes before. As the appointment progressed, her focus kept returning to the source of infection. I watched her growing animation as she detailed her previous negative tests to the doctor, the implications clear in her tone. Though she never directly named me, her meaning was unmistakable. The doctor's occasional glances in my direction suggested he'd pieced together our true relationship, seeing through the thin veneer of "friendship" we'd presented.

The professional facade I'd maintained throughout the appointment cracked as soon as we reached the car. The quiet anger that had been building finally broke through.

"That *was* humiliating," I said, my voice low but sharp as I gripped the steering wheel. "You introduced me as just a friend, then spent the entire time practically pointing fingers at me in front of him."

Elina turned to me, surprise flickering across her face. "What do you mean?"

"Don't," I cut her off, my jaw tight. "He wasn't blind, Elina. He could see exactly what was happening between us. And you kept pushing about the source, making it clear you thought it came from me, when we both know it was probably you all along."

"I needed to understand—" she began, but I interrupted again.

"You needed to understand? Or you needed to blame? Because it felt a lot like the latter." The words came out harsher than I intended, but the hurt and anger were real. "If you wanted to accuse me, you could have done it privately. Instead, you chose to do it through implications in front of a stranger."

I saw the impact of my words in how she drew back slightly, hurt replacing the defensive look in her eyes. The space between us in the car suddenly felt vast, filled with all the things we weren't saying.

"I shouldn't have come," I said finally, softening slightly at her expression. "This was a mistake."

She reached for my hand then, her touch tentative but determined. "I'm sorry," she whispered. "I was scared and I handled it badly. You're right - I shouldn't have done that to you in there."

The sincerity in her voice made some of my anger dissolve. I squeezed her hand back, knowing that in the grand scheme of things, this fight was small compared to what we meant to each other.

The journey back was quiet but different now, the tension gradually melting into something softer. Elina sat close enough that our shoulders touched, her fingers absently tracing patterns on her coat. I could see her processing everything - the diagnosis, our brief fight, the doctor's reassurances, the weight of it all.

When we reached my apartment, she hesitated at the door while I hung up my coat and loosened my collar. The remnants of our argument had faded, replaced by the familiar pull between us. I turned and gently took her hand.

"Come in, Elina. You don't have to act strong all the time," I said softly, the words now less a peace offering and more an acknowledgment of our shared vulnerability.

She exhaled and nodded, slipping off her shoes before following me inside. I had work to do, but I couldn't leave her alone with her thoughts. She curled up on the couch, hugging her knees, as I set up my laptop at the dining table.

"I'm fine," she said after a long silence, but her voice was barely convincing.

I looked up from my screen. "Are you?"

She sighed and shook her head. "Not really."

I closed my laptop. "Then let's talk."

She hesitated, then walked over and sat across from me.

"I know it's nothing serious," she admitted. "But it still feels... humiliating. Like I have something dirty inside me."

Our earlier anger forgotten, I reached across the table, taking her hand. "Elina, don't ever say that. This virus—it's nothing about you. It's common. It's life. And you heard what the doctor said, right? Just a yearly test and that's it."

She nodded slowly, but her eyes were still troubled. "It just makes me feel like I—like we—did something wrong."

I tightened my grip on her hand. "You didn't. We didn't. Don't let this define you."

She gave a weak smile, but I could see the weight still on her shoulders.

That night, she didn't go back to her place. She often stayed at my apartment, though some nights she would return to her studio, saying she needed her space, her own clothes, her own things. I never questioned it. She was still adjusting to this life, to us, to the fragile reality we were building together.

Mornings were our small battleground, a gentle war of priorities and desires. I was always in a hurry, jumping out of bed the moment my alarm went off, already thinking about work and everything else I needed to do. Elina, on the other hand, had a different rhythm, one that reminded me to slow down.

Every morning, she would pull me back into bed, wrap herself around me, and whisper, "Stay just a little longer." Her voice would be soft, still heavy with sleep, but filled with a contentment that made my hurried thoughts pause.

And every morning, I'd groan, laugh, and try to escape, but she'd tighten her grip, her warmth making the outside world seem less urgent.

"One more hug," she'd bargain. "Just one."

"Elina, we have to work."

"We always have to work," she mumbled into my chest. "But what if we just stayed like this forever?"

I smiled, pressing a kiss to the top of her head. "Then we'd starve."

She laughed but didn't let go right away. And so, I learned to pause—just for a moment. Because, even in the rush of our uncertain future, she was right. These moments mattered.

A week later, the doctor called. Elina answered, putting the call on speaker so I could listen, her hand finding mine instinctively.

"Your test came back positive," the doctor said. "But there's nothing to worry about. Just keep monitoring it with a yearly check-up. There's no immediate action required."

Elina exhaled, her grip on my hand tightening. "So... it won't get worse?"

"There's a very low risk. Just be consistent with your tests, and you'll be fine."

She nodded and thanked the doctor before hanging up. A beat of silence stretched between us.

Then, suddenly, she laughed, the sound carrying both relief and lingering anxiety.

I raised an eyebrow. "You okay?"

She looked at me, shaking her head in disbelief. "I was so scared... but for what? It's nothing."

I smiled, drawing her closer. "Told you."

She exhaled. "Thank you for being with me through this. I mean it."

I pulled her into a hug. "Always."

That night, I called Nadia, keeping it to voice only as I'd been doing lately. I told her my internet wasn't set up properly yet—a convenient excuse that let me avoid seeing her face while I held Elina in my arms. The lies were becoming easier, but the guilt never lessened.

Shared Moments

Elina's family called frequently. She had a special place in my apartment where she would sit, making sure her background looked unfamiliar so they wouldn't suspect she was staying with me.

One evening, after she ended a call, she turned to me with a look I couldn't quite read.

"You love her," she said.

I blinked. "What?"

She sat on the couch, pulling her knees to her chest. "Nadia. You still love her. I can feel it."

I opened my mouth to argue, but the words didn't come. Because she was right. Every time I went somewhere new, I expected Nadia to be by my side. We had been best friends, and she had been woven into every part of my life.

But I loved Elina. She was my passion, my obsession, the fire in my life. I wanted to be with her, even as part of me still waited for Nadia's understanding.

Elina sighed. "It's okay," she said. "I just hope... I hope I'm not here because of competition. I hope it's real."

I sat beside her. "It is real."

She nodded but didn't say anything else.

That week, she stayed with me every night, curling into my arms like she was afraid of something slipping away. I noticed the change in her after her test results. The easy intimacy we'd shared had become hesitant, careful.

One night, as we lay in bed, I finally said it. "You've been distant."

She hesitated, then whispered, "I thought maybe... maybe you wouldn't want to touch me anymore."

My heart clenched.

I turned to her, brushed a strand of hair from her face, and kissed her softly. "Don't ever think that."

She exhaled shakily. "Really?"

I nodded. "This virus isn't going to come between us."

That night, she fell asleep faster than she had in weeks. Less stress, fewer restless movements, her body finally at peace.

And in the middle of the night, in that space between dreams and wakefulness, she whispered something.

"You are my life, Darian."

I held my breath. She had said these words before, in moments of passion or tenderness, but this was different. This wasn't a conscious declaration or a response to my touch. This was her unconscious truth, spoken from that vulnerable place between dreams, when all our careful walls come down. The words had slipped from her lips as naturally as breathing, revealing what lay in her deepest heart.

In the morning, when I told her, she frowned.

"I said that?"

I nodded.

She smiled, pressing a sleepy kiss to my shoulder. "Well... it's true."

Her simple confirmation touched me differently now. Because I knew it wasn't just something she said - it was something she felt so deeply it emerged even in her sleep. Through all our complications, the guilt, the uncertainty, her unconscious mind had revealed what was absolutely certain: I had become her anchor, just as she had become mine.

Elina's landlord was from Parin, a woman who balanced kindness with curiosity in equal measure. While she meant well, her frequent unannounced visits and personal questions created a delicate situation that Elina navigated with grace. The landlord would often appear at Elina's door with traditional dishes, a gesture that spoke of both hospitality and the desire to maintain cultural connections in this new land.

But what struck me most was how Elina transformed these moments into something uniquely ours.

"Try this," she would say, her eyes bright with anticipation as she placed the warm container on my table. "She made it fresh today."

I would catch her watching me take the first bite, waiting, sharing this piece of her world with me before experiencing it herself. It was these small gestures that began weaving us closer together, creating a tapestry of shared moments that felt increasingly significant.

One Sunday morning in mid-January, Elina was at my place, the winter sun streaming through the windows, casting a gentle glow across the room. We had spent the morning in comfortable silence punctuated by conversation, the kind of easy companionship that feels both new and familiar.

"You know, we're so close to the sea," I said, stretching my legs. "We came to a beach town, and we've never even seen the beach."

The way her eyes lit up at the suggestion made something stir in my chest. Her excitement was contagious, pure and unrestrained.

"You're right! Let's go today!" she exclaimed, already moving with purpose.

We grabbed our bikes and layered up against the cold, Elina leading the way through a small forest that opened up to vast dunes. The wind whipped around us, fierce and wild, but it only added to the adventure. The beach was nearly empty, save for a few brave parasurfers dancing with the waves.

"Shall we mark this place as our first common beach?" I asked, watching how the wind played with her hair.

"Yes," she smiled, linking her arm with mine, the warmth of her body a stark contrast to the cold air.

The moment felt weighted with possibility, but as we walked along the shore, my thoughts drifted to Nadia. She had always loved places like this - wild and untamed. For over a decade, we had discovered such beauty together, and that history couldn't simply vanish with the tide.

I found myself by the dunes, watching the waves crash against the shore. When Elina noticed my distant gaze, she gave me space, understanding without words the complexity of the moment. Her quiet acceptance only deepened my growing feelings, even as they confused me.

The ride home was colder, but inside, we quickly fell back into our rhythm - playing cards, laughing, teasing. Yet something had shifted, subtle but undeniable. Each shared glance, each moment of comfortable silence, seemed to carry more weight than before.

The day had changed something between us, adding another layer to our evolving story, even as I struggled with the echoes of my past with Nadia and the undeniable pull I felt toward Elina. It was a complex dance of emotions, one that would only grow more intricate with time.

Patterns of Trust

In mid-January, Elina and I settled into a comfortable routine. Our mornings were filled with purpose—she attended Dutch classes while I immersed myself in writing at the library. The evenings belonged to us, marked by competitive card games, playful banter, and moments of genuine connection that made everything else fade away.

Yet beneath this surface of normalcy, three haunting truths gnawed at my mind: what I now knew about her past with a married boyfriend of one year, the way she and I had started our own story while I was with Nadia, and the revelations about her family history. Each piece added to a puzzle I wasn't sure I wanted to complete. Sometimes, in quiet moments, I caught myself wondering if she had some unconscious attraction to married men.

During this time, Elina began branching out socially, meeting a couple through her language classes. Her eyes lit up whenever she spoke about these new friendships, and I found myself caught between happiness for her independence and a deep-seated unease. The patterns were becoming harder to ignore.

"Mehmet promised to help me find a job," she mentioned one evening, her fork pushing around the pasta on her plate. "It could be really good for my career here."

I nodded, watching her carefully. Something in her enthusiasm triggered all those familiar warnings. Three different stories, all pointing to the same conclusion—her complicated relationship with boundaries and truth.

Then came the afternoon when Elina casually mentioned meeting both Mehmet and his wife at the library. The careful way she said it, almost too casual, made me look up from my work.

"I'll come with you," I said, closing my laptop with more force than necessary.

Her smile faltered, just for a heartbeat. "Oh... well, okay."

That slight hesitation echoed in my mind as we sat side by side at the library, the silence between us heavy with unspoken thoughts.

When Mehmet arrived alone, the surprise that flickered across both their faces told me everything I needed to know. Elina recovered quickly, her professional mask sliding into place. "Mehmet, this is Darian, my co-founder and business partner," she said, her voice carrying a forced lightness that only I would notice.

I watched their interaction with growing certainty—the way she leaned forward when he spoke, how his eyes followed her movements, how she seemed to forget I was there. Each moment confirmed what I had feared.

Back at the apartment, we moved through lunch in tense silence. The clink of forks against plates felt too loud, the space between us too wide. Finally, as we cleared the dishes, I couldn't contain it anymore.

"Why did you lie to me?" My voice cut through the artificial peace.

Elina's hands stilled on the plate she was holding. "What?" she asked, but her eyes gave her away.

"You told me we were meeting a couple." I kept my voice steady. "There was no wife there."

She sighed, shoulders tensing. "I didn't know she wouldn't come. Mehmet didn't tell me."

"And you didn't find that strange?" I stepped closer, the frustration building.

Her eyes met mine, defiant. "Darian, you're overreacting. It was just a meeting. He's married."

A bitter laugh escaped me. "Oh, so that's the excuse? He's married?" I moved closer, the hurt transforming into anger. "So am I, Elina. That didn't stop you."

The silence that followed was deafening. Her face paled, composure cracking.

"You know why I don't trust you?" I continued, each word carefully chosen. "Because I see patterns, Elina. Your year-long relationship with a married man, the way you and I started, your own history... Maybe this is just who you are."

Her expression hardened. "You think I'm like that?"

"I think you're drawn to what you shouldn't have," I said, the words coming out sharper than intended. "Maybe one man is never enough for you. Maybe you're attracted to married men without even realizing it."

She recoiled as if struck, hurt and anger warring in her eyes. "If that's what you think of me, then I don't belong here."

Grabbing her coat, she moved toward the door. "I won't stay in your home anymore."

I watched her go, pride and pain keeping me rooted in place. The door closed behind her with a finality that echoed through the empty apartment.

I let her go.

That night, memories of Nadia flooded my mind - how we built our relationship on unwavering trust. I remembered the early days, when my jealousy surfaced over that doctor from her hospital who'd shared her flight. Instead of dismissing my feelings, she'd shown me through her actions that I was the only one in her heart. Over the years, our bond had grown into something I thought was unbreakable. Yet here I was, watching that precious trust crumble through my own actions. My growing feelings for Elina had created cracks in what Nadia and I had built together, and I found myself torn between the love I'd built over years with Nadia and these intense, unexpected feelings for Elina that I couldn't seem to control.

The next morning, I woke up with Nadia's photo still visible on my desk. Her smile, captured in that moment from happier times, made my heart twist with guilt. The weight of my argument with Elina pressed against my chest, and I chose to let the silence stretch between us. Maybe distance would help clear my mind of this confusion.

I spent the morning immersed in my work, focusing on the final chapters of my book. The manuscript was almost complete—just a few more revisions before closing this chapter of my life. Each word I wrote felt like a step away from the person I used to be, the man who had built a beautiful life with Nadia, and toward something unknown and terrifying.

Then, amidst my inbox full of unread messages, I saw Elina's name.

She had sent a formal business email—something that felt jarringly different from our recent intimate conversations. It was direct, professional, focused entirely on our startup. The contrast between this detached tone and our heated exchange from the night before made my stomach clench.

I stared at the email, reading between the lines of her carefully chosen words. Despite everything, she remained committed to our shared vision. The startup we were building together still mattered to her, even if everything else between us was complicated.

The emails evolved into messages on our company chat platform. At first, we maintained the professional facade, but gradually, the walls began to crumble. Business talk softened into personal concern. A tentative "How are you holding up?" A careful "I've been thinking about what you said."

By late afternoon, the weight of unsaid words became too heavy. I called her.

When she answered, her voice carried a warmth that made my pulse quicken. "Hi."

"Elina..." I breathed her name, feeling the familiar conflict rise in my chest. "About last night—I shouldn't have lost control like that."

"I understand," she interrupted softly. "We both said things we didn't mean."

The silence between us felt electric, charged with possibilities and uncertainties.

"Can I come over?" she asked, her voice barely above a whisper.

"Yes," I replied, even as Nadia's picture seemed to watch me from the corner of my eye.

When Elina arrived, something had shifted between us. The anger had dissolved, replaced by a magnetic pull I couldn't deny anymore. She stood in the doorway, her presence filling every corner of the room.

"You know," she said, her eyes meeting mine with an intensity that made my breath catch, "I see the way you struggle with this—with us."

I remained silent, caught between what I had and what I wanted.

She stepped closer, her hand finding my face, fingers tracing my jaw with a gentleness that made my defenses crumble. "When you're ready to see what's really here between us, just look at me. Really look at me. You'll understand."

Her gaze held a promise I couldn't ignore—a future I hadn't allowed myself to imagine. The pull between us had grown stronger than my guilt, stronger than my memories of Nadia.

I drew her into my arms, holding her close, knowing that this moment marked a point of no return. My heart raced with equal parts excitement and fear, understanding that choosing this path meant leaving another behind.

For now, in this moment, I allowed myself to embrace the complexity of what we were becoming.

Two days later, Elina was at my apartment, sitting cross-legged on the couch with her laptop balanced on her knees. The afternoon sun cast a warm glow through the windows, highlighting the concentrated look on her face as she worked. When my phone rang, displaying the Immigration Office number, the peaceful moment shattered.

I answered, listening as the officer requested additional documents for Nadia's visa application. My fingers tapped nervously against the desk as I wrote down the requirements, already mapping out what needed to be done. After hanging up, I immediately started gathering the paperwork, my movements mechanical and precise.

I felt Elina's gaze before I saw it. She had stopped typing, her eyes following my movements with an intensity that made my skin tingle.

"So... Nadia is coming?" she asked, her voice carrying a weight I hadn't heard before.

"Yes," I replied, focusing on the form in front of me, afraid of what I might see in her eyes if I looked up.

The silence between us grew thick with unspoken words. I could feel the weight of her stare, searching for answers I wasn't ready to give.

Finally, I let out a deep breath and leaned back. "I don't know why she hasn't left me," I admitted, the words hanging heavy in the air. "After everything I've done to her."

Elina rose from the couch, her movements deliberate as she crossed the room. She knelt before me, her warm hands on my knees, eyes burning with an emotion that made my heart race.

"Ask me," she whispered, her voice full of certainty. "If anyone has questions about loving you, I'm the one who can answer that."

Looking at her, I saw everything I'd been trying to deny - the depth of her feelings, the strength of our connection, the complexity of our situation.

She leaned in, her lips meeting mine in a kiss that felt like both a question and an answer. "Because you," she murmured between gentle kisses, "are the loveliest person I have ever known."

Her words wrapped around me like a warm embrace, but beneath them lay a truth I wasn't ready to face. Love, in all its complicated glory, had a way of revealing paths we never expected to find.

As days passed, I noticed subtle changes in Elina. Her smile carried whispers of uncertainty, her touch lingered longer, as if trying to understand what we were becoming.

One afternoon, while biking through the city streets, she suddenly stopped. I pulled up beside her, watching as emotions played across her face, raw and unguarded.

"Elina..." I said softly, my chest tight with the weight of everything unsaid between us.

That night, as moonlight filtered through my bedroom window, something shifted between us. Her tears came quietly at first, then in soft, trembling breaths. I lay beside her, close enough to feel her heartbeat, but didn't reach out.

Sometimes love means sitting with the questions we're not ready to answer.

Because in that moment, we both knew.

The future held possibilities we hadn't dared to imagine, and uncertainties we weren't ready to face.

Dissonance in Düsseldorf

Late January arrived, marking the much-anticipated trip to Düsseldorf for the concert. Elina had been looking forward to this for months, and I knew how much it meant to her. For her, it wasn't just about the music—it was about the experience, a once-in-a-lifetime event she had dreamed of attending. I wanted to match her excitement, but my mind was preoccupied with work, finishing my book, and the looming uncertainty of our future.

The night before, she came over to my apartment so we could start the journey together in the morning.

"We should get up early," I told her while packing the last of my things. "It's a long way, and if we leave on time, we'll have a chance to settle in before heading to the concert."

Elina, lounging on my couch, scrolled through her phone absentmindedly. "Mmmhmm."

I glanced at her. "I mean it. The earlier, the better."

She finally looked up, resting her chin on her hand. "I think we should sleep longer and just be fresh for the concert."

I sighed. I knew her habit of sleeping late—sometimes until ten or even later. Pushing her on this would only lead to tension, so I let it go. "Fine. But let's not be too relaxed."

She grinned, clearly pleased, and reached for my hand. "Don't worry, my love. It'll be fun."

The next morning, we started later than I wanted, leaving around ten. We took the tram to Riverton's central station and caught the train to Düsseldorf. On the way, Elina was glued to her phone, recording videos of the scenery, taking pictures, and marveling at the changing landscapes.

"Look at these clouds," she whispered excitedly, nudging me.

I glanced up briefly from my laptop. "Yeah, I see them."

"You don't appreciate these little things," she teased. "Always working."

I smirked, typing away. "Deadlines."

She pouted dramatically. "And I'm here making memories."

The journey took longer than expected. We changed two trains, then boarded a bus in Venlo for the final stretch. By the time we reached Düsseldorf, it was late afternoon, and we were starving. The snacks Elina had packed weren't enough, so we stopped at a small restaurant for a late lunch.

After eating, we took another tram and a bus to get to the apartment we had rented for the night. We arrived about an hour and a half before the concert, thinking we would quickly check in, drop our bags, and freshen up before heading to the venue.

As we rang the bell, a large man with an Eastern European accent and full of tattoos opened the door and gave us a puzzled look.

"Yes?" he asked, his gaze shifting between me and Elina.

I pulled up the booking confirmation on my phone. "We rented this place for tonight."

The man shook his head. "No, no. There are guests here already."

"What do you mean there are guests?" I frowned. "We booked this."

Elina glanced at me with uncertainty. The man pulled out his phone and made a quick call, speaking in a language we didn't understand. After a few minutes, he hung up and looked back at us.

"The booking is for May 27th. Not January 27th," he said.

Elina and I stared at each other in disbelief.

We had booked the wrong date.

It took a moment for it to fully sink in. We had no place to stay.

Elina looked stricken. "Oh no," she whispered.

I exhaled sharply, trying to suppress my frustration. "We need to find a hotel."

She nodded quickly, already scrolling through her phone, searching for available places.

As we walked back toward the concert venue, tension crackled between us. The stress of the day finally boiled over.

"This is exactly why I wanted us to leave earlier," I snapped. "I've been through this before. Nothing ever goes according to plan with you."

"What's that supposed to mean?" Elina's voice rose slightly. "You're blaming me for the booking mistake?"

"If we had left early like I wanted—"

"Oh, so everything would have been perfect if I just did exactly what you wanted?" Her eyes flashed with anger. "You always do this. Always trying to control everything."

"Because you never think things through!" I shot back. "You just float through life expecting everything to work out!"

"At least I try to enjoy life instead of constantly worrying about every little thing!"

The argument was escalating, and in that moment of heated frustration, I said the words I would instantly regret: "Don't worry. You know we're separating soon anyway. You'll get rid of me and won't have to deal with my 'controlling' nature anymore."

The moment the words left my mouth, I regretted them.

Elina's eyes widened, and her entire expression collapsed. Tears welled up almost instantly, and her breath hitched. Then, before I could react, she started crying, right there in the middle of the line.

My heart clenched.

People around us turned their heads, shifting uncomfortably at the scene unfolding between us, but I didn't care. I immediately pulled her into my arms.

"Shh," I whispered, stroking her back. "I'm sorry. I didn't mean that."

She gripped my jacket, her body trembling. "You know I can't be separated from you," she choked out. "And you choose today, of all days—the day of the concert I've been dreaming about my whole life— to say something like that?"

Her words hit me like a punch to the chest.

Guilt surged through me. "Elina," I murmured, cupping her face. "I'm an idiot. I shouldn't have said that."

"You always say things like this," she sobbed. "Like you're preparing me for something awful."

I tilted her chin up so she would look at me. Her tears shimmered under the streetlights. Without thinking, I leaned in and kissed her.

It wasn't just a kiss—it was desperation, an apology, a plea to make everything right again.

The line moved forward, but for a moment, we stayed locked in that embrace, lost in each other.

"We'll figure it out," I whispered against her lips.

She sniffled, wiping at her eyes. "Please, let's just enjoy the concert. No more bad thoughts tonight."

I nodded, squeezing her hand. "No more bad thoughts."

We stepped into the venue together, the weight of unspoken words still hanging between us. The tension lingered, but for now, we had the music. And maybe, just maybe, that would be enough.

As we handed over our jackets and bags, Elina's excitement shimmered through the cracks of our earlier argument. She had been waiting for this moment for so long, and despite everything, her energy was contagious.

The balcony seats we had chosen were perfect—no obstructions, just a direct view of the stage, a space carved out for us amidst the crowd. She practically bounced in her seat, her eyes darting around the grand hall, absorbing every detail.

"I can't believe we're finally here," she whispered, squeezing my arm.

I simply nodded, watching her, letting her enthusiasm soften the rough edges of the evening. The tension was still there, lingering beneath the surface, but in this moment, as the lights dimmed and the first notes filled the air, all that mattered was the music.

She took her seat eagerly, her hands gripping the armrests as if bracing herself for the experience. I settled in next to her, leaning back in my usual way—the relaxed, confident posture she always commented on. She had told me before that she loved the way I sat, that it made me look effortlessly in control.

As the lights dimmed, the singer appeared on stage, and the concert began. The moment the first notes filled the hall, Elina shot up from her seat, standing, swaying, singing along with an excitement that was contagious. She didn't even glance at me—she was completely lost in the moment. I smiled, watching her enjoy herself, but I remained seated, absorbing the music in my own way.

She once came to me and told me this song is about our story. The whole time during that song she had tears in her eyes and was looking at me while she had half of her eyes on stage. The song was about separation of two lovers.

A few songs into the concert, two girls arrived late and took the empty seats beside me. They were just as excited as Elina, dancing and singing along, but what I didn't expect was how one of them—the one sitting directly next to me—began to move in closer, swaying her body in my direction.

At first, I ignored it, focusing on the performance. But it was impossible to ignore her presence. She was singing loudly, occasionally brushing against my arm as she moved. It was clear she had noticed me with Elina, but that didn't stop her from being overly friendly.

Then came the break.

Elina, without hesitation, turned to me with bright eyes. "I have to find the singer and take a picture with her!" she exclaimed, already moving toward the exit.

I sighed. We had argued about this before. I had told her how much I hated the idea of begging for pictures or autographs, that people should carry themselves with a level of self-respect where others seek them out—not the other way around. It was a difference in mindset, in self-esteem. I wanted the woman I was with to have a presence that commanded attention, not one that chased it.

But Elina, in her excitement, completely forgot about me and dashed off.

As soon as she left, the two girls beside me turned their attention toward me.

"You're not dancing?" the one next to me asked, leaning in.

I smiled politely. "I'm enjoying it in my own way."

Her friend, the one who had come from France, laughed. "He's the silent, mysterious type," she teased.

I chuckled, keeping the conversation light. "Something like that."

The girl beside me tilted her head. "Are you here alone?"

I shook my head. "No, my girlfriend's here."

She smirked. "Well, if you want to join us for the after-party, you're welcome to ditch her for the night."

I raised an eyebrow. "No, thanks. I have a hotel booked with my girlfriend."

She leaned in closer, lowering her voice. "You can get rid of her for just one night."

I felt a flicker of annoyance but kept my expression neutral. "No," I said firmly.

The conversation ended there, but I was left with a strange feeling—a mixture of amusement and irritation. When Elina was gone, I had been reflecting on something deeper. Watching her run off to chase a celebrity made me question things. The mother of my child, my life partner, should be someone who carries herself with a certain level of dignity. Someone who doesn't seek validation from others but rather inspires admiration from those around her. I didn't want someone who begged for attention—I wanted someone who naturally drew it.

Just as I was lost in these thoughts, Elina came running back, her face glowing with excitement. Without hesitation, she threw herself into my arms. I took her face in my hands and intentionally kissed her—making it very clear to the two girls beside me that I was with her.

The second half of the concert began, and I tried to shift my focus back to the music. But the girl next to me seemed determined to keep my attention. She started dancing more provocatively, swaying her hips, moving in front of me until she became a direct obstacle between me and the stage.

I could feel Elina glancing at me occasionally, but she said nothing. I kept my eyes on the performance, but there was no denying that the girl was putting on a show—one clearly meant for me.

As the concert ended, I quickly booked a hotel nearby, and we grabbed a cab. The moment we were alone in the car, I turned to her.

"You disappeared during the break," I said.

She smiled, still riding the high of the concert. "I had to!" She excitedly pulled out her phone and showed me.

I nodded, forcing a small smile. "And while you were gone, that girl was all over me."

Elina's expression didn't change much. Instead, she looked at me with that knowing look she always had. "I was watching you," she said simply.

I raised an eyebrow. "Yeah? And?"

"The way you sat there, looking like a gentleman, was exactly why people are drawn to you," she said. "That's why she was trying so hard. And that's why I love you so much my love!"

I let out a short laugh. "You think so?"

She smirked. "But I also saw you watching her ass."

I turned my head toward the window, shaking my head. "I was trying to watch the singer, but she made herself the view."

She laughed softly, resting her head on my shoulder. "At least you're honest."

I sighed, running a hand through my hair. "You know how I feel about things like this, Elina."

"I know," she said, tracing circles on my arm. "But you don't have to worry. You're mine, and I know that."

I didn't respond right away. The night had been chaotic, from the booking mistake to the concert tensions. But one thing was clear—Elina and I were entangled in a way that neither of us knew how to escape. She came to my arm, smiled and slept peacefully.

***

The morning after our last night in Düsseldorf was unexpectedly peaceful. The tension from the previous day had dissolved into the quiet intimacy of the night. Elina had fallen asleep in my arms, her body warm against mine, and for a few hours, it felt like none of the arguments, none of the lingering doubts, had ever existed.

As the first light seeped through the curtains, I felt her stir beside me. She shifted slightly, her breath soft against my chest before her eyelashes fluttered open.

The first thing she did was smile—a sleepy, genuine smile that made my heart ache. Without a word, she leaned up and kissed me, her lips soft and slow against mine, as if trying to hold onto the moment just a little longer.

"Good morning, my life," she whispered.

I brushed a strand of hair from her face. "Morning."

She stretched lazily, her fingers tracing idle patterns on my arm. "I don't want to get up yet."

I smirked. "That's because you always sleep late."

She laughed. "That's because I love staying in bed with you."

For a moment, we just lay there, wrapped in warmth, ignoring the fact that we had to check out soon. It was one of those rare mornings where we weren't fighting, where there was no unspoken tension hovering between us—just the simple comfort of each other.

But eventually, hunger won, and we made our way downstairs to the hotel's breakfast lounge. The air smelled of fresh bread and coffee, and as we settled at a small table near the window, Elina looked at me with a glint of mischief in her eyes.

"I know we fought a lot on this trip," she said, stirring her coffee.

I raised an eyebrow. "You don't say."

She rolled her eyes but smiled. "But I wouldn't have wanted to come with anyone else."

I sighed, watching her spread a thick layer of jam onto her croissant. "Even with all the chaos?"

She smirked. "Especially with all the chaos. It wouldn't be us without it."

I chuckled, shaking my head. "You might be right."

She reached for my hand across the table, her fingers warm against mine. "We had a good night, didn't we?"

I met her gaze, remembering the way she had curled into me the night before, how everything else had disappeared in that moment. "Yeah, we did."

Before we left, I told Elina I needed to step outside for a moment. She didn't ask why—she already knew.

"Go," she said simply. "I'll finish packing."

I stepped out into the crisp morning air and dialed Nadia's number. She picked up after a few rings.

"Hey," I said.

"Hey," she replied, her voice calm but distant.

I hesitated before speaking. "Just checking in."

There was a pause. "You sound tired."

"I am," I admitted.

She didn't ask where I was or what I was doing, but I could feel the silent understanding between us.

"How are things on your end?" I asked.

"Same," she said softly. "Work, life, waiting."

I sighed. "I'll be back soon."

She didn't respond right away, and when she did, it was only a quiet, "Okay."

When I returned to the hotel room, Elina was standing by the window, scrolling through her phone. She didn't look up immediately but asked, "Ready to go?"

"Yeah," I said, grabbing my bag.

We checked out of the hotel and decided to take our time heading back to Riverton. The morning was cold, but the sun had finally broken through the heavy clouds, casting a pale glow over Düsseldorf.

"Let's explore a little before we leave," I suggested.

She smiled. "I'd like that."

We wandered through the streets, walking past old buildings and along the river. Elina snapped pictures, capturing small details that caught her eye—an old bookstore, a row of bicycles, a graffiti-covered alleyway.

For a moment, it felt easy, like we were just two people traveling together, free from the weight of everything else.

But as we started the journey back, reality crept in again. I opened my laptop and got to work, losing myself in emails and notes, while Elina sat quietly beside me, scrolling through her phone.

"You're working already?" she asked after a while.

"Yeah, I need to catch up," I said, not looking up.

She sighed and leaned her head against the window. "You never stop."

I glanced at her. "You knew that before we even got here."

She didn't argue. Instead, she closed her eyes and dozed off, her head resting against my chest. Slowly, I felt the dampness spread—she was crying again, quietly, her body trembling slightly.

I didn't say anything, just held her closer.

The train rattled on, carrying us back, but it felt like we were going nowhere at all.

When we arrived in Riverton, another argument sparked over something as trivial as which tram line to take. The exhaustion and frustration boiled over, and by the time we got to my apartment, it had escalated into a full fight.

"You always have to be right!" she snapped as we reached the door.

"You just love arguing over nothing," I shot back.

"Then maybe I shouldn't stay here anymore," she said, her voice shaking.

"Maybe you shouldn't," I said coldly, stepping aside to let her leave.

She stared at me for a long moment, her eyes searching for something—maybe for me to take it back, maybe for proof that I still wanted her to stay.

And then, she turned and walked away.

I stood in the doorway, watching her disappear into the night, feeling the weight of her absence settle in before I even closed the door.

The Weight of Unspoken Things

The next morning, as soon as I woke up, I called Elina. The previous night had been heavy, but with daylight streaming through the window, I felt the familiar pull toward her—the same pull that always brought us back together, no matter how much we fought.

She picked up after just one ring.

"Hi," she said softly.

"Hi," I replied, my voice still groggy from sleep.

There was a pause—a silence that wasn't uncomfortable but carried the weight of everything left unsaid.

"I missed you," she finally admitted.

I sighed. "I missed you too."

And just like that, the frustration of the night before faded into the background.

"I'm sorry," I said.

"So am I," she whispered.

A few hours later, she was at my apartment. She walked in without a word and wrapped her arms around me. I held her close, breathing her in, feeling the warmth of her body against mine. It was always like this—no matter how much we hurt each other with words, we couldn't resist finding our way back.

That afternoon, we existed as if nothing had happened. We played cards, made coffee, and watched rain drizzle against the window. The tension from the previous night had melted away, leaving only the comfort of being in each other's presence.

I leaned back in my chair and sighed. "You know, we never had a normal relationship. From the beginning, we were always hiding, always under pressure. It's never been simple."

Elina put her cup down and looked at me. "I know," she admitted. "I wish things were different."

I watched her, waiting, sensing there was more.

"If I could put you in my social life, introduce you to my friends, bring you to family gatherings," she continued, "maybe you'd trust me more. Maybe you'd never question me."

She paused before exhaling deeply. "But you were out of your mind, Darian. You got married. You made things so hard for us." She said this like a joke, a phrase repeated so often it became part of our rhythm. In reality, we both knew that when I got married, we had never even known each other.

I ran a hand through my hair. "I know. We met at the wrong time, in the wrong place in our lives."

She reached for my hand across the table, lacing her fingers through mine. "But despite everything, I wouldn't change meeting you."

I squeezed her hand gently. "Neither would I."

The reality of our situation was undeniable, but in that moment, none of it mattered. We still had each other—at least for now.

***

It was February 9th, cold and quiet—the kind of winter day that carried a strange stillness. Elina sat beside me, watching as I worked on my book, her chin resting on her knees, her fingers tracing invisible patterns on my sleeve. She had planned to leave that evening, but when she learned about the expected delivery—a print copy of my book before publication—she insisted on staying.

"I can't leave before your book arrives," she had said, smiling. "This is something big. I want to be here when you hold it for the first time."

Her enthusiasm should have made me happy. Instead, it made me uneasy.

I didn't want her to see the book.

I knew what was inside.

I had poured everything into this project—months of work, countless hours spent watching and documenting a family of falcons I visited daily, their lives unfolding through my telephoto lens. It was a world that had belonged to Nadia and me. She had been there, by my side, sharing in the quiet wonder of it all.

And the dedication...

The book was dedicated to Nadia.

Elina was in it too—acknowledged in a way only she and I would understand, under our chosen nickname for her. A small place in my world, but not the place she wanted.

When the package arrived, my chest tightened as I ripped it open. The weight of the book in my hands was heavy—not just in its physical form but in everything it carried within its pages.

I flipped through quickly, trying to pass the dedication page before she could notice.

But Elina saw it.

Her eyes scanned the page, and in an instant, her breath hitched.

She went silent.

For the first time in a long time, she had nothing to say.

And that silence was louder than anything she could have spoken.

****

Our lives had merged into a comfortable routine, centered in the familiar space of my apartment. The days blurred together, filled with work, card games, and quiet companionship. But beneath it all, there was an undeniable tension, a weight of words left unsaid that neither of us dared to address.

In the midst of it, I finally ordered my new bow. Elina helped me select the color, her genuine enthusiasm temporarily bridging the growing distance between us. For a moment, sharing that small decision felt like a glimpse of what we could be. A fragment of normalcy.

When the bow arrived, Elina eagerly offered to join me for pickup. I agreed, expecting a simple errand. But even something as mundane as choosing a route home became a proxy for our deeper conflicts.

"This way is faster," she said, gesturing at her phone's map.

"It's literally a one-minute difference," I replied, exhaling heavily.

"But if it's shorter, why not just take it?"

I gritted my teeth. "Because I know this route. It's familiar."

She persisted the entire way back, her irritation crackling in the space between us. I snapped back, she retaliated with calculated precision, and before we knew it, we were both caught in a familiar dance of provocation, neither willing to yield.

It was always like this now. Even our card games became minefields of potential conflict. We understood why. But awareness didn't grant us immunity.

The Accident

The evening air had a bite to it when I decided to head to the archery club alone. Elina was staying home, wrapped in her favorite blanket with a book—something she'd been looking forward to all week. I almost envied her cozy setup, but the pull of practice was stronger. The streets were quieter than usual, my bike wheels humming against the pavement, until everything changed in an instant.

He appeared like a ghost—a tourist lost in his own world, AirPods gleaming in his ears, phone pressed to his face as he stepped directly into the cycling path. His expensive camera swung carelessly from his neck, the strap tangling with his gesturing hands as he laughed at something on his call.

Time compressed into microseconds.

My hands clenched the brakes instinctively, but physics had other plans. I swerved hard, the world tilting at impossible angles. The tourist's oblivious figure blurred past me as my balance failed, and gravity claimed its prize.

The impact came in waves: first my hip, then my shoulder, and finally my head snapping back against the pavement. The bike clattered beside me, its wheel spinning uselessly in the air like a fallen insect.

For what felt like an eternity, I lay there, my breath coming in sharp gasps. The sky above me seemed to pulse with each throb of pain from my ankle. A constellation of aches bloomed across my body, but my ankle screamed the loudest.

The tourist finally noticed—barely. He turned, phone still pressed to his ear, and offered a dismissive "Sorry, mate" before continuing his conversation, disappearing around the corner as if he hadn't just upended someone's entire evening. His voice faded into the distance, still chattering about dinner reservations and tourist spots.

Pride and stubbornness—my two most faithful companions—pushed me to my feet. My ankle protested with each movement, but I gritted my teeth. The archery club wasn't far, and I'd already come this far. Besides, what was a little pain? I'd shot through worse.

I picked up my bike, wincing as I tested its condition. Like me, it was scraped but functional. The ride to the club was a blur of contained gasps and white-knuckled determination.

The hour of practice that followed was an exercise in denial. Each step across the range sent jolts of pain through my ankle, but I pushed through, telling myself it was nothing. The familiar rhythm of draw, aim, release became my meditation, each arrow a distraction from the growing discomfort.

It wasn't until I started the journey home that reality caught up with me.

The pain transformed from a dull throb into something alive and vengeful. Each pedal stroke sent lightning bolts of agony through my foot, the winter air seemingly crystallizing around the injury. By the time I fumbled with my apartment keys, tears were threatening to spill over, my hand shaking from both pain and the lingering shock of the fall.

I collapsed onto my couch, finally allowing myself to really look at my ankle. It had swollen to twice its size, angry purple bruises blooming across the skin like watercolors.

Nadia's number was already pulled up on my phone before I fully committed to calling her. She was a doctor, yes, but more importantly, she was the voice of reason I often ignored. We'd been friends since university, and she'd patched me up more times than I cared to admit.

"Let me guess," she answered, her voice carrying that familiar mix of concern and exasperation. "You've done something stupid again?"

I explained what happened, trying to downplay it, but Nadia had known me too long to fall for that.

"You need to bandage it and rest for a week. No pressure on it, Darian," she said, her tone brooking no argument. "If you keep walking on it, it'll only get worse. And knowing you, you're already planning how to ignore this advice."

I exhaled heavily, staring at my swollen ankle. "A whole week?"

"You want to heal properly or not?" Her voice softened slightly. "I know you hate being sidelined, but this isn't something you can push through."

"Fine," I sighed, defeat coloring my voice. "I'll do it."

"Just keep your foot elevated. And don't be stubborn about this." She paused, and I could practically see her concerned frown. "Promise me you'll actually rest?"

"Yeah, yeah," I muttered, both of us knowing I was exactly the kind of person to ignore medical advice. It was part of why we'd become friends in the first place—she'd caught me trying to train through a sprained wrist during university archery practice.

The call had barely ended when my phone lit up again. Elina's name flashed across the screen, and something in my chest tightened. She was supposed to be having her quiet evening at home, but the moment I told her what happened, her voice changed, worry threading through every word.

"I'm coming over," she said, no room for discussion in her tone.

"No, it's fine. I can manage—"

"I said I'm coming." The line went dead before I could argue further.

Less than an hour later, my doorbell rang. Elina stood there, cheeks flushed from the cold, her hair windblown, clutching a pharmacy bag. She must have rushed out immediately after our call, searching through the city's few open pharmacies on a Sunday night.

"Everything was closed," she said, pulling out a roll of bandages and some anti-inflammatory cream. "I had to check four different places before I found one with an after-hours window. But I got what you need."

Something caught in my throat as I watched her, this woman who had interrupted her peaceful evening to hunt down medical supplies for me. Her dedication hit harder than the fall had.

"You didn't have to do that," I murmured, overwhelmed by the simple act of care.

She frowned, kneeling in front of me with the supplies. "Of course I did. Now, let me see that ankle."

Her hands were gentle as she examined the injury, her touch careful and precise. She worked in silence, applying the cream before starting to wrap the bandage, her fingers moving with surprising expertise.

"Tell me if it's too tight," she whispered, focused entirely on her task.

I swallowed, watching her. "It's perfect."

When she finished, she sat back on her heels, exhaling slowly. Her eyes met mine, dark with an emotion I couldn't quite read.

"I hate seeing you hurt," she said quietly, her hand still resting lightly on my leg.

Words failed me. Instead, I reached for her, pulling her into my arms. She came willingly, fitting against me like she belonged there, her warmth seeping into my tired muscles. We stayed like that for a long while, saying nothing, letting the silence speak for us.

What followed was a week of Elina's determined nursing. She appointed herself my caretaker, enforcing Nadia's orders with gentle but uncompromising authority.

"You're not putting weight on that foot," she'd say, standing between me and whatever task I was attempting to do myself. Her small frame somehow managed to block entire doorways when she was being protective.

"I can handle it," I'd protest, trying to maneuver around her.

She'd fix me with a look that was both stern and tender. "No, you can't. You're resting. Doctor's orders." Then she'd guide me back to the couch or bed, making sure my foot was properly elevated.

She transformed my apartment into a sanctuary of recovery. Coffee appeared at my elbow before I could ask for it, my favorite meals materialized at regular intervals, and she seemed to have a sixth sense for when I was about to try something foolish like walking to the kitchen unaided.

At night, she stayed, curling up beside me in bed. Her presence became a different kind of medicine, her steady breathing next to me more soothing than any painkiller.

"You're spoiling me," I told her one evening, as we sat on the couch, my foot propped up on pillows she'd arranged with scientific precision. Her head rested on my shoulder, her hair tickling my neck.

She chuckled softly, the sound vibrating against my skin. "I like taking care of you. Even if you are the world's worst patient."

"You'd make an incredible nurse," I said, meaning it despite my teasing tone.

"Please," she scoffed, but I could hear her smile. "I'd never survive in a hospital. Too many rules, too many patients. But for you?" She tilted her head to look at me. "For you, I'll make an exception."

I looked down at her then, really looked at her. At the way she fit against me, at the careful way she'd been tending to me all week, at the quiet strength in her dedication. Something in my chest constricted, a feeling too big for words.

"I don't deserve you," I whispered, the truth of it aching more than my ankle.

Elina shifted, sitting up to face me properly. Her eyes met mine, soft but unwavering, filled with a certainty I wished I could borrow.

"Yes, you do," she said simply, as if it were the most obvious thing in the world. Her hand came up to brush through my hair, the gesture achingly tender. Then she leaned in, pressing a gentle kiss to my forehead, her lips lingering for a moment.

And somehow, in that moment, surrounded by her care and wrapped in her certainty, I started to believe her. Maybe I did deserve this—deserve her. Maybe sometimes love isn't about deserving, but about accepting what's freely given.

My ankle would heal, eventually. But something else had been mended in that week—something I hadn't even known was broken until Elina's gentle hands put it back together.

****

A few days later, as my ankle was finally starting to improve, we received another message from Martha—there were more letters waiting for us at the cottage. This would probably be the last time we needed to pick them up, a small but symbolic end to yet another chapter.

Before heading there, I carefully wrapped one of my framed bird photos—a gift for Martha and Johan, a small token of appreciation for all they had done for us. That place had been our first shelter in this new country, and though temporary, it had given us warmth when we needed it most.

The bike ride was careful and slow, mindful of my healing ankle. As we arrived, Martha greeted us with her usual kindness, accepting the framed photo with genuine delight. She ran her fingers over the glass, studying the details of the bird in flight.

"This is beautiful," she said, smiling. "You really took this?"

I nodded. "Yes. I wanted to give you something as a thank-you for everything. You and Johan helped us more than you know."

She looked at Elina and me, her expression soft, almost motherly. "You two have really built something here. A home, a life."

I exchanged a glance with Elina. She didn't know. They didn't know. They had no idea that we were living separately now, that our situation was more complicated than they could imagine.

Martha hesitated for a moment before asking, "So, you don't live together anymore?"

I saw the curiosity in her eyes—not judgment, just genuine surprise. I smiled lightly and shrugged. "Things are always changing."

She nodded, not pressing for more. Maybe she sensed that our story wasn't one easily explained.

After picking up the letters and saying our goodbyes, we biked back through a route we had never taken before. The road curved gently past open fields, leading us to a quiet place—a bench in front of an old windmill, overlooking a vast, endless landscape of green and golden hues.

We stopped there, leaning our bikes against a nearby post, and sat down. The silence between us was comfortable, the kind that doesn't demand words.

Elina sighed, gazing at the scenery. "Why haven't we been here before?"

I smirked. "Because we were always too busy running."

She smiled but didn't argue. It was true. We had spent so much time moving, searching, figuring things out, that we rarely just stopped to be still.

We had brought tea, but neither of us reached for it. We just sat there, taking in the moment.

Then, in the distance, we saw a willow tree. Its branches swayed gently in the wind, its roots firmly planted in the land.

Elina looked at it, then at me.

"It's beautiful," she said.

"It is," I agreed.

But as much as we loved willows, this one wasn't ours. It wasn't the willow—the one that had witnessed our love, our laughter, our stolen moments. The one that had stood beside us in Baharvan, watching as we built something we could never quite hold onto.

Elina seemed to read my thoughts. She reached for my hand and squeezed it gently.

We sat there for a long time, in front of that unfamiliar willow, knowing it was time to let go—of places, of moments, and maybe, of each other. The week of her taking care of me after the accident had been beautiful, a reminder of what we once had, but perhaps it was also a goodbye in its own way—gentle and loving, just like us.

****

As February neared its end, everything felt like it was accelerating toward something inevitable. Special dates loomed on the horizon, events we had spoken about in passing but never fully prepared for.

My phone rang. Nadia's name appeared on the screen.

I had been expecting this call.

"Hey," I said.

"Hey," she replied. "I got my visa."

We both knew what this meant, but hearing it out loud made it real.

"That's great," I said. "Congratulations."

"I couldn't have done it without you," she said. "And... I booked my ticket. March 16th."

That was sooner than it felt in my mind.

"I want you to come to Parin," she said. "Help me pack. Fly back with me."

I should have known she would ask this.

"Nadia..." I started. "I'll have to see how busy I am. There's a lot going on here, and—"

"I know you're busy, Darian. But this isn't just about packing."

We both knew why she wanted me there.

"I'll think about it," I said.

Elina's Reaction

Later that night, we were lying in bed, her head resting on my chest, my fingers idly tracing patterns on her back.

"Nadia got her visa," I said.

"And?" she asked.

"She booked her ticket for March 16th. She asked me to go back to Parin. Help her pack. Fly back with her."

Elina lifted her head, frowning as she sat up in bed.

"No." Her voice was sharp. "You shouldn't go."

"Elina, it's not—"

"No, Darian." She shook her head. "She can pack her own bags. You don't need to be there."

"I didn't say I'm going for sure. I just said maybe. I might need to bring some of my stuff too."

"Darian, come on. You know she doesn't need you there. She just wants to pull you back in."

I knew Elina had a point, but at the same time, there was something unfinished between me and Nadia, something I felt like I owed her.

"I haven't promised anything," I said.

She threw herself onto me, holding me so tightly that I could feel the tremor in her arms. Her embrace spoke of fear, of knowing what might come next, of trying to hold onto something that was already slipping away.

We lay there in silence, the weight of unspoken words hanging between us. Maybe we both knew what would happen when Nadia arrived.

New Home

Elina had been facing growing tension with her landlord, the kind but intrusive woman who treated her more like a daughter than a tenant. What had once seemed like warmth and care had turned into constant interference, making her feel suffocated. With Nadia's arrival approaching, she had been desperate to find a place of her own.

One morning, after breakfast, as she was about to leave for her place, I stopped her, my thoughts briefly drifting to Nadia before I pushed them aside.

"Why don't you check the real estate agency down the street?" I suggested.

She sighed, her eyes meeting mine with quiet trust. "I've checked everywhere, Darian. It's impossible without a long waiting list."

"Just try. You never know."

Reluctantly, she agreed, and miraculously, they had an available studio. She called me in disbelief, her voice full of excitement and relief that made my heart warm unexpectedly.

"I got it," she whispered as if she couldn't believe it herself. "They gave me the key!"

By March 1st, she was officially moving in. I went to the agency to collect the key, then headed to her old place to help her move. She was riding her bike to the new place, while I took care of the heavier boxes, loading them into the van. Something about her independence both drew me in and reminded me of Nadia's strength.

At one point, as I carried two large boxes at once, Elina frowned.

"Darian, don't overdo it," she scolded, reaching for one of them. "I don't want you hurting yourself!"

I smirked, trying to ignore how her concern affected me. "You worry too much."

She rolled her eyes. "And you don't worry enough!"

The apartment was a cozy studio on the fifth floor, with a stunning sunset view and a small balcony. It was perfect for her—small, warm, and entirely hers. I found myself imagining her making it into a home, then caught myself wondering why that image felt so right.

That night, she decided to stay in her new place. I returned to mine, though part of me wanted to linger longer.

The next morning, before she even woke up, I went to the supermarket and did a full shopping for her—fresh bread, eggs, coffee, fruits, and some essentials. I wanted to make sure she had everything she needed, just as I'd always done for Nadia in our early days. The parallel wasn't lost on me.

When I arrived, I found her waiting, her space already neatly arranged. As I set the bags on the counter, she smiled in a way that made my chest tighten.

"You know, I love that you can come to my place now. No more sneaking around, no more feeling trapped."

I nodded, looking around, trying to maintain some distance. "It suits you, Elina."

She stepped closer, wrapping her arms around me. "You made this easier for me."

We stood there for a moment, the morning light streaming through the windows. For the first time in a long while, she seemed truly content—and I found myself torn between the comfort of this moment and thoughts of Nadia.

After Elina settled into her new apartment, we spent the next few days making it feel like home. The first thing we did was buy flowers and flower boxes for her balcony. She had always loved plants, and watching her work with them showed me a side of her that made my feelings grow more complicated.

"You know," she said as she patted the soil around a fresh batch of seeds, "gardening feels kind of magical. You put something so small into the earth and just trust that it will grow."

I watched her fingers carefully pressing the seeds into the soil, remembering similar moments with Nadia in our garden. "Kind of like us," I said, half-joking, though the words held more truth than I wanted to admit.

She glanced at me, a small, knowing smile on her lips. "Maybe."

Over the next few days, we continued building her space together, each moment drawing us closer in ways I tried not to acknowledge. One afternoon, we went downtown to buy a coffee machine. It was a small thing, but for Elina, it was essential. She wanted me to be there to help her choose, and I couldn't say no.

"I need one that makes real coffee," she said, scanning the shelves. "Not just something that drips like an old man."

I laughed, grateful for these light moments that made me forget my complicated feelings. "So you want something strong, powerful... like me?"

She rolled her eyes. "More like something that won't break after a few months—unlike your jokes."

We finally settled on a sleek espresso machine, and she was thrilled. "Now I can make you real coffee when you visit," she said proudly. The domesticity of her words stirred something in me that I tried to ignore.

Another day, we went out to buy her a pair of shoes. She had been needing new ones for a while, but had been holding back because of money.

"You don't have to come with me," she said at first, hesitant.

"But I want to," I insisted, even as I wondered why I felt such a need to be part of these small moments in her life.

After looking through several stores, she finally found a pair she loved—but hesitated at the price.

"You should get them," I told her.

She frowned. "They're expensive, Darian. I can find something cheaper."

I insisted on paying half, knowing how much she needed them. It took some convincing, but in the end, she accepted—not because she wanted help, but because she understood my desire to support her.

"You're too kind to me," she murmured as we walked out of the store, holding the bag in her hand.

"You just deserve good things," I said simply, though the words felt weighted with unspoken meaning.

Before heading home, I surprised her with a small speaker for her apartment. It was the kind of gift I'd given Nadia early in our relationship, and that thought gave me pause.

"Elina, you need this," I said as I handed her the box. "You can't live in silence."

She looked at the speaker and then at me, her eyes softening in a way that made my heart race. "You always know what I need before I do."

***

The first weekend of March, Elina and I planned a full day of shopping at the largest home goods store in town. The morning air was crisp, and I found myself looking forward to spending time with her in a way that made me slightly uneasy.

We took the bus together, our shoulders occasionally brushing as the vehicle swayed. Each time it happened, I felt a small jolt of awareness that I tried to ignore. The store sprawled before us, aisles filled with possibilities and the promise of turning spaces into sanctuaries.

"You should get this," I suggested, picking up a small bedside lamp, trying to keep my voice casual. "Your place is too dark at night."

She met my eyes with that knowing look that always seemed to see right through me. "You just want me to keep the light on so I don't fall asleep before you text me."

I smirked, caught in the truth of how much our nightly conversations had come to mean to me. "Caught me."

As we wandered through the aisles, she stopped abruptly in front of the tools section. She picked up an electric screwdriver—one I had mentioned wanting weeks ago. The fact that she remembered such a small detail made something twist in my chest.

"This one's for you," she said with quiet determination.

I raised an eyebrow, uncomfortable with the intimacy of the gesture. "Elina, you don't have to—"

"I want to," she interrupted, her eyes holding mine. "You always fix things, build things. Let me do this for you."

We spent hours selecting items together—a carpet, kitchenware, storage boxes, and decorations. Each choice felt weighted with meaning, with the way her eyes would seek my approval, how she'd lean close to show me patterns or colors she liked.

The cab ride home was a study in unspoken tensions. The backseat was filled with bags, the rolled-up carpet barely fitting inside. Our driver, a cheerful man with kind eyes, started chatting with us.

"You two just moved in together?" he asked, glancing at our purchases.

I grinned, trying to diffuse the intensity that had been building all day. "No, no, we're just friends."

The driver chuckled. "Ah, friends. Are you sure?"

I laughed, my heart racing as I said, half-jokingly, "She's actually my second wife."

Elina turned to the driver, and her voice carried a weight that made my breath catch: "It's my dream to be his wife."

Her words cracked something open inside me. This wasn't a joke—it was a truth she'd been holding close. I turned to look at her, but she was already gazing out the window, the city lights playing across her face.

The cab driver smiled knowingly. "That's how love works," he said, and I felt the words settle heavily in the space between us.

At her apartment, I insisted on carrying the heavier items despite her protests. The carpet, the bags—I needed the physical activity to ground myself.

"You need to let me help," I said, trying to keep my tone light.

"I just don't want you to get hurt," she murmured, her concern making my chest tight.

She had always noticed things about me—how I moved after archery practice, the way I favored my right side after a long day.

Once everything was inside, she looked at me with hope in her eyes.

"Stay," she said softly.

I shook my head, needing space to think. "I have work to do."

She accepted my excuse with grace, though disappointment shadowed her features.

"The coffee machine we ordered is coming tomorrow," she reminded me. "Come over, and we'll unpack everything together?"

I nodded, already knowing I wouldn't be able to stay away. "Of course."

That night, in my apartment, I couldn't shake the weight of her words in the taxi. They echoed in my mind, reminding me of Nadia, of promises made, of the growing complexity of my feelings.

It's my dream to be his wife.

The words haunted me because part of me wanted to hear them again.

***

The next morning, I woke before dawn, my mind still swimming with thoughts of yesterday. The supermarket's fluorescent lights felt too harsh as I carefully selected fresh pastries, fruits, and coffee beans— things I knew she loved. Each item I chose felt like a small confession.

When I arrived at her apartment, she was waiting by the door, and something in her expression made my heart stutter. The soft morning light caught in her hair, and her smile held a warmth that made me forget, for a moment, about everything else in the world.

"You bought all this?" she asked, her eyes widening at the bags in my hands. There was wonder in her voice, as if such a simple gesture was something extraordinary.

I nodded, trying to keep my voice steady. "You didn't have anything left in the fridge."

She shook her head, a gentle laugh escaping her. "You really do take care of me, don't you?" The question held layers of meaning I wasn't ready to explore.

I shrugged, fighting the urge to reach out and touch her face. "Someone has to."

She pulled me inside, her fingers lingering on my wrist for a moment too long. Her apartment had transformed overnight—she had arranged everything we bought, creating a space that felt both new and familiar. The morning light filtered through her curtains, casting warm shadows across the room.

"I'm happy you can come to my place now," she said, looking around with pride, but her eyes kept finding their way back to me. The words seemed to carry a deeper invitation, one that made my pulse quicken.

We moved to unbox the coffee machine together, our hands brushing as we worked. The simple domestic task felt charged with meaning— each shared glance, each accidental touch, each quiet laugh building something between us that I couldn't name. Or perhaps didn't want to.

Standing in her kitchen, watching her figure out the settings on the machine, I realized we were creating more than just a comfortable space. We were building moments, memories, possibilities that both thrilled and terrified me. The scent of fresh coffee filled the air, mingling with the morning light and her presence, making everything feel intensely real.

That night, I stayed. The decision wasn't conscious—it felt as natural as breathing, as inevitable as the way my heart raced when she smiled. And somehow, that was the most frightening part of all.

My Birthday

The morning of my birthday arrived in quiet stillness. Nadia had called at exactly midnight—00:00, down to the minute, her punctuality a remnant of all our birthdays together. Her voice, warm and familiar through the phone, marked the start of this day just as it had marked so many others before. Now, as morning light filtered through the windows, the day stretched ahead, not demanding grand celebrations, but holding the weight of unspoken possibilities.

As I stepped into Elina's apartment, the familiar warmth of her space enveloped me, carrying the subtle scent of vanilla and coffee that had become uniquely hers. There, sitting neatly on the small table, was a beautifully wrapped gift, its shape unmistakable against the morning light.

The morning of my birthday arrived in quiet stillness. Nadia had called at midnight, her voice carrying the warmth of our shared past, a tradition now tinged with something bittersweet. The day stretched ahead, not demanding grand celebrations, but holding the weight of unspoken possibilities.

As I stepped into Elina's apartment, the familiar warmth of her space enveloped me, carrying the subtle scent of vanilla and coffee that had become uniquely hers. There, sitting neatly on the small table, was a beautifully wrapped gift, its shape unmistakable against the morning light.

She had bought me the coffee machine.

I had been eyeing it for weeks, always putting it off, telling myself I didn't need it, that it was just another unnecessary indulgence. But she had noticed. The way she noticed everything about me, with an attention that made my heart race and my thoughts tangle.

She stood there, watching me carefully, her green eyes filled with something deeper than just birthday excitement. The morning light caught in her hair, creating a halo that made her seem almost ethereal.

"I know you've wanted this for a while," she said softly, her voice carrying a warmth that settled deep in my chest. "For mornings when you need a moment for yourself." The words hung between us, heavy with meaning.

It wasn't just a coffee machine—it was a piece of her, a tangible reminder of how deeply she'd come to understand me. The thought of morning coffee would forever be intertwined with her now, with this moment.

I swallowed the tightness in my throat and looked at her. What could I say to express the storm of emotions her simple gesture had unleashed?

Instead, I pulled her into my arms, holding her close, longer than necessary, letting my silence speak for me. She melted into my embrace, her fingers gripping the fabric of my shirt as if anchoring herself to this moment. The scent of her shampoo, the warmth of her body against mine, the slight tremor in her breathing—everything felt amplified, significant.

That night, she cooked a meal she knew I loved—a dish that carried the taste of care and growing intimacy. The apartment was dimly lit, the glow of candles flickering against the walls. She had decorated the room with small fairy lights brought from her old home, weaving them softly around the space, creating a world that existed only for us.

We sat across from each other, eating in a silence that wasn't empty, but full—full of growing feelings, of changing hearts, of futures reimagined. Every now and then, she'd glance up at me, a small, tender smile playing on her lips that made my heart skip.

After dinner, she disappeared into the kitchen, returning with a homemade cake. The care she'd put into every detail of this day overwhelmed me.

She placed it gently on the table and, in the softest voice, whispered, "Happy birthday." The words carried more than just wishes—they held promises, possibilities, the whisper of something deeper growing between us.

We lit the candle, and I made a wish, one that surprised even me with its intensity.

We played cards, laughing between moves, the space between us charged with an electricity that made every accidental touch feel like sparks against my skin. For those moments, we let ourselves just be—two people discovering something beautiful and terrifying.

Later, as her body curled into mine in bed, I felt the weight of everything shifting between us. She held me tighter, her face buried against my chest, her heartbeat echoing mine. I ran my fingers through her hair, pressing a kiss onto her forehead, drowning in the overwhelming tenderness of the moment.

"This was the best birthday I've ever had in my life," I murmured, meaning every word.

She didn't speak immediately, just held me closer, as if trying to press this moment into memory. The night wrapped around us like a cocoon, holding us in this perfect moment where everything felt possible.

And maybe, in some way, it always would be.

TEN

THE LAST STATION

The countdown had begun. One week until Nadia's arrival. The good news was that I hadn't gone back to Parin to bring Nadia myself. The bad news was that this was the end of us.

Neither Elina nor I spoke about separation—not directly, not in words. But we both felt it looming, a shadow hanging over every moment we spent together. We clung to each other, stealing time as if we could hold back the inevitable. Some nights, she was at my place. Some nights, I was at hers. There was no pattern, no logic—only the unspoken urgency to be with each other before everything changed.

Elina knew. She knew I hadn't divorced Nadia. She knew Nadia was still fighting—not just for our marriage, but for me. Nadia had confronted me multiple times, her eyes filled with both anger and love, refusing to let go of what we had. "Ten years, Darian," she had said during our last call, her voice breaking. "Ten years of building a life together. I won't let you throw that away." The weight of those years pressed against my chest, while my heart ached for the woman who had shown me a different kind of love—fierce, unexpected, and transformative. Nadia had even flown to see me twice, fighting with everything she had to keep me. She knew me better than anyone—or at least, she had, until Elina came into my life.

And yet, Elina didn't ask questions. She didn't make demands. Instead, she loved me harder, as if her love could bridge the impossible gap between what was and what could have been.

The last week, Elina poured everything she had into me. She cooked for me, took care of me, made me coffee every morning—as if she could leave pieces of herself behind in these small gestures, as if by doing so, I would never forget her. Each moment became a treasure we couldn't keep, but couldn't bear to let go.

One evening, she called her mother and asked for a special family recipe—something she had never made before. I sat on the couch, watching her on the phone, her voice trembling slightly as she jotted down instructions. Her hands moved with practiced grace, even as her eyes betrayed the storm within.

When she hung up, she turned to me with a soft smile that held worlds of unspoken words.

"I want to make this for you," she said. "Before I go."

She didn't say before we separate. She didn't have to. The words hung between us, heavy with everything we couldn't say.

She cooked with so much care, tasting the spices, adjusting the flavors, making sure everything was perfect. And when she finally placed the plate in front of me, she sat across the table and watched me eat, waiting for my reaction. Her eyes tracked every movement, memorizing the moment.

"This is amazing," I said, swallowing the first bite.

She exhaled, a mix of relief and sadness. "It's my childhood," she whispered. "I wanted to share it with you." In that moment, I understood—she wasn't just sharing a meal, she was giving me a piece of herself, a memory I would carry long after we parted.

I reached for her hand, squeezing it gently. "Thank you."

The other night, she made her special dish again—the one she had first cooked for me back in the cottage, the one I had fallen in love with just as much as I had fallen for her. Each bite was a reminder of how far we'd come, and how soon it would end.

Our Last Days

Everything changed in the last three days. The air between us grew heavier, the reality inescapable. Simple moments became profound— the way she helped me clean my apartment, how we found her hair everywhere, marking her presence in my space.

As we picked them up, she let out a small, broken laugh. "Even when I leave, I'll still be here," she said, twirling a strand around her finger before letting it fall. The simple gesture carried the weight of all our tomorrows that would never be.

We cleaned twice. As if erasing traces of her presence would make leaving easier. But how do you erase someone who has become part of your soul?

Every evening, she asked me to come to her place. One night, as we sat together on her couch, she pulled out her phone and opened her gallery. Her fingers trembled slightly as she found what she was looking for.

"Remember this?" she whispered, pressing play.

The video transported us back to Baharvan, to that rainy afternoon in the coffee shop. The camera captured us, sitting close together, rain pattering against the windows behind us. We were laughing, completely lost in our own world. Then, unexpectedly, we had started talking to our future children, making promises about the life we would give them, the love they would grow up in. "Your dad is the kindest man," Elina had said to our imaginary children, her eyes shining with joy. I had played along, telling them how their mother's smile could light up the darkest days.

Watching it now, in the heavy silence of her apartment, felt like looking through a window into a future that would never be. Elina's hand found mine, squeezing it tight.

"I have to live with these memories now," she said, her voice barely steady. "All these beautiful moments, all these dreams we had..."

I pulled her close, feeling her tears soaking through my shirt. Every evening, she cried in my arms. The first time, I tried to be strong—holding her, kissing the top of her head, whispering reassurances I wasn't even sure I believed myself.

But as the nights passed, it became harder. The second night, she clung to me tighter. Her breath was shaky, her voice barely above a whisper.

"I don't know how to do this," she admitted. "I don't know how to wake up one day and not have you."

I swallowed hard. "You will," I said. "You're strong."

She shook her head. "Not when it comes to you."

Her fingers dug into my back, desperate, unwilling to let go. Each touch was a plea, each embrace a prayer for time to stop.

The third night, it broke me. She didn't speak at first—she just curled into me, her face buried in my chest, silent tears soaking my shirt. Then, finally, she lifted her head and looked at me, her eyes holding galaxies of emotion.

"I love you," she said, her voice raw. "You know that, right?"

I cupped her face, my thumb brushing away the tear that slid down her cheek.

"I know," I whispered. "I know."

She held my hands against her face, pressing my palms into her skin, as if trying to memorize their warmth.

"Tell me you love me," she pleaded.

I kissed her forehead, then her nose, then her lips.

"I love you."

Her breath hitched. "Say it again."

I wrapped my arms around her.

"I love you, Elina."

That night, we didn't sleep. We just lay there, in the dim glow of her apartment, holding on to each other like it was the last time. Because maybe it was.

The Last Sunset

The evening of March 14th, I stayed. The sky outside her window was painted in hues of red and gold, the last embers of the day casting their glow across the city. The sunset turned everything into fire—our skin, the walls, the reflections in the glass. Elina sat nestled in my arms, her body sinking into mine, as if she could stretch this moment into eternity.

She picked up her phone, scrolling absently through Instagram. A shared post caught her eye—one of those "add yours" prompts. She stared at it for a while, fingers hovering over the screen. Then, as if the weight of reality had finally settled on her chest, she lifted her phone, took a picture of us—our silhouettes against the burning sunset—and typed just three words.

"Maybe life is this."

Her words hung in the air, and I felt the weight of them. Maybe life was this—just moments like these, fleeting and fragile, slipping through our fingers no matter how tightly we tried to hold on. There was something bittersweet about it. We both knew this was one of those moments we'd remember long after everything else had faded.

The next morning, March 15th, she made me coffee and breakfast. She lay on the couch putting her head on my lap, while I sipped from the cup, as if she was trying to memorize the feel of me—one last time. I tried to make her laugh. I always did. And she did laugh—but between her tears.

"Stay tonight," she pleaded softly, her voice barely above a whisper.

I kissed her forehead, lingering there for a moment. "I can't. I need to shower, change, and get ready for tomorrow."

She didn't argue. She just nodded, understanding even in her heartbreak.

And when I stood at the door, ready to leave, she hugged me so tight that I could feel the tremor in her fingers, hear the uneven breath she was trying to control.

We kissed—slow, heavy, painful. Each second stretched into infinity, each touch a goodbye we weren't ready to say.

Then, I walked away.

The Last Night

I had barely been home for two hours when my phone lit up with her name. It was 8 PM, and I was still trying to gather myself to start packing and preparing for tomorrow. When I saw her message, my heart clenched.

"Could you come back and stay tonight? Please?"

She wasn't just asking me to return. She was begging. I could feel her pain through those simple words on the screen. And despite having just left her, despite knowing I needed to prepare for tomorrow, I knew I had to go back. Because how do you deny the last request of someone whose heart is breaking?

When I arrived, she threw herself into my arms. Her entire body trembled with the force of emotions too big to contain.

"Thank you," she whispered over and over again, her voice breaking. "Thank you for coming."

That night, she cried like I had never seen her cry before. Loud, raw, relentless.

"I was thinking," she sobbed into my chest, "what kind of kindhearted person I'm losing."

She clutched at my shirt, gripping it as if I would slip away if she let go.

"I love you," she choked out. "The way you sit. Your smell. Your behavior. Everything. And I'm losing you."

I held her tighter, knowing nothing I said would ease the pain. Because how do you comfort someone when you're the reason for their pain?

And in those hours, we didn't sleep. She just cried. And I just held her, memorizing the weight of her in my arms, the scent of her hair, the sound of her breathing.

The Final Goodbye

The morning came too soon. She made me breakfast, just like she always did. She watched me eat, silent, memorizing every second. Then, as I picked up my bag, she said the last thing I expected.

"I'm coming with you."

"Elina—"

"Just to the station," she interrupted, her voice barely steady. "Just until the tram."

I nodded. I didn't want to say no. Not to this. Not to her.

We walked through the streets in silence, the weight in our chests making every step heavier. At the station, I had to take Tram Line 3.

We stood there, face to face, eyes locked, as the tram approached. And that was when she broke. Her eyes filled with fresh tears, her breath hitched, and suddenly, she was sobbing again—right there, in front of everyone.

She shook her head violently, as if she could somehow stop time.

"Please. Stay for the next one," she whispered, barely able to speak.

Her voice was small, desperate. I glanced at the tram. I could still make it in time if I waited for the next one.

"Okay," I whispered.

The doors slid open, people shuffled in, and we let it go. She buried herself in my arms again, shaking uncontrollably. I kissed the top of her head.

"I'm not going to die," I murmured, trying to soothe her. "We still have the company. We'll still see each other."

But she just shook her head.

"It's not the same."

Her fingers gripped my jacket tighter, and when she looked up at me, her face was streaked with tears. In that moment, I realized this wasn't just separation - it was the end of something that had grown beyond either of our control.

"I need you to know," she whispered, her voice breaking, "that loving you wasn't a mistake. Even if this is how it ends."

The next tram approached, its wheels screaming against the tracks. This time, we both knew I couldn't stay. I wanted to tell her that she had awakened something in me I thought had died with my father - a capacity for feeling that both thrilled and terrified me. That even though I was choosing Nadia, she had changed me in ways I couldn't undo.

Instead, I stepped onto the tram, carrying the weight of unspoken words. As it pulled away, I slumped into a seat and opened my wallet with trembling hands. There, carefully preserved between the folds, was a single strand of her hair—the one she had given me in Baharvan. I held it gently between my fingers, this delicate piece of her that she had pressed into my palm with a laugh, saying "Now you'll always have a part of me with you." The strand lay delicately against my palm, golden-brown like her eyes on all those mornings we'd shared together.

Through the window, I watched her figure grow smaller until she disappeared from view. The rain blurred everything outside, and suddenly, my mind was flooded with memories. I saw her smile in the mornings at Nextera Labs. I heard her laughter over double-burgers. I saw her small hands sewing my torn gloves. I remembered the time she came to pick me up in her brother's funny small pickup. I remembered how she drove me to the mechanic when I needed Titanus. I saw her emerging from the confectionery with a smile, cake and balloons in hand in Baharvan. I saw our willow. I felt her breath. I heard her voice.

Every moment of us played in my mind like a movie—one that had just reached its final scene. Each memory a reminder of what we had built, what we had shared, and what we were losing.

And as the tram carried me to the airport, as the rain blurred everything outside the window, I whispered her name. But only the rain heard me.

In that moment, I understood that some loves aren't meant to last forever. Sometimes, they're meant to change us, to show us parts of ourselves we never knew existed. And even though I was going back to Nadia, to the woman who had fought so hard to keep me, who had crossed oceans and moved mountains to save our marriage, a part of me would always belong to Elina. Even as Nadia's determined love pulled me back to our shared life, to the decade we had built together, I knew that Elina had changed me forever. She had shown me what it meant to love without conditions or demands, and that kind of love leaves an indelible mark on your soul.

The rain continued to fall, washing away the last traces of what might have been, leaving behind only memories of a love that had burned too bright to last.

ELEVEN

THE NOTE TO THE SEA

For eight months, she was still here. Not in my life, not in my days, but in the air, in the places we had been, in the streets where our footprints had long faded into the concrete's memory.

We hadn't spoken since that night at the tram station. Not a call, not a message. Nothing but the echo of her last breath against my chest, the ghost of her fingers slipping away from mine.

And yet, she remained in my mind, like an old song I couldn't forget, its melody playing in the quietest moments of my days. I wasn't looking for her, but I saw her everywhere. In the woman adjusting her scarf at the corner, her movements so familiar they made my heart skip. In the girl at the bookstore flipping through pages with careful fingers, the way she used to do. In a silhouette in a crowded tram that made my breath hitch for just a second—until I realized it wasn't her, could never be her again.

Then, one evening, without meaning to, I found her. Not in a place, not in a conversation, but on LinkedIn. She had moved. A new city. A new job. A new life. And just like that, it was real. She was gone, not just in spirit, but in every possible way.

That night, I drove to her apartment.

I stood outside her door, my fingers tightening around the fountain pen in my pocket. That pen—I had brought it to give to her, my precious pen, the same one she had used that day in the coffee shop. I remembered how her eyes had lit up when she first wrote with it, how she had smiled at the way it glided across the paper. Now I wanted her to have it, to take this piece of me into her new life, to write her own story with it.

I had come thinking, maybe, she hadn't packed everything yet. Maybe she was still in the process of leaving. Maybe I wasn't too late.

But I was wrong.

I rang the bell. Silence answered. I rang again. Nothing but the hollow echo of emptiness.

And then, I saw it. On the balcony, in the corner, was the plant she had saved. The one I had helped her arrange, our hands brushing as we adjusted its placement just right so it would catch the best light. We had talked about how it would grow, how its leaves would spread, how it would still be there in the changing seasons—just like us.

It was still there. But she wasn't.

The lights were off. The apartment was empty. She had left. And I had come too late.

When I arrived home that night, I cried. More than I had in a long time. I cried for the loss, for the finality of it. For all the words that would never be said, all the moments that would never be shared, all the dreams that would remain just that—dreams.

And then, I thought of my wife. The woman who had stayed through everything. The one who was still here, still beside me, while I had spent so many nights grieving someone who wasn't. The one who fought for me, even with me, her love never wavering even when I had given her every reason to let go.

I knew that I couldn't carry this weight forever.

A few days later, I drove to the sea.

The storm had come without warning, as if nature itself understood the turmoil in my heart. Lightning split the sky, illuminating the angry waves that crashed against the shore with devastating force. The wind howled, a mournful song that seemed to carry all my unspoken goodbyes.

Rain pelted my face, mixing with tears I didn't bother to wipe away. The waves stretched endlessly before me, dark and powerful, as if they had always known how to take things away, how to pull them into the depths and never return them. They rose like mountains, fell like avalanches, each crash against the shore a reminder of how small we are in the face of time and tide.

In my hand, I held a small glass bottle. Inside, a single strand of her hair—the one I had carried with me for too long, a real piece of her that had rested against my heart through all these months. And a note.

I had written it with the same fountain pen she once held, her fingerprints somewhere beneath mine on its surface.

"I remember the day that I took it from you and put it in my wallet. It has been with me all these days. But now it's time to let it go. May the waves protect it and bring peace to our lives! ...and to remember it all too well..."

Below the words, I signed only the title: **Maybe Life Is This.**

And at the bottom, I sketched a willow tree—its branches reaching downward, touching the earth, as if whispering its own quiet goodbye to the secrets it had kept for us.

I rolled the note, sealed it inside the bottle, and stepped closer to the shore. The waves roared before me, their fury matching the storm that had raged in my heart for eight months. For eight months, I had carried the weight of her presence in her absence. For eight months, I had searched for her in the faces of strangers, in the corners of rooms, in the spaces between heartbeats.

Thunder cracked overhead as I drew back my arm. The bottle caught a flash of lightning, gleaming for one brilliant moment like a star fallen to earth. Then it arced through the rain, through the wind, through all the words we'd never say.

The sea took it with a violence that felt like mercy. I watched as the waves claimed it, as the storm pulled it deeper and deeper, until it disappeared into the darkness. The bottle would join other lost things in the depths—other memories, other loves, other lives that had slipped away.

And then, finally, I turned away. The rain continued to fall, washing away the salt of tears from my face. Each step back felt lighter than the last, as if the storm was cleansing more than just the air.

Behind me, the waves crashed on. Before me stretched a different kind of life—one where memories would fade like footprints in sand, where love would change like seasons, where pain would heal like all wounds do.

And as I walked away, I understood what she had meant that night against the sunset.

Maybe life is this: not the forever we dream of, but the moments we're given. Not the love we hold onto, but the love we learn to let go.

Maybe life is this.